### Praise for *My Highland Spy*

"An exciting Highland tale of intrigue, betrayal, and love."

—Hannah Howell, *New York Times* bestselling author of *Highland Master*

"A master of Highland romance... [A] love story that transcends time and place. *My Highland Spy* is the first in a new series, and I'm eager to read the next one."

—Becky Condit of *USA Today*

"This book begs to be read and reread."

—*RT Book Reviews*

### Praise for *To Wed a Wicked Highlander*

"Roberts has created the baddest boy of the Highlands. This action-packed romance has everything Roberts' fans adore: a strong heroine who meets her match in a to-die-for hero, deception, betrayal, love, and redemption."

—*RT Book Reviews* Top Pick!

"Victoria Roberts knocked it outta the ballpark with this one! It is Highland romance at its best. I couldn't put it down."

—*Night Owl Reviews*, 5 Stars, Reviewer Top Pick

## Praise for *X Marks the Scot*

Winner, *RT* Reviewers' Choice Award, Best
Medieval Historical Romance

"For a complex story brimming over with pride and
passion, betrayal, trust, and most of all the power to
make a bad boy a hero, pick up this read."

—*RT Book Reviews*

"This is one author who just keeps on getting better…
One of the most exciting Highland romances I have
read. Definitely worthy of five stars!"

—*Night Owl Reviews*, 5 Stars, Reviewer Top Pick

## Praise for *Temptation in a Kilt*

"An exciting Highland adventure with sensual and
compelling romance."

—Amanda Forester, acclaimed author of *True
Highland Spirit* and *A Midsummer Bride*

"Well written, full of intrigue and a sensual, believable
romance, this book captivates the reader immediately."

—*RT Book Reviews*

"Roberts's debut features appealing characters and
an interesting background of ancient clan feuds and
spurned lovers."

—*Publishers Weekly*

# KILTS
## AND
# DAGGERS

# VICTORIA ROBERTS

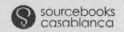
sourcebooks
casablanca

Published by Sourcebooks Casablanca, an imprint of Sourcebooks, Inc.
P.O. Box 4410, Naperville, Illinois 60567-4410
(630) 961-3900
Fax: (630) 961-2168
www.sourcebooks.com

Printed and bound in Canada.
MBP 10 9 8 7 6 5 4 3 2 1

*To Michelle Spak, my beautiful sister, who knows the true meaning of family. I love you because you're my sister, and I laugh because God knows there's nothing you can do about it.*

*Suspense is worse than disappointment.*
—Robert

# One

*Sutherland, Scottish Highlands, 1610*

"SCOTLAND. THE LAND OF BARBARIAN FOOLS, AND NOW my sister is among them," said Lady Grace Walsingham.

"What is done is done, my dear. There's nothing you can do now except offer your felicitations and place a smile on that beautiful face of yours. If you'll pray excuse me, I'll take my leave to consort with the enemy. May I suggest you do the same? We cannot be rude to our gracious hosts."

If Lord Daniel Casterbrook wasn't her betrothed, she would've chided him right where he stood. He pulled her close to his side, more than likely to prevent her from fleeing, and they walked together into the crowd. Unlike the tall and disheveled kilted men, Daniel sported a pair of tan breeches and wore a slashed doublet with paned sleeves. His tall boots turned over at the top, and his brown hair was pulled back into a lovelock that hung over his shoulder. His shoulders weren't nearly as wide as those of the other men in attendance, but his features were so perfect that he was almost too beautiful for a man.

As Daniel stopped and huddled with Uncle Walter in deep conversation, boisterous sounds of laughter filled the air. But Grace couldn't have been more miserable as she pulled the laced bodice of her emerald gown away from her damp skin. The heat was so unbearable that sweat was dripping between her breasts and down her back. She gazed around the room filled with men, women, and flowing ale and wondered if her sister had gone mad.

Kilts, daggers, and men in the throes of battle—that's what she tried to overlook while standing in the great hall of her brother-in-law's home. Granted, the kilts and daggers belonged to the Sutherland clan, but she couldn't understand why her sister hadn't taken down those dreadful tapestries before her wedding day. Why would someone want to display the ghastly scene of warriors on the battlefield, especially on such a celebratory occasion? That was not something she would permit on the day of her own wedding, but her sister was blissfully happy, and Grace supposed that was all that mattered.

When the men paid her no heed, Grace turned and left them. She could take a hint that she wasn't wanted. She stepped around the bagpiper, placing her hands briefly over her ears to shield them from the dreadful performance. The kilted man tapped his foot while he played the ungodly instrument, which sounded a great deal like pigs in the midst of being slaughtered. If his actions were any indication, he clearly thought he was engaged in some kind of lovely

erted her eyes. The rogue made her feel
ays knew her thoughts, and she couldn't
about him. She jumped when a familiar
oice spoke beside her.

apologies. I didn't mean to startle you. I'm so
ou decided to stay with us for a while."

race waved her sister off. "Ravenna, you have
e so much for our family. Postponing my wedding
as the least I could do. Furthermore, this will be a big
transition for Elizabeth and Kat. Living in the Scottish
Highlands will be a lot different than they're used to.
And I cannot lie; I will miss you all so terribly. Before
I go, I want to see my sisters settled into their new
home, and I'd really like to spend some time with all
of you before I become Lady Casterbrook. There's
plenty of time for that later." She bumped her sister in
the arm with her elbow. "Truth be told, I'm counting
on you to tell me all the secrets about married life, Lady
Sutherland. Although I had grown rather fond of Lady
Ravenna Walsingham—or even 'Mistress Denny'—I
do find your new name suits you quite well."

Ravenna shook her head. "I'd rather not be
reminded about 'Mistress Denny.' But how could
I forget that you were the one who traveled from
Edinburgh and gave my true identity away? Everything
turned out for the best, but I certainly hope you've
learned a valuable lesson from your careless actions."

"Rest assured, Lady Sutherland. Now that I know
you're a spy for the Crown, I will never be so foolish
as to place you in harm's way again."

"Lower your voice. And I told you... I've retired
from service."

Scottish melody. She di[...]
music, if she could e[...]
headache as big as Lon[...]

God, she felt like she [...]
Sutherlands. She said a silent [...]
the bagpiper finally ceased his [...]
head was pounding. She thought p[...]
make an early escape to her chambe[...]
raised voice stopped her in her tracks. Al[...]
man was rarely comprehensible, she'd recogn[...]
voice anywhere.

"He is such an arse. Ye do know when he tells the tale, he was naught but a mighty fine warrior. Anyone who knows him recognizes the truth. I donna even think he remembered to grab his sword before he cowered and ran away like a dog with his tail between his legs."

The men around him laughed in response, and Grace chided herself because she couldn't resist a peek. When her eyes met Fagan Murray, the captain of Laird Sutherland's guard, for some unknown reason, her heart started hammering in her chest and she found it difficult to perform the simplest of tasks—like breathing.

The captain's dark hair hung well below his shoulders, and he had a smile that grated on her nerves. Although he had the craggy look of an unfinished sculpture, he exuded masculinity in a way that unsettled her. He wore a kilt of green, black, blue, white, and orange, the Sutherland tartan. When the man caught her staring, his eyes twinkled, and a smile played on his lips.

Grace rolled her eyes. "So you and Uncle Walter continue to say, but how does one simply *retire*? Are you ever really done trying to protect our king and country? Who knows? Perhaps Uncle Walter will give me my first assignment when I go back to England. With your instruction, I'm more than ready."

"Grace," Ravenna said with impatience, "we never agreed that you'd take my place."

"I think what you mean to say is that *you* never agreed."

Ravenna rubbed her hand over her brow. "It takes far more than a handful of my words and guidance to be ready to work for the Crown. And you're getting married in a few months. What about Daniel?"

"What about him? He'll never find out. I never knew you worked for the king either."

"Yes, and look what good that did me," her sister snapped. "Do we have to have this discussion right now, especially on my wedding day?"

"You do look beautiful."

Ravenna's smooth ivory skin glowed. Her red hair dangled over her shoulders in loose waves that hung down her back. She wore a light-blue wedding gown, and her skirts were split and tied back to reveal the gold silk brocade beneath.

"I have to ask you this again. Are you sure you want to stay at the manor house and remain in England? I know Uncle Walter will watch over you, but—"

"Oh, I'm quite certain. I'll only live there until Daniel and I wed." Grace didn't miss how her sister had quickly changed the direction of the conversation. Looking around the great hall at Ravenna's new family only further confirmed that Grace's decision was the right one. "I know your husband's family…er, clan, suits you, but this life is not for me. My home is in England, and frankly, I want to be around people I can clearly understand."

A deep voice interrupted the conversation.

"Are ye keeping my wife all to yourself? 'Tis time to give her up for a wee bit, lass."

"Pardon?" asked Grace.

Laird Ruairi Sutherland was definitely not a man Grace would like to encounter in a dark alley in London in the middle of the night. Her sister's head only reached the middle of the massive man's chest. His brown hair had traces of red and was fairly straight. He had a powerful set of shoulders and looked like a bloody mercenary, as though he could kill someone with only a stare. In Grace's humble opinion, Ravenna was more elegant and graceful when she was with the brawny Highland laird. Grace had a difficult time understanding why her sister couldn't have found a more suitable mate in England, but she had to admit that Ravenna looked quite content.

When her brother-in-law lowered his head and devoured her sister's mouth, Grace didn't mind taking her leave to find a solitary wall on the other side of the great hall. That was until someone found her and she realized she should've sought her chamber after all.

"'Twas a bonny day for a wedding, but ye donna look as though ye're enjoying yourself. Why is that?"

She lifted her eyes to find the captain of Laird

Sutherland's guard and couldn't stay the sigh that escaped her. Fagan Murray, kilted barbarian and Scottish miscreant, stood before her with a gaze that was sharp and assessing. The man was just as big and imposing as Laird Sutherland. The way he stood there and continued to gape at her, Grace supposed he was waiting for a response. She held her head high because she didn't feel like giving the brute the time of day.

"What is amiss, *bhana-phrionnsa*?" He spoke slowly, and she knew he mocked her. "Do ye nae understand my words?"

"Oh, I heard you. I want to know what you called me."

"The name suits ye. I called ye 'princess.'"

"Don't call me that." She looked around nervously in the hope that someone would rescue her from this *man*, and that was a term she used very loosely because he was certainly no gentleman.

His smile broadened when he realized he'd unnerved her, which irked her even more. If she was going to stay in Scotland for the next few weeks, she couldn't let this Highlander get the best of her. Grace carefully masked her expression because most of the time the rogue saw right through her nervousness and used her weakness to his advantage.

She spoke lightly and cast him a tight smile. "You know, Mister Murray, I seem to remember my fist fitting perfectly into your eye. If you don't want me to blacken your other one, I suggest you leave off. Please let me know if you need me to speak more slowly because I want to make sure my words are understood perfectly."

❧

Fagan scowled.

When Lady Grace had shown up out of nowhere, insisting Ravenna was a lady—not governess "Mistress Denny" as Ravenna had claimed to be—what the hell was he supposed to have done? He was the captain of Ruairi's guard, for God's sake. What did the English chit think? That she could make such a declaration and he'd simply turn his cheek? She was a daft lass if she'd thought as much.

He continued to study Princess Grace, who stood there with her oval face pointing daintily in the air. Her brownish-gold hair was pulled up on the top of her head, and loose tendrils softened her face. He knew not to be fooled by the suggestion of supple curves beneath her emerald dress. She was a temptress but had a bite that could bring a man to his knees. She was nothing but trouble. The lass had a smug look on her face, like she knew she'd gotten the best of him, but it would take a lot more than the words of some English wench to tear down his stone walls.

"Och, your words were perfectly clear, *bhana-phrionnsa*." He lowered his voice, barely speaking above a whisper. "But truth be told, I've seen ye watching me, staring. Your eyes tell me what ye are thinking." When she stiffened, he leaned in closer. "I think ye wonder what lies beneath my kilt. If ye ask me nicely, mayhap I'll show ye. But ye'll have to say please."

Grace's face reddened as he knew it would. As she huffed and walked away from him with her chin still pointed in the air, Fagan couldn't stay his smile. He rather enjoyed her discomfiture and found perverse pleasure in ruffling her English feathers. When he felt a tug on his sleeve, he looked down.

"Fagan, ye must help me. Kat is following me everywhere."

"Torquil, she's nae used to having a lad around. She only wants to get to know ye." With his reddish-brown hair, green eyes, and pale skin, the boy was the picture of Ruairi.

"Aye, well, I didnae ask to have so many lasses about. Why couldnae I be blessed with lads? 'Tis so unfair."

Fagan placed his hand on the boy's shoulder. "Your father talked to ye about this. Ye know Elizabeth and Katherine will live here. This is now their home, too."

"I know, but could ye at least tell Kat to stop following me everywhere? Why are lasses so annoying?"

Fagan smirked. "Believe it or nae, lad, there will come a time when ye will enjoy the company of a lass." When the boy looked at him as though he had three heads, Fagan chuckled.

"That will ne'er happen."

No sooner were the words out of Torquil's mouth than the wee lass came up behind him, her golden curls bouncing with each step. The lad spun on his heel and was gone before Kat had a chance to catch up.

"Where did Torquil go?"

Fagan bent down and looked into her bonny blue eyes. "He's truly glad that ye're here, lassie, but ye might want to leave him be for a wee bit. Ye see, Torquil's nae used to having so many lasses around. Why donna ye give him some time to get to know ye?"

He knew she was thinking about his words by the expression on her face, and then her eyes lit up. "That's a great idea. I'll go and talk with him so he gets to know me better." Before he could stop her, Kat's blue dress wound around her small frame as she turned to track Torquil down, just like a little spy for the Crown.

Although Ruairi had told Fagan that Ravenna was no longer a spy for the English, Fagan still had his doubts. He'd be sure to watch Ruairi's back to make certain Ravenna didn't stab it in the middle of the night. When he looked over at the couple, he knew his suspicions were misplaced. Even though he hated to admit it, Laird Ruairi Sutherland had fallen in love with an English lass. Truth be told, Fagan knew the woman felt the same way about his friend. A blind fool couldn't miss the way the two of them looked at each other.

As Fagan turned, Torquil ran out of the great hall with Kat and Angus nipping at his heels. Even the black wolf was taking a liking to all the lasses underfoot. Fagan was always ready to protect and defend Ruairi against their fiercest enemy, but no one could have readied him for the day when their home was invaded by the fairer sex.

"I've ne'er seen so many bloody English," said Laird Ian Munro in his best English accent. "Be sure to keep them here, and whatever ye do, donna let them cross the border to my lands. I beg ye." Ian smoothed his long, red hair, which practically reached his elbows and was secured at the nape of his neck.

"Aye. I couldnae agree more. Most will be taking

their leave on the morrow. Thank God for small favors." Fagan nodded to Lady Grace. "Unfortunately, some will be with us for a while."

Ian lifted a brow. "I donna see how that is a problem for ye. The lass is rather pleasing to the eye. Mayhap ye will find yourself enjoying the pleasure of her company after all, eh?"

"Och, aye, I enjoy the pleasure of her company until she opens her mouth and words escape it. Besides, she's betrothed, poor bastard." Fagan pointed across the great hall. "And look. The lass isnae the only one who makes a man daft. Set your eyes upon poor Torquil."

The boy approached them, looking over his shoulder. He placed his fingers to his lips in a conspiratorial gesture. "Shhh…donna tell Kat ye've seen me. I believe that I lost her somewhere in the bailey. I think I'm safe now."

Ian slapped Fagan on the shoulder. "I think it will be good for all of ye to have some women under the Sutherland roof. I'm certain ye'll take a liking to having them around."

"I donna think that will ever happen." Fagan folded his arms across his chest, realizing at the last moment that he was sounding much like a certain boy he knew.

Ian gave him a knowing look. "I've learned to ne'er say ne'er, my friend."

If it wasn't bad enough that the castle was under siege by the Walsingham sisters, now Ruairi and Ian were taken by the wily ways of the women, English women no less.

❧

A sour look crossed Kat's face as she approached Grace in the great hall. Kat bowed her head, rounded her shoulders, and leaned against the stone wall.

"I don't understand why he runs from me. I didn't do anything to him."

Grace patted Kat on the top of her head. "No one understands why boys do what they do. Why don't you leave him alone for a little while?" When Kat shrugged, Grace realized she needed to keep her sister occupied with something other than the laird's son. "I find myself needing a bit of fresh air. Do you want to walk in the gardens with me?"

"Shall I find Elizabeth? Perhaps she'll want to come along."

"Yes. I'll meet you both by the door."

A cool breeze brushed the small tendrils of hair on the back of Grace's neck. As she gazed out into the courtyard, she couldn't help but notice the many colored kilts and the brawny men who wore them. At least she was able to make out the Sutherland clan colors now. She'd seen the tartan more often than not, and frankly, she'd had enough of it and the men who wore it.

A rich voice spoke against her ear. "Have I told you lately that you look very lovely, my lady?"

She spun around and smiled. "You have, and I thank you again, my lord."

"Are you certain you don't want to return with us on the morrow? It's not too late to change your mind." Daniel leaned in closer. "I know you don't feel at ease here. You could always come back and marry me now."

"I appreciate your concern, but you know I want to be here for—"

"Your sisters."

"Yes. I know this is difficult for you to understand, but I wanted to make sure they—"

He brushed his hand lightly on her arm. "What is there to understand? Take all the time you need, my lady. I have no intention of going anywhere, and family is most important. Now if you'll please excuse me, I do believe I could use another drink. Could I bring you anything?"

"No, thank you. I'm taking the girls for a walk in the garden."

Daniel brushed a brief kiss on the top of her hand. As Grace watched him walk away, she was aware that her relationship with her sisters was hard for him to grasp. With her mother and father passed, Grace only had Ravenna, Elizabeth, Kat, and of course, Uncle Walter. Her family meant everything to her, and they were all close in the way families should be. Her parents had raised them well.

But now she had Daniel.

The last she wanted to do was make him feel as though she was keeping him at arm's length. After all, the man was going to be her husband. Lady Grace Casterbrook sounded lovely, if she did say so herself. Lost in her reveries, she turned and continued to watch the bustling courtyard. She thought perhaps she should start to look for the girls because they were taking longer than expected, but then someone pulled on her skirts.

"I found Elizabeth, Grace."

"Perfect. Let's go then."

Grace watched the girls amble along the garden path. She loved them with all her heart and had a hard time trying to imagine her life without them in it. She didn't blame her sisters for wanting to stay in Scotland and knew they thought of Ravenna as more of a mother figure. At nine and fifteen, Kat and Elizabeth needed stability in their lives. And although Grace was reluctant to admit it, Ravenna's new home was the best place for the girls right now, even if that meant they were far away from England and her.

When Kat and Elizabeth stopped to study a rose, Grace realized none of her siblings had a singular trait that distinguished them as being a Walsingham. Kat had beautiful blond locks, while Elizabeth had reddish-brown hair. Ravenna had long red hair, and Grace's was a warm-colored brown with golden strands, compliments of the sun. Then again, no one had thought their mother and Uncle Walter looked like brother and sister either. Her mother had pale skin and Uncle Walter's was much darker. Frankly, the man looked like a bloody pirate with his dark looks and cool demeanor. He had an air of command about him, as if he were the captain of a ship on a stormy sea.

Grace made her way over to a stone wall about waist high. Orange and yellow flowers lined the stone path, and the scent of roses wafted through the air. A few buds were in bloom and the garden was lovely. Stretching her neck, she leaned forward and looked over the wall. She found herself smiling with pleasure. Laird Sutherland had a fine home.

The blue waves of the ocean crashed onto the

rocky shore below. She closed her eyes, and the sound was so peaceful, so soothing. Although she detested many things about the Highlands, she enjoyed the sea wholeheartedly. She couldn't imagine waking up to this view.

A shrill scream rang through the air, and she froze.

"Grace!" yelled Elizabeth.

Tiny stones crushed under Grace's feet as she lifted her skirts and darted along the path. When she reached the girls, she found Elizabeth kneeling on the ground beside her sister as blood dripped from Kat's forehead and into her blond curls.

"I told her not to run. She tripped and hit her head on a big stone."

Tears fell down Kat's cheeks. "Look at my dress. There's blood all over it." Her voice wavered with panic.

Grace lowered herself to the ground and tried unsuccessfully to wipe the blood away from Kat's gash with her hand. "There, there, everything will be all right."

"What happened?"

When Grace looked up, Ruairi's captain was standing there, towering over them with a look of concern. She didn't understand how the man had arrived so quickly, but she was glad he did. "Kat fell and hit her head on a rock."

Without hesitation, Fagan unsheathed his dagger and cut a piece of cloth from his tunic. He knelt down and pressed the material to Kat's head. When she whimpered, he gave her a compassionate smile and smoothed her hair.

The man was so gentle with her sister that Grace was taken aback by his kindness. "Should we try and get her to stand?" she asked.

"Nay. Leave her still for a moment." As Kat's sobs became louder, Fagan added, "Ye only have a wee bit of a scratch. Donna worry upon it."

Although the gash bled like a raging river, Grace understood his look telling her not to frighten Kat. He continued to apply pressure to the wound to stop the bleeding. After a heavy silence, she heard approaching footsteps and the laird's son appeared. His expression became serious, and for a moment he paused.

"What happened to her?"

When Fagan answered the boy in what Grace presumed to be Gaelic, Torquil sat on the ground beside Kat. The boy took her hand in a gentle gesture. "I know the blood may frighten ye a wee bit, but ye'll be all right. I've fallen and hit my head before too. Do ye want to see the scar?" When Kat nodded, Torquil lifted his hand and separated a section of his hair with his fingers. "Do ye see that?"

Kat gulped hard. "Yes. It's very big."

Torquil turned back and smiled at her. "And ye see I'm all right."

When Kat nodded, Fagan spoke to Grace. "Hold the cloth firmly to her head, and I will seek the healer. I want her to take a look at your sister's wound. We may need to patch that up. Keep her here and donna attempt to move her."

He started to walk away, and Grace called after him. She wasn't sure what she was going to say, but when the steely captain turned and his eyes met hers, she smiled her thanks. He bobbed his head in return, and she didn't understand how a single look from the man could make her feel like there wasn't anything in the world he couldn't handle. For some odd reason, she was slightly comforted by the thought. As her mind wandered, she barely noticed that Fagan had passed Daniel on the path. Her betrothed reached her side and glanced down.

"What the bloody hell happened to Katherine?"

"Daniel," Grace chided him. "She hit her head on a stone." Grace shifted and glanced at her fingers, which were now covered with blood. "I need another piece of cloth. Blood has soaked clean through."

Daniel looked around. "I don't have anything."

"Mister Murray used a piece of his tunic," said Grace. To her surprise, Daniel lifted a brow and then gazed down, studying his courtly attire. The man's clothes could be replaced. Her sister could not. "Please, Daniel, I need something quickly."

He felt around his chest pocket and pulled out a handkerchief. When he attempted to give her the material he used to blow his nose, Grace scowled. With her free hand, she attempted to pull her dagger from under her skirts. She'd cut her own clothing to help her sister, but she didn't have to. Torquil ripped the bottom of his tunic and handed her the material.

"Thank you, Torquil."

She shot Daniel a cold look and thought perhaps she may have even growled. Who'd have thought a twelve-year-old boy would have more sense and compassion than her husband-to-be?

# *Two*

GRACE BARELY SURVIVED THE NIGHT FROM HELL. FOR heaven's sake, she couldn't even roll over. Elizabeth had an elbow in her back and Kat had a knee in her gut. Perhaps having her two sisters sleep in the same bed with her wasn't one of her best ideas. Not that she had any particular desire to be tortured in the middle of the night by flailing arms and legs, but she wanted to keep an eye on Kat and had thought this was the best way to do it.

When the sun finally cast rays of light through the slits in the curtains, Grace freed her hand from under the blanket and rubbed her tired eyes. She tried not to think any more about Daniel and his behavior last eve, but what unsettled her even more was that she couldn't get Fagan out of her mind. No matter what she did, she couldn't banish the images of the brawny captain. How could she possibly erase the memory of the man who'd kindly held her sister's hand as the healer placed three stitches into the girl's head? And Daniel... He had simply stood there. At least he had moved out of the way, because he'd been no help whatsoever.

Her sisters finally rose, and once everyone was dressed, they descended the stairs to the great hall to break their fast. Grace was about to ask Kat for the hundredth time how she was feeling when her sister started talking about what mischief she and Torquil were going to get into today. Kat's wound was all but forgotten. That's when Grace reached the conclusion that her youngest sister wasn't going to have any problem adjusting to life in the Highlands, as long as the laird's son was around.

Grace placed her hand on Elizabeth's arm. "Is everything all right?"

When they reached the last step, Elizabeth stopped. "Can I ask something of you?"

Grace nodded. "Kat, why don't you go on ahead? We'll catch up to you." Grace smiled at Elizabeth. "What is it?"

"Do you think I'm too young to wed?"

"Yes," replied Grace without hesitation. "You're fifteen and have your whole life ahead of you." She took a deep breath and sighed. "I have a feeling I'm going to regret this, but why do you ask?"

Elizabeth shrugged. "Ravenna didn't wed until she was twenty-six. Granted, you'll soon be nineteen when you wed Lord Casterbrook... Who do you think will be my guardian, Laird Sutherland or Uncle Walter?"

"Since you'll be staying with Ravenna, I'd have to say Laird Sutherland, but you know our sister will look after you. What are you worried about?"

"When the time comes, do you think Ravenna and her husband will arrange a marriage for me with someone back in England, or do you think perhaps I'll be wed to a man here in the Highlands?"

Grace smirked. "I should hope not."

"Why not?" Elizabeth suddenly couldn't look Grace in the eye.

"What's the matter with you?"

"Nothing. I just… Now that you'll be wed, I know I'm next. If Laird Sutherland wanted to arrange a marriage for me, I would like to say that I do think Laird Munro would be rather pleasing."

Grace couldn't help it. Her jaw dropped. "Wait a moment. Laird *Ian* Munro? Are you telling me that you fancy Ruairi's redheaded neighbor? The one who looks like some kind of unruly Scottish vagrant?"

"Shhh…lower your voice. I think he's very handsome, and he doesn't look like a vagrant."

"He's nearly twice your age." Grace placed a patient hand on Elizabeth's shoulder. "When the time comes for you to wed, I'm sure you'll find a more suitable mate than Laird Munro." She looked around to make certain no one was near and then lowered her voice to a whisper. "Elizabeth, these Highland men lack comportment. Don't you want to find a man from your own country who's refined and doesn't sport a kilt? Wouldn't you rather wed someone who understood your beliefs and customs, someone like Daniel perhaps?"

Elizabeth looked at Grace in surprise. "Like Daniel?"

"This is really not the best place to have this conversation. Why don't you go and break your fast? I'll be along shortly."

Grace watched Elizabeth walk away, and then she

closed her eyes and squeezed the bridge of her nose with her fingers. Her best decision yet was deciding to stay. Her sisters—well, one sister in particular—needed her guidance now more than ever. Ravenna may have fallen in love with a Highlander, but there was no way Grace would allow Elizabeth to be so foolish.

After finally composing herself, Grace entered the great hall and tried to mask her discomfiture. Ruairi's clan was already seated for the meal, and no remnants of the prior evening's festivities were left to be seen. As she approached the dais, Grace noticed that Ravenna simply glowed. For a slight moment, Grace was envious of the love her sister had found with Ruairi. Although the man lived and breathed everything Scottish, his actions showed that he adored Ravenna as he placed an errant curl behind his wife's ear and cast a warm smile.

"Niece, come and sit beside us."

Uncle Walter and Daniel both stood upon her approach, but her steps slowed when she saw Fagan sitting at the other end of the table. He didn't stand, but one corner of his mouth turned upward as he tossed a piece of biscuit into his mouth. When his eyes met hers, he gave her a brief nod, and her lips puckered with annoyance. The beastly man had no manners whatsoever, but she was trying to overlook his poor behavior, especially after his kind actions with Kat last evening.

"Good morning, Uncle Walter, Daniel." Grace was about to address Ravenna, but her sister and her husband were too busy exchanging wooing looks with each other. Daniel pulled out Grace's chair, and she sat between Daniel and Elizabeth and across from her uncle. She refused to glance toward the unrefined folk at the other end of the table. "Stop it, Grace," she said under her breath.

"Stop what?" asked Daniel.

She waved him off. "Oh, nothing. Please forgive me. I'm merely talking to myself."

"There is nothing to forgive. Did you sleep well?"

"Yes, thank you. And you?"

"I will certainly sleep much better when I'm back under my own roof. Are you certain you don't want to return with us?"

"I'm certain." She took a bite of oatmeal.

"I'll make sure the manor house is ready upon your return," said Uncle Walter.

"Thank you. I only intend to remain in the Highlands for about a month at the most." She lowered her voice. "I think that is all I'm able to bear."

Uncle Walter chuckled, and Daniel leaned in close, whispering in her ear. "I admire your courage and determination, my dear. If you change your mind and want to come home sooner, I can always send a carriage for you."

Grace pulled back and smiled. "Thank you, but I don't think that will be necessary. I'll be fine."

"Kat, stop! *Thalla dachaigh!*" Torquil bellowed.

As the boy ran behind Grace, she turned on the chair and held out her arm to stay her sister. "Kat, you know better than to give chase to Torquil. Your behavior is not very ladylike. Now I want you to stop."

"Torquil, *thig an seo*," ordered Fagan in a steely

tone. He grabbed the boy by the tunic and pulled him close. Grace didn't know what Fagan said, but he and Torquil continued to speak in hushed tones at the other end of the table.

"Lady Katherine, why don't you come with me to the courtyard while the horses are readied?" asked Daniel, standing. "Lady Elizabeth, would you care to come along?"

"Yes, thank you."

"I think I'll join you," said Uncle Walter. He walked around the table and placed his hand on Grace's shoulder. "We'll leave you to eat in peace."

Grace gazed around the table, realizing she was the only one left of the group. "I hope it's not my company."

"Of course not. Take your time. There is no need to hurry."

"Thank you." Grace turned to Kat and gave her sister a stern look. "I want you to listen to Uncle Walter and Daniel. Do you understand?"

Kat let out a heavy sigh. "All right."

While the men escorted Kat and Elizabeth out of the great hall, Torquil dashed off in the other direction. Once Grace had a chance to talk privately with Ravenna, the two of them would need to make certain that rules were in place for Kat in regards to the laird's son. The thought barely crossed Grace's mind before another followed. Unsuccessfully, she tried to suppress a sudden giggle. She knew men often chased skirts, but this was the first time she'd ever encountered a female chasing them.

"What do ye find so amusing?"

She lifted her eyes to find Ruairi's captain across from her. "Mister Murray…" She didn't remember extending an invitation for the man to sit, but this was another example of his total lack of comportment. Shaking her head with displeasure, she gestured to the chair on which he already sat. "Please, why don't you join me?"

He failed to notice her mocking tone and folded his arms on the table. "I see your sister is feeling much better this morn."

"Yes. I truly can't thank you enough for seeing to her last eve. Your kindness was most welcome."

Fagan's face reddened before he quickly changed the subject. "I donna want to trouble Ruairi and Ravenna since they are recently wed, but we need to do something about Katherine and Torquil."

She lifted a brow. "*We?*"

"Aye. The lass follows him relentlessly, and he's verra annoyed by it."

"Mister Murray, they're children, and I think they're simply getting to know one another. I understand this may be difficult for you to believe, but Kat's never done anything like this before. I think she's just not used to having someone around who's near her own age, a boy, and everything here is so new to her. She's left England, lives in a castle, and has people around her with whom she's not familiar, but I do understand your concern. What did Torquil say to her? I assumed his words were none too kind."

Fagan paused. "Ye assumed right. He told Katherine to stop, and then he told her to go home. I assure ye the lad will nae be speaking that way again to the lass, but can ye—"

"Yes, of course. I'll talk to Kat." Grace shook her head and spoke in a dry tone. "Frankly, I don't know what's wrong with her *and* Elizabeth lately."

"Elizabeth?"

When Grace realized her words were spoken faster than she could stay them, she looked down at her oatmeal. "It's nothing. I spoke before—"

He lowered his voice. "Ye had nay trouble telling me your sister wasnae a governess, but ye have an issue talking to me about what's wrong with Elizabeth?"

"Mister Murray, I don't feel at ease discussing these subjects with you."

"Then call me Fagan. Mister Murray was my father's name anyway."

Grace looked around and then softened her voice. "Now is that truly appropriate?"

"I told ye before. Ye're a long way from England, lass. Lest ye forget, ye're in the Highlands now. We do things differently here."

She lifted a brow. "How could I forget?"

"Ruairi said ye'll be staying with us for a few weeks. More to the point, I already call Ruairi's wife Ravenna." He turned up his smile a notch. "Ye and I are practically like family. Ye will call me Fagan, and I will call ye Grace, or I could always call ye *hhana-phrionnsa*. I'll be kind enough to give ye a choice."

"Ravenna may permit you to call her by her Christian name, but I certainly do not, Mister Murray. Although you do make me laugh, I'm afraid you and I are far from family."

જાજ

When Grace's eyes smoldered, Fagan knew he shouldn't get too close to the flame for fear of getting burned. There was still enough time to take his leave. Otherwise, he'd be verbally sparring with a lass in the middle of the great hall. Ruairi would no doubt have his head for causing mischief with his kin so soon after the wedding.

Fagan slapped both hands on the table and casually stood. Instinctively, he took another step back in case the lass suddenly had a strong urge to reach across the table and throttle him—or worse. Nevertheless, once she heard what he was about to say, the table wouldn't provide enough space between them.

"Verra well then. I think *bhana-phrionnsa* suits ye quite nicely." When Grace's cheeks turned scarlet, Fagan smiled. "Donna say I didnae warn ye. Remember I did give ye a choice." He winked at her and then turned on his heel.

"Wait!"

He had a hard time trying to mask his smile. He turned around slowly and lifted a brow. "Aye?"

Grace flew to her feet, walked around the table, and closed the distance between them. She lifted her head, and by the way she was unsteady on her feet, he swore the daft lass was standing on the tips of her toes in a futile attempt to look him level in the eye.

"England and Scotland have been warring for centuries, Mister Murray, yet somehow Scotland has never won." Lifting her skirts, she brushed his arm with her shoulder and took a few steps away from him.

That was until he called after her and stopped her dead in her tracks. "*Cuine a chì mi a-ris thu*, Grace?" *When will I see you again?* He made certain he said the words as though he spoke to his lover, which obviously had the desired effect because her whole body stiffened, and then she left him without a backward glance. Fagan's mood was suddenly buoyant. He wasn't exactly sure why he loved to unnerve Princess Grace, but he had one hell of a time doing it.

"What happened with Torquil?"

Fagan turned around and let out a chuckle. "My apologies, I didnae recognize ye without Ravenna strapped to your body, my laird."

Ruairi folded his arms over his chest. "Arse."

"Aye. The wee sister seems to have taken a liking to stalking the lad. Donna worry upon it. I talked to Torquil, and Lady Grace will speak with Katherine."

"Our home has certainly changed, has it nae?"

"Ye should've thought about that before ye decided to wed the lass. So many women under one roof will surely put us all in an early grave."

Ruairi chuckled. "Let me know if ye still see trouble brewing between Torquil and Katherine. Mayhap my lovely wife and I will have to have a chat with them. I cannae have a bloody war within my walls between my own kin."

Fagan followed Ruairi out into the bailey where the first round of Walsinghams was ready to depart. Lord Casterbrook, the unlucky betrothed of Princess Grace, and Lord Mildmay, Ravenna's uncle, would soon be nothing but a distant memory. Fagan had to admit that he was much fonder of the latter. There was something about the poor bastard who captured Grace's heart that Fagan didn't like.

He couldn't place his finger on anything in particular, but Casterbrook was odd. Then again, look who the man was marrying. Fagan didn't think a priest could handle Lady Grace's obstinate behavior any better. But what man in his right mind would agree to take on such a burden? That was truly a mystery, one Fagan had no interest in solving.

Noticing Elizabeth standing by herself against the wall, Fagan approached her. "Lady Elizabeth, how do ye fare?"

"Oh, I'm quite well. Thank you, Mister Murray."

"Ye donna have to stand on such propriety. Ravenna calls me Fagan. I would be honored if ye would call me the same." When she gazed around the bailey and a look of sadness passed over her face, he added, "Donna worry. Ye'll be able to visit your uncle, and I'm sure he will come to visit ye."

"Does Laird Munro ready his mount as well? I don't see him."

Fagan lifted a brow. "Ian? Aye. It will nae be long before all are out from underfoot."

"And does Laird Munro come here often? I heard Laird Sutherland say that he doesn't live that far from the Sutherland border."

"First of all, Ruairi would be cross with ye if he heard ye call him Laird Sutherland now. Ye are part of this clan. He is Ruairi. I am Fagan. Understand?"

Elizabeth smiled. "Yes."

"I know Munro may frighten ye with his fierce looks, but donna fash yourself over him. He will nae bother ye. Besides, ye are under Ruairi's protection. Ye have my word that nay harm will come to ye here. Ye are safe, Elizabeth."

The lass spoke in a rush of words, shaking her hands in a nervous gesture before her. "Oh, you misunderstand. Laird Munro doesn't frighten me at all. I was only wondering when he'd return."

Something in Fagan's gut cautioned him not to ask. Granted, he wasn't adept at reading the lasses, but he wondered what this was all about. Another disturbing thought came to mind. Surely the young lady wasn't pining after Munro. The idea was simply absurd.

*Dear God.*

Something clicked in his mind. Not only had wee Katherine taken a liking to Torquil, but now Elizabeth had her sights set on the neighboring laird. He'd definitely have to warn Ian to run hard and fast. When the Sutherland lands were invaded by an army of English lasses, Fagan had known the women would hold no prisoners in their wake, and his instincts were usually right.

"Pray excuse me, Fagan."

Elizabeth walked over to the waiting carriages. As all four Walsingham sisters stood in the bailey, Fagan leisurely made his way to Ruairi's side. He knew that he should lend moral support to his friend, but he walked slowly enough to make sure the man suffered just a little. From the looks of things, Ruairi was drowning in a pool of English—something he deserved for bringing such chaos into the clan.

"Uncle Walter, Ruairi and I can't thank you enough for coming to our wedding."

"I wouldn't have missed it. Your mother and father would've been proud, and you don't need to thank me, Ravenna. I'd do anything for you girls. You know that."

Grace entwined her arm with Ravenna's. "I hope you mean that, Uncle Walter, because when I return to England, you and I are going to have a little chat." Grace's eyes narrowed and something unspoken passed between them.

Lord Mildmay turned his head to the side, clearing his throat, while Fagan wondered what the wily minx was up to now. He couldn't wait until she returned to England because that would be one less problem he'd have to deal with.

Lord Casterbrook stepped forward and lifted Grace's hand, brushing a brief kiss across her knuckles. "My dearest lady, England will not be the same without your presence. I will count the days until your safe return."

With all Fagan's might, he tried not to roll his eyes. He truly did. But when a little smirk escaped him, Ruairi elbowed him in the gut.

"I'll send my own private carriage for you when you are ready to return, and my men will escort you safely home."

"Oh, that won't be necessary," Ravenna interrupted.

Lord Casterbrook lifted a brow. "Oh…and why is that, Lady Sutherland?"

"The captain of my husband's guard will be escorting Grace home."

# Three

THE DUST HAD BARELY SETTLED AS THE CARRIAGES departed through the gates, but Grace couldn't hold her tongue any longer. Fagan had stiffened as though Ravenna had struck him, and his mouth was clenched tighter now, if that was even possible.

"Why? Why would you refuse to let Daniel send someone to escort me home? Ravenna, the last thing I want to do is travel home with…your husband's captain." Grace was resentful that Ravenna hadn't consulted her first before volunteering Fagan's services. Not only could Grace see the man's discontent, but she could feel him seething with mounting rage. She'd made every effort to mask the look of disgust that she knew had crossed her face, but she wasn't sure if she'd succeeded. She was so angry with her sister that she really didn't care.

Ruairi placed his hand on Ravenna's shoulder. "Ye were supposed to let me talk with Fagan first."

"My apologies, but I thought you already had."

For several long moments, Ruairi stood huddled with Fagan as they spoke in Gaelic. When the conversation didn't appear to be ending any time soon, Grace's temper flared. How rude! The men knew she and Ravenna didn't speak a word of their savage tongue. By the tone in Fagan's voice, any fool knew that he didn't want to escort her, but when Grace heard "*bhana-phrionnsa*" fall from his lips for the hundredth time, she'd had enough.

"Laird Sutherland," she interrupted vehemently. "I can assure you this *princess* will be just fine escorted home by her betrothed's men." She looked at Fagan, and her eyes clawed him like talons. When he glowered at her in return, she turned and smiled at Ruairi. "Thank you for your kindness, but there truly is no need—"

"Och, lass, while ye stay in the Highlands, ye are my responsibility. Fagan will escort ye home, and ye have nay voice in the matter."

Ravenna placed her hand on Ruairi's arm. "I know you mean well, but what about—"

"Ye know better than that, Wife. Everyone under my roof is my responsibility. I have a duty to protect them. I will not leave your sister's safety to chance. Lady Grace will be escorted home by my captain and his men. Now there is naught else to be said on the matter."

Ravenna may have been silenced by her husband's dark expression, but Grace refused to let any man, especially a Highlander, decide what was best for her. She was about to speak when Fagan shot Ruairi a withering glance and something unspoken passed between them.

This time when Fagan spoke to Grace, the tone in

his voice was rather pleasant. In fact, the man even smiled, and when he did, Grace found his grin to be irresistible. Perhaps Ruairi had given his captain a good scolding, because it was about time someone brought that wild dog to heel.

In a desperate attempt to try to dismiss the strange aching in her limbs, Grace depicted an ease she didn't necessarily feel. At least that was her intent until Fagan stepped forward and she found herself taking a quick, sharp breath. He lifted her hand, and when their eyes met, she felt a shock run through her.

"My dearest lady, Scotland will nae be the same without your presence. It would be my pleasure to escort ye back to England." A devilish look came into his eyes. "I will count the days until your safe return."

What. An. Idiot.

God, how she wanted to say those words aloud. When Ruairi tried to cover Fagan's words with a cough, Grace realized she never should've assumed anything about Fagan Murray. As he stood there with his sparkling emerald eyes, so arrogant, mocking Daniel's words, she wanted nothing more than to wipe that bloody smirk off his face.

She closed what little distance was left between them and whispered, "Eyes are not the only thing I know how to blacken, Mister Murray." When he swallowed hard, Grace knew she'd won this particular battle.

"Grace!"

Ignoring Ravenna's reprimand, Grace pulled her hand from Fagan's grasp, lifted her skirts, and left them all standing in the bailey with their mouths agape.

"Please let me apologize on behalf of my sister. Sometimes Grace's behavior is rather—"

"Och, Ravenna, 'twas naught that wasnae deserved. I only wish my laird had spoken to me first about this quest." Fagan's angry gaze swung to Ruairi, and Ravenna placed her hand on Fagan's arm.

"I will take responsibility for that. With all the excitement of the wedding, I thought Ruairi had spoken to you. I know that was his intention all along."

"Aye, but I had hoped to get a few drinks in him before I told him," said Ruairi in a scolding tone. He gave Fagan a brief nod. "Ye know Ravenna's sister is under my protection. If Casterbrook—"

Fagan held up his hand. "Ye donna need to say anything more. I wouldnae leave the task to Casterbrook's men either."

"Truly?" Ravenna rolled her eyes and shook her head. "Daniel is a good man. He's good for Grace. Just because he's English does not mean—"

"It doesnae matter if he's English, Scottish, or French. In truth, I donna care what he is. Your sister is my responsibility, and until she's safely back in England where she belongs, I only trust my own men with her escort."

Ravenna tapped Fagan playfully on the shoulder, and then her eyes lit up as though she held a secret. "Then let me be the first to offer you a word of advice if I may. If you're going to be traveling with my sister the entire way from Scotland to England, learn to keep your mouth shut."

"More than likely wise words from the woman who knows her best. I'd heed my wife's warning if I were ye."

"Donna worry about me. I can handle Lady Grace just fine."

"Mmm... If you think that, you don't know my sister as well as you think you do. Pray excuse me." Ravenna took a few steps away from the men and then turned around. "And Fagan? I wouldn't get too close to her if I were you."

Not even aware of his actions, Fagan lifted his hand and rubbed his eye. He had to admit that being punched in the face by a woman was not a common occurrence.

"There, there," said Ruairi in a singsong voice. "At least your eye is nay longer black and blue."

"Arse."

"Aye. Thank ye for nae removing my head in front of Ravenna. I did want to talk to ye beforehand."

Fagan shrugged. "I'm nae thrilled to be in Lady Grace's company for that long, but ye did what was expected of ye. And I'll do what's expected of me. I'll see her back to England into the waiting arms of her betrothed. Howbeit ye'll owe me one hell of a favor, my laird."

"Duly noted. Now that everyone has departed, 'tis about time we get everything back to the way it should be around here—quiet. I think we could all use the peace."

"Peace? With four lasses under roof? Ye're truly praying for a miracle then."

"Do ye think 'tis too much to ask?"

"What I think is that the only safe haven right now is behind the closed doors of your study with a pitcher of ale in hand."

Ruairi slapped Fagan on the shoulder in a brotherly gesture. "Then let us have a drink, shall we?"

"Ye donna need to ask me twice."

The men made their way to Ruairi's study, but as soon as Fagan closed the door, they hesitated. A steady thumping noise was coming from across the room. Ruairi followed the sound, and when he slowly pulled out his chair, a black mass of fur dashed out from under the desk.

"Angus, what the hell are ye doing in here?"

Two massive paws jumped up onto Ruairi's chest, and Torquil crawled out from under the desk.

"'Tis only fair that I have somewhere to go where Kat will leave me alone. She's driving me mad, and I know this is one place where the lasses arenae allowed."

Ruairi lifted a brow. "Nor are ye."

"Aye, well, I'm your son, a Sutherland. Ye can make an exception, can ye nae?" Torquil folded his arms over his chest. "Will ye tell Kat that if she doesnae have man parts, she's nae allowed in? Ye're the laird. She has to listen to ye." Ruairi pushed Angus away, and the wolf moved to stand by Torquil's side. "Ye see? Even Angus agrees with me."

Ruairi sighed and rubbed his hand over his brow. "Sit down, Torquil."

The boy sat in the chair across from his father, and Angus lay down at Torquil's feet, ever the strong protector. The two of them had been inseparable since the wolf was a pup.

"Do ye want me to take my leave?" asked Fagan, not wanting to intrude on a private father-and-son moment.

"Nay."

Ruairi poured himself and Fagan each a tankard of ale. When Ruairi lifted the cup and downed its contents in one gulp, Fagan chuckled. His friend was a laird, warrior, and husband, but out of all the duties Ruairi had, Fagan thought that being a father had to be the most difficult. He couldn't imagine being solely accountable for another person, especially one so young.

"I know ye're nae used to having lasses around." Ruairi sat in the chair behind his desk and gestured for Fagan to sit. "This is going to take some adjusting on everyone's part, including ye."

Torquil's eyes widened. "Me?"

"Aye. Did ye ever think how the lassie must feel? She's a long way from England—the only home she knew, away from her friends and what is familiar to her." Ruairi placed his arm on the desk and sat forward. "Let me ask ye a question, lad. How would ye feel if I made ye leave Scotland, leave your friends, and live in a new home which wasnae familiar to ye?"

A serious expression crossed Torquil's face. "I wouldnae like it at all."

"And what if ye tried to make a new friend and that person didnae want to have anything to do with ye?"

Torquil gazed at the ceiling, pausing. "All right, Da, but I donna like her chasing me."

"Let me offer ye a word of advice," said Fagan. "If ye keep running away from the lass, she's only going to chase ye that much harder. Talk to her. Mayhap if ye take her to the stables, show her where ye and Angus run, and spend some time with her, she will nae want to hunt ye down all the time."

"I agree with Fagan. Ye need to try to spend some time with Kat. Not an entire day's time, mind ye. I'm certain she's feeling a wee bit alone, and I have faith that ye'll do the honorable thing. Ye're a Sutherland. Why donna ye take Angus, and ye two can go and find her now?"

"All right." Torquil stood, letting out a heavy sigh when Fagan placed his hand on the boy's shoulder.

"As I said, lad, show her some things ye like to do and places ye like to go. Make her feel welcome."

"Come, Angus." Torquil walked toward the door and grabbed the latch. "But if this doesnae work and she still gives chase to me, I blame the two of ye." He closed the door, and Ruairi and Fagan chuckled.

"I donna know how ye do it."

Ruairi shrugged. "Donna ye miss the days of our youth?"

"Aye. Although I wish I would've had Torquil's troubles. Who wouldnae want a bonny lassie chasing us around for a change?"

"There is that. I appreciate your help with him. I know this will take some time for Torquil too. But I want Ravenna and her sisters to feel at home, to be at ease."

"Aye. When Lady Grace takes her leave, it will be even more peaceful around here."

"Ravenna tried to warn me, but I asked myself how bad one lass could possibly be. Grace is verra bold, but at least she'll soon be wed. Let us hope Casterbrook doesnae come to his senses, lest I have another wily lass under my roof."

Fagan lifted his tankard in mock salute. "Ye donna have to worry upon that. The lass will ne'er leave her beloved England. Thank God for small favors."

❦

Grace sought the solace of the garden and resumed her favorite place against the stone wall. The sound of the sea soothed her nerves, and a warm breeze blew through her loose tendrils. What was she thinking when she told Ravenna she would stay here for a month? She wondered if she should've accompanied Daniel after all. She wiped her eyes with the palm of her hands.

The fault was Fagan's.

She didn't know why she let the man get under her skin, and that was a place he'd been more often than not. If he thought her a princess, she'd be more than happy to play the role because royals didn't concern themselves with the hired help, even if the dastardly man was her brother-in-law's captain.

"There you are." Ravenna moved to Grace's side and leaned her hip against the wall.

"Here to scold me, Sister?"

"I don't want to, but I wish you wouldn't be so... forward with Fagan. I know you don't care for him, but he's only doing as Ruairi commands."

"The man drives me completely mad. How is it that he seems to be the only one who knows how to grate on my nerves? He always mocks me when he gets the chance, and frankly, I don't know how you put up with him."

"I have to put up with him. He's the captain of my husband's guard. If Fagan annoys you so much, just overlook him. Don't pay him any heed and enjoy your time with us. As you said, you'll soon be Lady Casterbrook."

"I know you're right, but that's another reason why I didn't want the man escorting me home, Ravenna. You should've let Daniel's men—"

Ravenna held up her hand. "One thing I've learned from my husband is that they do things differently here in the Highlands."

"So I've been repeatedly told."

Ravenna placed her hand on Grace's shoulder. "Why don't we gather Elizabeth and Kat and I'll take you to a place where none of you have yet been? I promise that you'll love it."

Grace felt the corner of her mouth lifting into a smile. "When you say it like that, how could I possibly refuse such an offer?"

While Ravenna disappeared to ready herself for a brief excursion, Grace wandered around the castle looking for the girls. When she entered the library, she paused. The room was a welcome surprise.

A large table surrounded by six chairs sat in the center of the library. Two chairs were placed in front of a stone fireplace, and one wall was lined with several wooden shelves. When she spotted a tapestry of another bloody battle scene hung on the wall and encircled by shields and swords, she shuddered. Her brother-in-law's decorating habits left a lot to be desired. In spite of that, she turned her attention back to his vast array of books. Perhaps she had more in common with Laird Sutherland than she'd initially thought because she too would rather bury her nose in a book than share Fagan's company.

"Stop it, Grace."

"Stop what? What are you doing in here?" Elizabeth stood up from a chair in front of the fireplace and replaced a book on the shelf.

"I didn't see you there. Ravenna wants to take us somewhere. Do you know where Kat is?"

"I'm not sure, but I think I know where to find her. I've seen her following that wolf around." Elizabeth hesitated, looking deep in thought. "Why do they call the animal...Angus?"

"I don't know. I suppose they have to call him something."

"But Angus? Why not call him Shadow or something to the like? The wolf is as black as the night." They walked out into the hall, and Elizabeth closed the door behind her. When she turned around, she was still waiting for Grace's response.

"You're asking me? I never understand why men do what they do, let alone these men." She lifted a brow. "Why are we talking about the wolf?"

Elizabeth averted her eyes. "I don't know. I suppose I'm occupying my thoughts." She took a step away, and Grace grabbed her sister's arm.

"Please tell me those thoughts are not about Laird Munro." When Elizabeth hesitated, Grace briefly closed her eyes and sighed. "You must cease thinking about the man." Elizabeth was about to open her mouth when Grace added, "You want someone who will value you for you. You are a beautiful, caring person, and the man doesn't even know you exist. You're a lady, born in England. He's a laird, born in Scotland—the Highlands of Scotland, I might add. You share no common ground. I beg you to cease this sudden fancy you have for him, please. You're only going to be hurt, and I don't want to see that happen."

Elizabeth nodded, and they walked in silence to the great hall. Grace knew her sister was cross with her, but she refused to let Elizabeth believe a Highland laird was the man in her future. If her sister couldn't think clearly, Grace was determined to be the voice of reason.

They walked out into the bailey, where the stone walls of the castle cast more than half the courtyard in shade. For the first time since she'd been in the Highlands, Grace realized how massive her sister's new home was.

"Grace, are you coming with us?" asked Kat.

"Yes, Elizabeth and I were just searching for you."

"I was in the stable with Ruairi."

Ravenna approached with an apologetic look on her face. "I hope you don't mind, but Ruairi wanted to come along."

"Not at all. You two are recently wed. I only hope that we're not intruding."

"Of course ye arenae." Ruairi came up behind Grace and moved to her side. "Ravenna's clan...er, family is now mine too. I want all of ye to feel at home here."

"Thank you, Ruairi. That was very kind. So where are we going?"

Ruairi gave Ravenna a sly grin. "I'm nae ruining the surprise, but Ravenna told me how much ye like the garden view so I'm taking ye somewhere even better."

"Better than the garden? Oh, you definitely have my interest now. Let's go then."

Torquil ran through the bailey, and everyone looked surprised when the boy stopped in front of Kat. "Do ye mind if I come along?"

"You want to come with us?" Kat's eyes lit up. "Ravenna?"

"Of course he can come with us."

The stable master brought out the saddled horses, all of them fine-looking mounts. Ruairi and Ravenna led the way, followed by Kat, Torquil, and Grace. After they passed under the portcullis, Grace shifted her rump in the saddle and looked back at Ravenna's home. She couldn't help but sigh at the impressive sight.

What a formidable castle, with its round turrets and square watchtower. To her left were the steep cliffs and to her right was the lush forest. Ruairi's vast home was a bit staggering since Grace was more accustomed to her smaller manor house, but there was something definitely warm and enchanting here that her sister favored. Grace could almost see why—almost.

She turned back around, smiling to see Torquil in deep conversation with Kat. The boy wasn't as skittish as he had been before, even riding by her sister's side instead of fleeing the other way. Perhaps Kat wouldn't be so determined to stalk the laird's son if the boy paid her some attention.

The sound of thundering hoofbeats came from behind, hard and fast. When Grace looked over her shoulder, her eyes narrowed, and her lips puckered with annoyance. "Bloody hell."

"My apologies that I'm late. Ye didnae miss me too much, did ye, Grace?" Fagan had the nerve to smile.

## *Four*

FAGAN STOOD ON THE BEACH AND WATCHED THE ocean waves lap onto the sandy shore. The warm breeze whipped his hair against his cheek, and the sun bathed his face. He smiled as Torquil chased Kat around in the sand, their gentle laughter tinkling through the air. Ruairi and Ravenna sat on a blanket while Elizabeth ambled along the edge of the water. Grace had taken off her boots, lifted her skirts in her hands, and waded in the sea up to her knees.

When she turned and gazed over her shoulder, Fagan cleared his throat. For a brief moment, he had almost forgotten that the lass was Ravenna's sister. Wisps of hair framed Grace's face and brownish-gold ringlets curled on her forehead. She was a slim, wild beauty, even more so when he overlooked her obstinate behavior and venomous tongue. The way the sun cast her in rays of light made her look ethereal, reminding him of a water goddess, as if she commanded the vast sea itself.

Fagan turned on his heel, pulling a piece of dried beef from his sack before he lost his wits. He sat down on his blanket and tossed a piece of meat into his mouth. Torquil walked toward him with Kat, and they sat beside him.

"What can we do now?"

"Lad, ye have an entire beach and the sea all to yourself." When he glanced over Torquil's shoulder, Grace had her eyes closed and her face lifted toward the sun. "Lady Grace looks verra warm. Mayhap she needs to cool off, eh?" He winked at the boy, and seeing the amusement in Torquil's eyes, Fagan laughed. "Donna tell her I sent ye her way. She'll have my head. That means ye too, Kat."

The little girl raised her fingers to her lips to stay a giggle. "I won't."

"Come on, Kat. Let's devise a way to sneak up on her so she doesnae see us."

Fagan leaned back on his elbows and couldn't wait to see Grace get ruffled once more. At least this time he would not be the object of her displeasure. As Torquil and Kat stealthily made their way behind their unsuspecting victim, Fagan didn't even try to mask his smile. The two of them hastily cupped handfuls of water, soaking Princess Grace. He wasn't certain if it was the first, second, or the third time that Torquil and Kat's hands went in the water, but he knew it was only a matter of time before Grace lost her collectedness.

Just as Fagan had expected, the lass screamed and jumped.

"How dare you!" Grace whipped around, and a sudden chill hung on the edge of her words.

Fire lit her eyes in a sparkling display. Fagan jumped to his feet to come to Torquil and Kat's aid, but then he paused when the woman did something unexpected. She dropped her skirts in the water and her smile deepened to laughter. She cupped handfuls of water and tossed them right back at Torquil and Kat.

"Nay! Nay!"

"What's the matter, Torquil? You don't like to get a little wet?" When Katherine started to retreat out of the water, Grace grabbed the girl from behind. "And just where do you think you're going, Sister? Oh no, you don't."

Kat kicked in the water as Grace lifted her sister from her feet. "Stop, Grace! Stop!"

"But it's all right when you get me wet, eh?"

"It wasn't my idea! It was Fagan! It was Fagan!"

Torquil placed his hands on his hips. "Kat, ye werenae supposed to say that! Ye gave your word. Fagan will be cross with ye."

And that's the moment when Fagan realized he'd been sold out by a wee lassie with a big heart and a big smile.

❧

"I heard that I have you to thank for this." Grace grabbed a blanket from her mount. She was attempting to pat her hair dry while Fagan rested his arm on the saddle, trying to mask a smile.

"Ye seemed to enjoy yourself before ye found out I was the cause."

"Please don't misunderstand me, Mister Murray. The children do not bother me. *You* bother me. Why are you even here? Why aren't you out protecting Ruairi's lands or doing whatever it is you do?"

His eyes narrowed. "Ruairi is my laird. I go everywhere he goes. 'Tis my duty."

"A pity the poor man cannot even relieve himself alone."

"Ye're verra amusing."

"Contrary to what you might think, I am not here for your amusement."

He clenched his mouth tighter, and then he looked away from her. "I see Torquil and wee Katherine are getting along now. Mayhap ye can learn something from your nine-year-old sister."

Grace didn't miss the heavy sarcasm that dripped from his voice. How could she? She waited for him to look her in the eye. "Perhaps when you cease acting like a twelve-year-old boy, Mister Murray, you and I will get along just fine." She brushed past him, poking her elbow into his gut on the way by. "Pray excuse me."

As Grace approached her sister, Ravenna glanced up from the blanket. Ruairi sat beside her, leaning back on his elbows. "Please tell me you're not sparring again with Fagan." There was a strong hint of censure in Ravenna's voice.

"Of course not. What is there to spar about? That would mean I actually cared what the man thought of something."

When her brother-in-law chuckled, Grace had an underlying feeling that he was mocking her. "Pardon, Ruairi?"

Ravenna mumbled under her breath to her husband, and he gave his wife an appeasing nod in return. He fingered the material of his kilt as if he were trying to contain himself and hid a smile.

"Och, it wasnae anything of importance."

"I was wondering if I could have a moment alone with my sister." Ruairi was about to stand when Grace held out her hand to stay him. "Please don't get up. Ravenna, why don't you walk with me along the beach?"

"All right." Her sister stood, brushing down her skirts and shaking the sand from her day dress. She gazed down at her husband. Without warning, he reached up, smacking Ravenna on the bottom with the palm of his hand.

"Donna be too long, Wife."

When his eyes darkened like a summer storm, Grace grabbed her sister by the arm and led her away from her kilted husband. And to think she'd believed the wooing part of a relationship was over the instant someone was wed. The way Ravenna and Ruairi continued to behave, she'd begun to think they were an exception to that rule.

As Grace walked along the edge of the shore with her sister, her steps slowed and she moved her feet away from the water. She wasn't sure why, because she was already wet from being targeted by two little miscreants. She glanced at Ravenna, who looked as if her thoughts were off in some distant land.

"Marriage suits you."

Ravenna's smile broadened further. "I'd like to think so."

"I never thought I'd say this, but I believe this is where you're meant to be. You've spent far too much time being concerned about us, trying to care for everyone around you but yourself. This is your time to enjoy your life. You deserve happiness, and I'm glad you've found it with Ruairi, even if your life is now here in the Highlands." She made every effort not to crinkle her nose.

"Thank you for your kind words. You know how much I love you and the girls with all my heart, but being with Ruairi... I never realized there was something missing until I found it." She shook her head. "I'm sorry. Here I am prattling on like some silly chit, and I'm sure you know exactly what I mean because you feel the same way about Daniel."

"I was hoping to steal you away for a moment to talk to you about something."

"Of course. What do you want to talk about?"

Grace stopped and smoothed her hair as it whipped in her face. "I'm concerned for Elizabeth."

Ravenna sighed. "You don't think Elizabeth and Kat will like it here. I thought we talked about this. They only need time."

"Oh, no, it's nothing like that. Our sister told me that since you're wed and I'm soon to be, she knows she's next."

"Elizabeth shouldn't be worried over such things. Ruairi and I aren't going to make marriage arrangements for her anytime soon. She's fifteen. She has plenty of time."

"And I told her the same, but it seems our dear sister has come to fancy one of these Highland men."

Ravenna stared at Grace with astonishment. "What? *Who?* Please don't tell me she favors Fagan. That would be awkward."

"I don't think you have to worry about that. It's

not your husband's captain she favors." Grace lifted
a brow.

"If not Fagan, then who?"

"Laird Munro."

Ravenna's voice rose in surprise. "*Ian?*"

As her sister spotted Elizabeth walking alone on
the beach, Grace watched the play of emotions on
Ravenna's face. Grace was relieved to see that her
sister suffered from the same distress she did.

"What are we going to do?" asked Grace.

"I need a moment to think about your words
because I still can't believe them. Ian. I don't know if
they've ever said two words to each other." Ravenna
pulled back the hair that blew across her lips. "She's
only fifteen, and Ian is around Ruairi's age."

"Yes, I know. He's old."

"My husband is only thirty, and I suppose you've
forgotten that I'm twenty-six. You must think me old
as well."

Grace shrugged. "You did wait until you were
twenty-six to wed. I thought perhaps you were going
to die an old spinster."

"How refreshing," Ravenna said dryly.

"What are we going to do?"

"Nothing. I'm sure whatever Elizabeth is feeling
will pass. Furthermore, I don't think Ian has any
intention of paying Ruairi another visit anytime soon,
especially with all of us women under one roof. I tend
to think we frighten the men."

"With good reason, but Elizabeth was not my
only concern. We need to talk about Kat. She's been
following around that poor boy relentlessly. Between

you and Ruairi, Elizabeth and Laird Munro, Kat and the laird's son, I don't know what's wrong with all of you. It's as if you all suffer from the same Scottish ailment. I seem to be the only Walsingham sister left with any sense," Grace scoffed. "Don't you think that our mother and father raised us with higher standards than what these men have to offer?"

"Grace…"

She held up her hands in mock defense. "I know. I'll try to hold my tongue. I just do not understand why you would choose these *Highlanders* over a peer of the realm."

"That's not how love works."

Grace didn't feel like being the recipient of another of Ravenna's haughty lectures so she quickly changed the subject. "What are we going to do about Kat?"

"She's young and close to Torquil's age. This is all new to her, and I'm certain once she becomes more content here, she'll leave him alone. I'm sure she only wants a friend since she's left hers behind."

"I suppose you're right. I told Ruairi's captain the same."

"Good. Everything is settled then."

Grace folded her arms over her chest. "Not quite. I want to know when you're going to teach me more because I have every intention of speaking to Uncle Walter when I return home. I want to do this. I want to be a spy for the Crown."

❧

While the masses were gathered to return to the castle, Fagan grabbed the mounts and led them over.

Ruairi assisted Ravenna, and then he lifted Kat and Torquil onto their horses. Fagan helped Elizabeth, but when he turned to aid Grace, she held up her hand to stay him.

"I don't need your assistance. I can do it myself."

He backed away from her with raised hands. "Ye donna need to tell me twice."

Fagan swung his leg over his mount and waited for the Sutherland-Walsingham brood to depart. He trailed behind, following everyone up the sandy trail. When Angus darted onto the path from the field, Ravenna promptly removed both feet from the stirrups, lifting her legs onto her horse's neck.

"Ravenna, what are you doing?" asked Grace.

Ruairi looked over his shoulder and groaned. "Donna ask."

"I'm not giving Angus a chance to bite my feet."

"I thought the two of ye were now friends," said Fagan.

"And I believed you would've been over this foolish fear by now," said Grace. "It's been years since that dog bit you."

"I'm not afraid of dogs," said Kat.

"Angus isnae a dog. He's a wolf," said Torquil.

Ruairi raised his voice. "I've already learned that nay matter what ye say to my wife, words donna make any difference. She will do and believe what she wants."

"Of course she will. She is a Walsingham," said Grace, her voice laced with pride.

"So that explains everything," said Fagan under his breath.

Grace turned in the saddle and glared at him. "You do realize that I heard you, Mister Murray."

"And I heard ye, *bhana-phrionnsa*." He lowered his voice and gave her a roguish grin. "Fagan."

She whipped around in the saddle and tossed her locks over her shoulder in a defiant gesture. He suddenly had the impression this was going to be the longest month of his life.

They entered the bailey, not soon enough for Fagan, and he couldn't decide if he wanted to eat in the great hall or seek solace behind the closed doors in Ruairi's study with a tankard of ale in one hand. The latter would provide better company, but he knew Ruairi would chide him if he started making sudden disappearances from the clan.

As the lasses and Torquil went to their chambers to change their wet clothes, Fagan sat with Ruairi on the dais in the great hall. The tables below were filled with a score of Sutherland men and women, and for a blessed moment, the clan was back to the way it had been before the Walsingham sisters arrived and everything went awry.

"I think I'm going to ride out to the border after we sup," said Fagan.

Ruairi nodded. "To escape or truly check on the border?"

"Both."

"At least we nay longer have to fear the Gordon will be raising havoc, and Stewart and the Seton clan will nae be paying us a visit anytime soon, thanks to my wife."

"Aye, now if only we can keep the English at bay."

"Fagan, will you please stop with your references to the English?" Ravenna kissed Ruairi on the cheek, and Fagan stood. "There is no rule that you can't sit by my husband for the meal. Sit. I am perfectly capable of sitting by my English sisters, the enemy."

As she stepped around Fagan, Ruairi smacked his arm, gesturing for him to say something,

"Ravenna, ye know my words werenae meant for ye or your sisters—well, one sister mayhap, but nae ye."

She sighed. "That makes me feel so much better, Fagan. Thank you."

While Ravenna dismissed him, Kat, Elizabeth, Grace, and Torquil came into the great hall and sat down at the table. Fagan once again took his seat and cast Ruairi a helpless look. "I nay longer think I'm safe within my home."

"Arse."

Fagan shrugged.

"Ye already had one of them blacken your eye. Have ye nae learned a lesson? My wife even warned ye this morn. Learn to keep your mouth shut."

"As I said, my laird, after the meal I will ride out to the border."

"Will you take me along with you?"

Fagan's eyes widened as everyone looked at Grace.

When no one responded, she added, "I'd love to see your lands, Ruairi. If they're anything like the view from the garden wall or from the beach, I'm sure they're magnificent. Would you mind if I came along?"

Fagan received a swift kick to the shin from Ruairi

under the table. "Umm…nay, I wouldnae mind if ye came along, but I will nae be gone for long. Are ye sure ye want to—" When his shin ached from another hearty blow from his laird's foot, he quickly said, "We'll leave right after we sup."

❧

Grace wasn't sure why she asked what she did, but she wanted to see more of Ruairi's lands. She knew she could've asked her brother-in-law or Ravenna to escort her. But the arrogant captain was going to be her escort the whole way to England so she figured they both could survive the short jaunt to the border. When the meal was finished, Ravenna leaned in close.

"Are you sure you know what you're doing? You said you didn't want anything to do with Fagan, and with the way you've been speaking to him, I don't think he wants anything to do with you."

"Don't worry. Blood will not be shed. Although if there was, I'm sure your husband would have another fine tapestry made." When her sister's mouth clenched tighter, Grace said, "I wanted to see more of Ruairi's lands, and his captain was already riding out to the border. There is nothing more than that."

"Are ye ready?"

When Grace stood and brushed down her skirts, she didn't miss it when Ravenna lowered her voice to speak to Ruairi. "Do you think this is a good idea?"

Rather than wait for her brother-in-law's response, Grace walked with Fagan out into the courtyard. Neither one of them spoke, not that she was surprised.

The air was cooler than it had been that afternoon, but she had spent the day in a damp dress. He opened the door to the stable and she followed him.

At least twenty-five horses lined the stalls, their heads all turned toward her. Some of the animals pawed at the ground while others whinnied. There were huge wooden beams overhead and the smell of hay engulfed her senses. When she let out a loud sneeze, some of the horses shied, banging the wooden planks of their enclosures in response.

Fagan came out of a room with a saddle in hand

"Should we call for a stable hand?" she asked.

"Nay. I can saddle our mounts. 'Tis time for the stable hands to sup. We will nae take them away from their meal."

She approached him as he opened one of the stall doors and walked in. "Thank you for taking me with you. The beach was lovely." She was unable to see him past the massive brown horse he saddled, but she heard him grunt in response. "I talked to Ravenna about Kat and Torquil. I think it helped that Torquil came with us to the beach today."

"I said the same to Ruairi."

"Yes, well, we seem to have fixed the problem with my sister and the laird's son, Mister Murray."

He stepped out of the stall and patted the horse on the neck. He didn't look at her, didn't say anything in response, and she watched his broad back as it disappeared into the room again. While Grace stood in silence, she wrung her hands in front of her. After a few moments, he emerged with another saddle in hand and she quickly moved to get out of his way. The way he was behaving, she didn't think he would've waited for her to step aside.

While Fagan saddled the second mount, Grace ambled down the center aisle, studying the horses that lined the stalls. They stood tall and sturdy. She didn't know much about animals, but to her, they all looked like prize horseflesh. When she turned and made her way back to the stalls, the saddled mounts were no longer there. The beastly man couldn't even tell her that he was ready to depart.

She walked out and closed the stable door behind her. Fagan stood by the mounting block. "You could've told me you were waiting. I was only looking at the horses." She took a deep breath and knew she shouldn't have been so hostile toward him, but the man drove her completely mad. When she approached him, his steely gaze met hers.

"Earlier on the beach, ye didnae want my help. Do ye need my Scottish hands to assist ye, *bhana-phrionnsa*, or are ye capable of placing your English arse in the saddle yourself?"

# *Five*

LEAVES RUSTLED IN THE WIND. THE SUTHERLAND lands were beautiful with lush foliage, rocky cliffs, and mossy-green grass. The sky above had hues of purple and orange, and there was no other place Fagan would rather be. He never minded riding out to the border for that reason alone. For a slight moment, he had even forgotten Grace was with him because she'd been silent ever since they'd departed from the gates.

She sat on her mount, and her head whipped from left to right. "I find myself rendered speechless."

He had a quip ready on the tip of his tongue, but after his last remark about Grace's English behind, he decided he'd better heed Ruairi and Ravenna's advice and keep his mouth shut if he didn't want more trouble.

"How long have these lands been in the Sutherland clan?"

Fagan had heard Ruairi spin the tale of Sutherland clan history more times than he could count, and the lass had an eager look on her face. Perhaps she was interested in hearing a bit of history. When he hesitated and met her gaze, she nodded for him to talk.

"By the early tenth century, Norsemen had conquered the islands of Shetland and Orkney, as well as Caithness and Sutherland on the mainland. The Norse had control over Scotland beyond Moray Firth. The lower portion of the lands was called 'Suderland' because it was south of the Norse islands and Caithness. Ruairi and I share a common ancestor." When he noticed her eyes glazing over, he asked, "Do ye want me to continue?"

"Yes, please. I'm interested to hear about Ravenna's new family."

"A Flemish nobleman named Freskin de Moravia was commissioned by the king—David the First—to clear the Norse from the lands. De Moravia was a legend in his time, having killed the last breathing Norseman in Scotland. Some years later, the Sinclairs rebelled against the Bishop of Caithness over tithes he imposed, and once again, the Sutherland clan was charged with restoring law and order. These lands have been in the hands of the Sutherland clan for centuries. Ruairi's clan descends from Freskin de Moravia's eldest grandson, Hugh de Moravia, whereas the Murrays descend from the youngest grandson, William de Moravia."

"You must be very proud. Do you ride out here often?"

"My men make their rounds along the border."

"What's over that mountain pass? Can we go up there?"

"Nay. This is far enough. The lands beyond that field arenae our own."

She nodded. "Are they Laird Gordon's?"

"Gordon?"

"I thought I heard Laird Munro mention something about him. Perhaps I was mistaken. I had assumed the Gordons were a neighboring clan. Was Laird Gordon at the wedding? I don't remember meeting him."

"Nay. The Gordon is dead." Fagan wasn't going to tell her about the father of Ruairi's first wife. He also believed it unwise to mention that the land where Grace's mount now stood had been the site of a bloody battle between the Sutherlands and the Gordons not all that long ago.

"So who owns the lands beyond the mountain pass, Laird Munro?"

"Nay. They belong to the Gunns. Ian's lands are farther south."

Grace mumbled under her breath, but loud enough for Fagan to hear. "Let's hope they're far enough south that a certain someone won't decide to cross them."

"Lady Elizabeth mayhap?"

Grace glanced down at her reins, twirling the leather straps between her fingers. "Elizabeth? Why would you say that?"

"I think ye already know the answer to that question." He didn't miss it when Grace suddenly turned her head and promptly changed the subject.

"Do you mind if we stay here for a moment? There's so much heather in the field. I'd like to walk around."

"Nay, I donna mind." He dismounted, and by the

time he moved in front of his horse, Grace's feet were already planted on the ground. "If ye want to walk, give me your horse. I'll hold him for ye."

"Thank you." She handed Fagan the reins, spun on her heel, and was gone before he could say another word.

⁂

Grace stood in the middle of the field of heather, the skies lovely shades of purple, orange, and yellow. She needed a moment away from Fagan. How could the man know Elizabeth pined after Laird Munro? Was it *that* apparent? She caught herself glancing uneasily over her shoulder. Fagan had tied off the mounts and was walking toward her. She had a sneaking suspicion he was going to question her further and was uncomfortable with his ability to uncover her thoughts.

"For someone who hates the Highlands as much as ye do, ye seem to enjoy yourself."

"Oh, I do not hate the Highlands, Mister Murray. The people are rather questionable, but the lands are very beautiful."

"Is it true then? Is Lady Elizabeth trying to shackle Ian?"

Even though he spoke the truth, Grace wasn't daft enough to admit it. Girding herself with resolve, she kept her voice firm and final. "My sister is only fifteen. Why would she need to shackle anyone? Besides, she is beautiful and smart. She can have any man she desires. Why would she want someone like Laird Munro when there are plenty of English lords for her choosing?"

"I donna know, lass. 'Tis why I asked ye."

Grace straightened herself with dignity and smoothed her skirts. "Understand this… Elizabeth is a Walsingham, and we Walsinghams chase no man."

"Aye, well, I'll be sure to tell that to Torquil the next time I see him."

"We should return before the sun sets." Grace stepped around the wall that was Fagan. She started to walk back to the horses without him when a hand snaked around her waist. Suddenly, she found herself facing a very broad chest.

"The sun will nae set for another hour."

"What is it you want from me, and why do you *insist* on plaguing me at every turn?"

He boldly met her eyes. "Why is it ye always walk away from me when ye donna like what I have to say?"

She lifted a brow. "Pardon?"

"Donna be coy with me. Ye understand my words."

She huffed. "I don't like you, Mister Murray."

"So ye've said many times before, *bhana-phrionnsa*."

She gave him a hostile glare and clenched her teeth. "Will you quit calling me that?"

"Why? What are ye going to do? Punch me in the face again?" His expression was tight with strain, and he stood so close that she could feel his breath on her face.

"You are nothing but an arrogant, beastly excuse for a man and—"

Her last words were smothered because Fagan's mouth covered hers with a savage intensity that startled her. The punishment of his lips on hers made her knees tremble. Her emotions whirled and skidded. She couldn't think. She couldn't breathe. Her wild-beating heart was the only sound audible.

*Oh, bloody hell.*

Grace couldn't miss the musky smell of him as he pulled her closer. His hands locked against her ribs like steel bindings. She tried not to think about how hard and warm his body was against hers. When she felt blood surge from her fingertips the whole way to her toes, she knew this had to be a sin to feel so good.

His mouth did not become softer as he kissed her. His kiss was punishing, angry. He forced her lips open with his thrusting tongue, and she'd never felt more alive. She lifted her arms around his neck, and his long hair brushed her cheek. She could swear she felt the fierce pounding of his heart against hers, and she suddenly became deeply conscious of the heavy rise and fall of her chest against his.

God help her. She willingly complied. She knew she should deter his advances, but the passion between them consumed all thought. She returned his kiss with growing confidence, matching the thrust and parry of his tongue. What was wrong with her? She couldn't get enough. She succumbed all right, and she didn't do it in half measure but with fervor.

For some odd reason, she had no desire to back out of his embrace. She knew she should. This wasn't right. The kiss had to be so wrong. As if reality slowly crept back in, she arched her body against him, seeking to get free.

She pulled back and her mouth burned with fire.

She panted between slightly parted lips. "How. Dare. You. Kiss. Me." Then, in one forward motion, she grasped his jaw and reclaimed his lips with hers.

He crushed her against him, kissing her with no mercy. Without warning, he lifted his head and they parted by mere inches. "I. Donna. Like. English. Women." His voice was low and rough, as if he were in pain. With a primal growl, he lowered his lips to hers again, and she was made to endure the cruel ravishment of Fagan's mouth.

Her wild frenzy only seemed to increase his. He caressed her lips with demanding mastery. The harder and deeper he kissed her, the more she wanted. Grace had never dreamed a kiss from any man would feel like this.

Her hands explored the breadth of his shoulders and his powerful muscled chest. He was raw, primitive. He was a Highlander in every sense of the word and form. When an innocent moan escaped her, he pulled back.

There was a heavy silence.

Fagan disturbed her in every way. She knew an attraction to him would be perilous, but the idea sent her spirits soaring. As his gaze traveled over her face, she glanced down, pulling herself away from her ridiculous preoccupation with his emerald eyes. He lifted her chin gently with his finger, and his breathing was heavy.

"'Tis foolish for an English lass to fall in love with a Highlander. I donna want to see Elizabeth hurt."

Grace detected a thawing in his tone. She nodded, almost forgetting he was speaking of Elizabeth. "I thought the same."

"There could ne'er be anything between them."

"I know," she whispered.

He dropped his hand and cleared his throat. "Good. Now that that's settled, I'll get the mounts."

✺

Fagan was mindless with lust. It had taken all of his strength to pull away from Grace. He wasn't sure where he came up with the brilliant idea to kiss her, when all he had really wanted was for her to hold her tongue. He was tired of her and her raging ire toward him. When he had enough sense to stop kissing her, he felt humbled just looking at her. She'd given him the greatest of gifts.

Grace had been completely honest in her response to him.

He grabbed the reins to the mounts before he lost all sense of reason. She slowly approached him, and he didn't ask for permission before he had lifted her onto her horse. In that uncomfortable moment, she couldn't look him in the eye, and he wasn't sure what he would've said to her if she had.

They rode back to the castle without a spoken word between them. The sun had started to set, and before long, light would be lost. Fagan hoped it would be dark enough soon to mask the troubled expression that he knew crossed his brow, because he'd begun to wonder just what he wanted from Grace. When he quickly stole a glance, a look of tired sadness passed over her face. Her glowing, youthful happiness had faded. He knew he was the cause and that unsettled him.

They rode into the bailey, and as soon as the stable

hand took away their mounts, Grace approached Fagan. Uncertainty crept into her expression, and for a brief moment he was surprised she didn't flee.

"Thank you for taking me with you. Ruairi's lands are beautiful."

"As are ye, Grace." He wasn't sure why he said the words, but he wanted to see her smile return. He needed to bring her bright eyes back to the way they were before he snuffed out the light.

She looked up at him with an effort. Her voice was low, soft. "I don't understand what happened. What was that between us?"

Fagan paused. "I donna know, but we know it cannae happen again. 'Tis more than likely best nae to discuss it."

She waved him off. "Of course. I don't know what I was thinking. The kiss meant nothing." She choked on her words and spun on her heel as he reached out to stay her.

"Grace…"

He was too late. She was gone, and he was an idiot.

Fagan took his sorry self into the great hall where Ruairi and Torquil sat at a table. Only a few clan members remained, most of them having taken their leave for the eve. Ruairi looked up and greeted Fagan with a brief nod.

"How far did ye go?"

Fagan stared, speechless.

"How far did ye ride? I thought I'd have to send the men out to find ye."

He sat beside Ruairi on the bench. "We rode to the border."

"And blood wasnae shed?"

"Nay."

"And Lady Grace is still alive and whole?"

Fagan rolled his eyes. "Aye. We are both verra much hale."

"I'm glad to hear it. There may be some hope for the both of ye yet."

"What are ye and Torquil doing? I thought ye'd be with your lady wife."

Ruairi folded his arms and leaned on the table. "Torquil is drawing a picture of the beach for Lady Katherine. I think all his studies with Ravenna in the library have uncovered a hidden talent. Who knew we had an artist in the Sutherland clan?"

"'Tis verra good, Torquil." Fagan gave Ruairi a brotherly punch in the arm. "But I would think twice before ye tell his secret to the women. Before ye know it, they'll have your tapestries down and replaced with Torquil's drawings."

"My tapestries? Why? What's wrong with them?"

Torquil looked up from his project. "The lasses donna like the scenes of war and battle. They say there's too much blood and death on your walls. They want flowers or something of the like."

"Flowers? And how do ye know that?" asked Ruairi.

"They donna think I listen, but I do. Ravenna and Grace talk about the wall hangings all the time." For a brief moment, the boy looked deep in thought. "Well, mostly Grace talks and Ravenna listens." When he resumed his purpose, Ruairi and Fagan chuckled.

"I'll leave ye two to your task then."

Fagan stood and made his way to his chamber. He wanted to be alone to forget every single detail of Grace's face, and he needed time so that his blood no longer rushed from unbidden memories of holding her, touching her. And if that didn't work, he'd stay confined within the walls of his chamber until he could figure out what the hell was wrong with him.

✸

Grace moaned when she heard the knock on her door. "Kat, you and Elizabeth were placed in a separate chamber for a reason."

The door opened and Ravenna walked in. "It's only me." She closed the door behind her and sat on the edge of the bed. "You're already in bed?"

"For being a spy for the king, you're not very observant. Tell me. What gave me away?"

"You're certainly in a foul mood. Is everything all right? Did Fagan return with you, or did you leave him out there somewhere in an unmarked grave?"

Grace tried to suppress a sigh. "Everything was all right. Are the girls in bed too?"

"Kat was falling asleep at the table. She's in her chamber now, and Elizabeth's in the library."

"I thought you'd be with Ruairi."

Her sister's eyes lit up at the mention of her husband's name. "He and Torquil are doing something in the great hall. Are you sure you're all right? You look flushed."

Grace punched the lumps out of her pillow and tried not to picture Fagan's face. "Don't be ridiculous.

I'm fine. Do you think we can set up a few targets on the morrow? I'd like you to teach me to throw my blade so that I can actually hit something for a change."

"Why do you want to practice throwing your dagger?"

"You know how to throw a blade proficiently, and I need to be able to defend myself when I work for the king."

Ravenna's face clouded with uneasiness. "Yes, but if I recall correctly, you seemed to do very well with your fist when you rammed it into Fagan's eye. Besides, I value my life. I've seen you throw your dagger, remember?"

"You're very amusing, Sister."

"We'll see. I'll leave you alone to get some sleep." Ravenna rose.

"I'll see you in the morning."

The door closed, and Grace nestled deeper into the blankets. She felt empty. She knew she and Fagan had gone too far, but that did not stop her from feeling a dull ache at the thought of him. Her face burned as she remembered his mouth on hers. His face still haunted her, smiling, serious, wanting nothing more than she was able to give.

For heaven's sake, she was betrothed. What kind of woman had she become to give in so easily to wanton desires? Fagan was a Scot, everything she was born to despise. And what about Daniel? If Fagan opened his bloody mouth, Daniel would never wed her and her chances of becoming Lady Grace Casterbrook would be null. She didn't understand how she had come so close to ruining her entire life in one heated moment.

She tried to dismiss the mocking voice inside that wondered why she had done something so terrible. Fagan hated the English, and now she'd given him reason to believe that she could act like a harlot. For a brief moment, she wondered how she compared to his other conquests—then chided herself.

Why was she having such thoughts? She shouldn't be. She. Was. Betrothed. She needed to remember that. Her last thought before she drifted to sleep was that Fagan was nothing more than a rogue, another arrogant Highlander who thought he was so much better than the English.

When Grace rose in the morning, she welcomed a new day. She washed her face, donned her day dress, and combed her hair, determined not to let her momentary lapse in judgment interfere with her sanity. She walked through the halls and studied the portraits, shook her head at the tapestries, and then descended the stairs to the great hall. She needed to keep herself busy.

Everyone was already seated on the dais, and Fagan didn't bother to look up from his trencher. She sat down next to Elizabeth and pasted a bright smile on her face.

"How are you this morning, Elizabeth?"

"I'm well, and you?" Her sister finished what was left of her biscuit.

"Ravenna and I are going to set up targets this morn. Perhaps you'd like to come along. She's going to show me how to perfect my aim with my blade."

Grace leaned forward, gazing down at the other end of the table. "Mister Murray, I'd like to try my luck with some moving targets. Would you like to stand in?"

The conversation at the table fell silent, and Grace heard Ravenna sigh.

# Six

FAGAN DIDN'T SAY A WORD. HE HAD KNOWN OF THE fiery passion that lay within Grace from the first time he'd met her, but now, any desire she'd felt for him was snuffed out like a candle in the rain. And in no time at all, she'd managed to fill that void with her disapproval of him again. Not that he blamed her. He would've expected the type of behavior he'd shown from one of those English curs she so blatantly admired, but not from him. He continued to chide himself for his poor judgment.

When everyone had left the table except for Ruairi, his friend cleared his throat. "What the hell is the matter with ye? Ye look like a whipped dog."

Fagan lifted a brow and ran his finger along the rim of his tankard. "Aye, well, I did something I'm nae verra proud of and I'm trying to think of a way to mend it."

Ruairi sat back in the chair and studied Fagan intently. "What did ye say to Grace now? Ye do realize that everything ye do or say to the lass will be told to my wife. Ravenna will continue to hound me if she doesnae approve, and I will ne'er hear the end of it. Now is the time that I'm supposed to be enjoying my wife in my bed. How can I do that if all the lass wants to do is speak of ye and what ye did or said to her sister?"

There was no way Fagan was daft enough to open his mouth to his friend, and he couldn't overlook the fact that Ruairi was his liege. Fagan was aware he'd have to pray long and hard that Grace wouldn't mention their little indiscretion to Ravenna because God only knew what the English spy would do to him once she found out. More to the point, he didn't think Ruairi would be in a very forgiving mood either.

"I might've said something about Grace placing her English arse in the saddle."

Ruairi chuckled and then hastily tried to mask his expression with a frown. "Fagan…"

"What can I say to that? The lass seems to know exactly how to fire my…ire." He was about to say "blood" and caught himself at the last possible moment.

"Be that as it may, she will only be here for a few more weeks. Can ye nae keep the peace until then?"

Fagan rolled his head from side to side. "If I must."

"Come. Let us practice swordplay with the men."

Ruairi and Fagan walked into the bailey. The sun's rays managed to make an occasional appearance between the gray clouds, but at least it was not raining. About a score of men had already started to gather against the northern wall. Perhaps this was just what Fagan needed to banish Princess Grace from his mind. And if that didn't work, he'd let Ruairi beat the foolishness out of him.

Fagan unsheathed his sword and stood at the edge of

the circle of men. He watched Ruairi best two of his guards with minimal effort. When the last man stepped out of the circle defeated, Fagan entered. He twisted his sword arm, cutting through the air in front of him.

"Think ye can best me, my liege?"

Ruairi shrugged with indifference and walked up to Fagan with a grin of amusement. "It wouldnae be the first time, nor will it be the last."

When the men chuckled in response, Fagan lifted his sword casually and studied the edge of the blade. "Mmm... I thought mayhap ye'd grown soft since ye said your vows. I know ye've been practicing your swordplay, my liege, but I donna think that particular sword will do ye any good here."

"Arse."

"Aye."

Fagan easily deflected Ruairi's blow as the sound of clashing metal rang throughout the bailey. When his heart raced, his blood pumped, and his senses came into full awareness, Fagan smiled easily. He took a deep breath and let the air fill his lungs. There were no women in sight, only men who beat each other senseless in the bailey. This was going to be a good day after all.

❧

When her sister conveniently disappeared after the meal, Grace was perfectly aware of what Ravenna was doing. And she didn't need to be a spy of the Crown to figure that one out on her own. After several unsuccessful attempts to thwart Grace from mastering spy craft, Ravenna had turned to avoiding her. But if

Ravenna believed for one moment that she'd be able to deter Grace from wanting to follow in her father and her sister's footsteps, she was a fool. All Grace really wanted to do right now was keep busy. And if that meant throwing a sharp blade at the targets as she pictured Fagan's face, so be it.

Grace found the unwilling Ravenna in the library and led her toward the courtyard.

"I told you before. I don't think any amount of practice will improve your aim. You've been trying this for years to no avail."

"In all fairness, you and Father never gave me a chance once you saw my aim was poor. And you know very well that I've never had as much instruction as you."

"All right, all right. You win." Ravenna stopped and pointed her finger at Grace. "But I'm giving you fair warning. The moment you cause me grief, I will no longer instruct you. Do you understand?"

Grace nodded. "I understand."

A look of discomfort crossed Ravenna's face as they turned and made their way silently through the halls. The quiet moment ended as soon as they walked into the courtyard and Grace heard a loud commotion against the far wall.

Men stood huddled around something neither she nor Ravenna could make out. The sound of clashing swords echoed through the air. From what Grace could decipher from the heavy Scottish accents, taunts were being thrown like stones. It sounded like there was a bloody battle in the bailey. Without hesitation, the sisters moved closer to the chaos.

The Sutherland guard encircled Ruairi and Fagan, who had swords drawn at the ready. Sweat glistened on their muscled forms and their bare chests heaved. Again to her surprise, Grace found herself drawn to only one man.

She knew she should've thought of Daniel, but she didn't. She couldn't. How could she when Fagan's kilt rode low on his lean hips and her mind suddenly burned with the memory of his hard body pressed against hers? She even had a hard time trying to keep her gaze riveted on the man's face. She tried. She truly did, but then she found her eyes moving slowly down his frame and dreamed once again of being crushed within his embrace. She made no attempt to hide that she was watching him, and then his gaze met hers.

The man looked like a warrior god sent from the heavens above. She was entranced and did not want to tear her attention away from him. He was so compelling, his magnetism so potent. Entranced by his strong chiseled jaw, emerald eyes, broad shoulders, and long flowing hair, she swore that her heart skipped a beat. Sweat beaded on his brow and his chest glistened. Her fingers just ached to touch him again.

When he looked at her enigmatically, she felt a shudder run through her. She turned her head away when Ravenna's gentle nudge brought her back from her woolgathering.

"Are you all right? They are only practicing their swordplay. You know they're not really fighting."

Grace heard herself swallow. "Pardon? Oh yes, let's go then." When she stole another glance at Fagan, he had resumed his sparring with Ruairi.

The mossy field was a lush, rich green, and the sound of ocean waves called to her in the distance. Grace took a deep breath as the smell of salt air and pine wafted through the air. When they approached the tree line, Ravenna bent down, pulling back the brush and uncovering a large piece of wood. She propped the target against a tree and brushed her hands together.

"That should do it. I used this to practice when Ruairi wanted to test my skill with my blade—before he found me out."

Grace dismissed her sister's snappish remark. "I assume you didn't hesitate to put him in his place, but then again, I don't know many men who can best you with a blade."

Ravenna shrugged. "I didn't want to do all that well, because then he would've been suspicious of me."

The sound of breaking branches came closer, and when Angus emerged from the woods, Ravenna froze. She spoke through gritted teeth. "Why can these animals always sense when you're not fond of them? He stalks me and no one else."

Grace waved her sister off. "He does this because you continue to act the way you do. Think of Angus as you should most men. Pay him no heed. When you dismiss him, he'll go away and leave you alone."

"That's what Ruairi said."

"Mmm… Then you should listen to me and your husband."

The wolf took a step toward them, and Ravenna placed her arms out in front of her. "Shoo, Angus!

Off with you!" Angus hesitated, and then the animal turned and walked toward the castle.

"Or you can just bellow at them."

Not paying any attention to Grace's comment, Ravenna walked back a few feet from the target. "Come stand right here."

"That's not very far away. You're not instructing Kat, you know."

"No, but you need to learn how to throw your blade first." Ravenna lifted her skirts and pulled out the dagger strapped to her leg while Grace did the same. "If you want to know all there is to know, I'll teach you." Ravenna held out her blade flat-handed as she gave pointed instruction with her other hand. "There are three types of blades: blade-heavy, hilt-heavy, and one that is equally balanced. Since you really haven't practiced, blade-heavy or hilt-heavy would work best. Fortunately, the blade you carry is hilt-heavy. My blade is equally balanced."

"All right, but how do I throw it?"

"Since your blade is hilt-heavy, you'll throw it by the blade." When Grace raised her arm with dagger in hand, Ravenna grabbed her forearm. "But before you're ready for that, we'll need to talk about your grip."

"I won't drop it."

Ravenna shook her head. "It's not that simple. You want a firm grip but also need to be able to maintain a delicate hold on your blade. Too much grip will hamper your release, while not enough might cause your dagger to fly out of your hand when you don't want it to."

"So how do I hold it?"

"Give me your blade." Grace handed Ravenna her dagger, and with a sudden flick of her wrist, her sister whipped the blade into the ground. "Now hold out the palm of your hand." Ravenna molded Grace's hand into place and then picked up the dagger from the ground and slid it into Grace's hand.

"You want the handle pointing away from you like this. Place the blunt edge of the blade into the crease you have created because you want the tip to line up with the bottom of your thumb. Now pinch the blade without pressing against the point or the sharpened edge."

"Like this?"

"Yes, exactly like that. Now turn around. You are fairly close to the target."

"Do you want me to move back?"

"No." Ravenna grabbed Grace's arm. "Bend your wrist back toward your forearm. The dagger will be able to turn over in the air more quickly. Now I want you to place your weight on your right leg and keep your left leg slightly forward. Be sure to keep the blade a safe distance away from your face so you don't cut yourself when you throw."

Grace rolled her eyes. "Can I just throw it already?"

"Grace… Now you're going to shift your weight from your right to the left leg at the same time you swing your forearm forward from the elbow so that your arm is straight out in front of you. At that point, you release your dagger." Ravenna stepped back. "Go ahead and aim."

Grace released her blade into the air and it landed in the tree, several feet above the target.

"It's important to remember to keep your entire movement fluid." Ravenna lifted her dagger and threw it dead center into the target. "Like that."

"So I see."

Grace walked over and pulled the daggers from the tree and the target. She returned Ravenna's blade and moved back to where she'd initially thrown hers. Grace gave her sister a brief nod. She turned and studied the target intently, trying to remember everything Ravenna had told her. She paid close attention to the way she held her blade, moved her body into the appropriate position, and lifted her dagger. When she felt ready, she tossed the blade at the target and let out a heavy sigh. At least the first time she'd managed to hit the darned tree. When she realized her dagger had missed the target and the tree entirely, she looked at her sister.

"Just try again, Grace."

Grace walked over to the target and looked next to the tree. Lifting her skirts, she turned her head over her shoulder. "It landed somewhere in the brush." With a carefully placed step, she walked into the heavy thicket, careful not to tear her day dress. She slid her boot along the ground in the hope she could feel her dagger. Behind her, she could hear the sound of her sister's blade as it hit the target with a thump, without a doubt dead center as it always was.

Not being able to see her dagger, Grace took a few more steps into the brush and spotted the hilt. She picked up the blade, and when she stood, she jumped. She couldn't help but place her hand over her heart to make sure the darned thing stayed put.

"What are you doing there? You startled me."

❧

Fagan's arm ached, his back pained him, and his muscles screamed from the strain of heavy swordplay. He and Ruairi had both refused to yield, his liege being just as—if not more—stubborn than he was. Only when it was time for the noon meal did both men agree there was no winner or loser. That was the only way either one of them would have stopped. As Fagan walked through the bailey with Ruairi, his friend lowered his voice.

"I didnae say anything in front of the men, but God's teeth, were ye trying to kill me?" Ruairi lifted his arm, pressing his shoulder and moving it around, at the same time Fagan rubbed his aching back.

"I could say the same to ye. My body feels as though 'twas through a bloody battle."

When they reached the great hall, about a score of clan members had already taken their seats for the meal. To Fagan's surprise, no one was seated yet on the dais. The sight pleased him because this day kept getting better and better. He couldn't help but wonder when his luck would run out.

They sat at the table, and Ruairi growled. "My wife is going to kill ye."

"Donna blame this all on me, my liege. Ye know I'm the better swordsman. Ye could have yielded some time ago. Ye're far too proud, Ruairi."

"Arse."

"Aye."

Their brief solace was interrupted by a wee lass with golden curls. "Ruairi, have you seen Ravenna or Grace?"

"I think they went for a walk. I'm sure they'll be back for the meal."

Kat sat down in the chair beside Fagan. "I saw you and Ruairi fighting in the bailey."

"We werenae fighting, lassie. 'Twas only a wee bit of swordplay."

She lifted a brow. "Why?"

If she'd folded her arms over her chest, Fagan would've sworn he was talking to a smaller version of Grace. "Ruairi and I have to maintain our skills to defend the castle. If we donna practice, we lose our skill and will nae be able to keep the clan safe."

"But I don't understand. Why would the two of you need to defend the castle? I know you have guards. Don't they do that for you?"

Fagan couldn't help but smile at Kat's innocent questions. He didn't want to give her all the details of what being a Highland captain entailed, but perhaps her curiosity would be satisfied with a bit of the truth. "I am the captain of the Sutherland guard and responsible for protecting Ruairi and this clan. I defend the castle with the guards. Do you understand now?"

She shrugged with indifference like someone else he knew. "I suppose."

"Where are Torquil and Elizabeth, Katherine?" asked Ruairi.

"Oh, Elizabeth was in her chamber, and Torquil and I were in the library."

"It makes me proud to see the two of ye getting along. Were ye reading together then?"

"No. After we saw you and Fagan draw swords on

each other in the bailey, Torquil and I were practicing swordplay of our own."

"What do ye mean ye were practicing swordplay of your own?"

"Torquil gave me my own sword and I was defending the castle too."

"And where did my son get this sword?"

Kat stared at the ceiling and tapped her finger to her lip. "Umm… I think he pulled one of the swords off the wall. Don't worry though. I knew it was far too big for me. Torquil used that sword and gave me one of the daggers."

# Seven

THE MAN WITH THE LONG, BLACK HAIR STOOD SILENTLY and stared back at Grace. He wore a black tunic and a dark-colored kilt, and he had a large scar over his left eye that traveled down the length of his jaw. Thank goodness he was one of Ruairi's men because she would've been frightened if she'd met him somewhere out on her own. When she repeated her question and asked him again what he was doing there, he turned and disappeared into the trees, but not before she spotted a shiny sword sheathed in a belt at his waist.

"Did you find it? Do you need my help?" asked Ravenna, calling to Grace in the distance.

Grace hesitated and only when she didn't see or hear any further sign of the man did she respond. "No, I found it! I'm coming!" She untangled her skirts from the brush and stepped into the clearing. She approached her sister, tapping the hilt of the dagger in her hand.

"Do you want to try again? I can help you with your stance."

Grace stood again in front of the target, and then

she looked at Ravenna. "Yes, but I need to say something first. I truly don't know how you're ever going to get used to these Highland men. I find them so odd."

"I've heard enough from you," Ravenna snapped. "You decided to stay to spend time with us, but all you've managed to do thus far is complain about Ruairi and his clan. He's a Highlander. Yes, he's different from us, Grace, but what did you expect? He's my husband. You're starting to insult me with your harsh words."

Grace placed her hand on her sister's shoulder. "Oh, Ravenna, I'm sorry. That's not what I meant at all. When I searched for my dagger in the woods, I saw one of Ruairi's guards there. I asked him what he was doing, and the man didn't even have the decency to respond. He just stood there staring at me like a dolt. Granted, the only one of Ruairi's men that I know is Fagan, but even he speaks when you ask him something—well, most of the time anyway."

Ravenna gazed at the tree line and spoke lightly. "I think that's enough instruction for today. Let's return to the castle. It's time for the noon meal anyway."

As they walked back to the castle, Grace could have sworn something was troubling Ravenna. Her sister kept stealing a glance at the woods and indiscreetly fingering the hilt of her blade through her skirts, which was a pretty good indication that Grace's instincts were right. Times like these made Grace wonder how Ravenna could've ever been a spy because her sister had seen Angus make his way back to the castle. The wolf was not in the woods, yet Ravenna continued to search for the animal, as if she waited for the beast to spring from the trees and attack her at any moment. And Ravenna didn't believe Grace had what it took to be a spy for the Crown! Grace was confident that she'd be mastering spy craft before her sister knew it.

When they entered the great hall, they both sensed something was wrong because Ruairi scowled, Elizabeth played with the food on her trencher, Fagan was quiet, and Kat and Torquil had their heads bowed.

"What's the matter?" asked Ravenna, taking her seat on the dais.

Ruairi took a drink from his tankard. His face was clouded with anger. "I think your sister and my son are now getting along too well. I donna know which is worse—Katherine giving chase to Torquil or having the two of them spar with each other in the library."

"Whatever do you mean?" When Ruairi took too long to respond, Ravenna looked at Kat for an explanation.

Ruairi cleared his throat. "Somebody saw Fagan and me in the bailey and decided to have a wee bit of sport." He shook his head. "While I practiced swordplay with the captain of my guard, Torquil practiced swordplay with your sister in the library. My son pulled a sword from the wall and gave Katherine a dagger to wield."

Grace couldn't stay the giggle that escaped her. When Ruairi's eyes met hers, she turned to Kat. "Kat, you know better than that, and you're not to take something without permission."

Kat folded her arms across her chest. "I didn't need to ask permission. Torquil gave it to me."

"And my son should've known better. One of ye could have been hurt."

"Aye, Da," said Torquil in an appeasing tone.

Ravenna gave Grace a knowing look, and Grace knew her sister had the same thought. They remembered when their father used to scold them for playing with his set of daggers in the study. Granted, no one was ever hurt, but getting into mischief had to be something that ran in the Walsingham family.

"I'm certain they meant no harm, Ruairi. They'll never do it again," said Grace. "Isn't that right, Kat and Torquil?"

The children both nodded at the same time. Grace had just turned back to her meal when she heard Ravenna whisper to Ruairi. *"Na bi fada."*

He looked over his shoulder and then back to his wife. "And where would I be going, lass?"

A heavy sigh escaped Ravenna. "That's not what I was trying to say. I'm never going to learn the Gaelic language." She lowered her voice again. "I need to talk with you."

"I'm finished with my meal. Do ye want to go to my study?"

Ravenna grabbed a biscuit from the table, stood, and turned to Grace. "I'll see you and the girls later."

Grace briefly wondered if that was secret code for her sister and brother-in-law to disappear and enjoy their nightly ritual in the middle of day. Grace closed her eyes and shuddered at the thought, pondering if Daniel would ever expect her to do such a thing.

"I'm finished too," said Kat.

As Torquil and Kat stepped away from the table,

Grace grabbed her sister's arm. "Be sure to stay away from sharp weapons on the walls."

"We know, Grace."

When Grace turned slightly, she caught Fagan staring at her. Her heart thumped erratically, but she managed to regard him with impassive coldness. She had to. She needed to shut out any awareness of him. The man had a way of muddling her thoughts every time he crossed her mind. She cleared her throat, pretending to be unaffected.

"You should've come with Ravenna and me, Elizabeth. I'm getting better with my aim."

Elizabeth lifted her eyes from her trencher. "Yes, I really should've taken a walk today, but I do find it hard to believe you've improved your aim so quickly. Where did you practice?"

"We set up a target in the field. Why?"

Elizabeth's eyes sparkled. "At least you weren't anywhere near the gardens. The poor blooms would've never survived your attempts for sure."

Fagan chuckled, but Grace didn't pay him any heed. "I can't wait to see how you do when Ravenna shows you how to wield a blade."

"I'm certain your sister will become more skillful, the more she practices, and one day be as skilled as Ravenna."

"One can always hope," said Elizabeth.

Grace barely heard Elizabeth's words because she was too stunned by Fagan's. This was the first time she could remember the man actually paying her a compliment instead of pulling some snappish remark out of his mental arsenal to use against her. She knew she shouldn't get too used to this type of behavior because the more she thought he was nothing more than a Scottish rogue, the easier her feelings were to control.

&#8667;

Elizabeth stood. "Pray excuse me."

"And me as well, Mister Murray."

If Fagan wasn't watching Grace, he would have missed the momentary look of discomfort that crossed her face when she jumped to her feet as though her English arse was afire. Elizabeth had already walked away from the table, and he grabbed Grace's wrist as she turned.

"There ye go again walking away, *bhana-phrionnsa*." He lowered his voice. "I would think by now that ye'd call me Fagan. Didnae we discuss this?"

She looked down at his restraining hand. "Be thankful I don't call you something much worse. Now please let go of my arm before somebody sees us." When he released her, she paused. "I see your men follow your example."

He lifted a brow. "What do ye mean?"

"Always around when you don't want them to be. If you're going to keep that wild dog out in the woods, perhaps you could learn to place him on a leash."

"Donna tell me ye're afraid of Angus too."

"Angus? No, Ravenna is the only one who harbors that fear. I'm talking about your guard who seems to be at a loss for words. Perhaps someone should help him find his tongue because apparently he's lost it."

Fagan shook his head, confused. "My guard? What the hell…er, what are ye talking about?"

She sighed in exasperation. "Your guard in the woods. When my dagger landed in the brush, the man stood there gaping at me. I asked him what he was doing, and he didn't even respond. He could've at least warned me he was standing there. He startled me."

"What did he look like?"

"I don't know. He looked like a Highlander. He had long hair, wore a kilt, and had a large sword. Frankly, all of you look the same to me."

"Grace…"

"I told you. I don't—wait a moment. He did have a large scar over his left eye. Do you know him?"

Fagan stood. "I'll have a conversation with him. And Grace, I donna want ye or Ravenna going near the forest again until I've had a chance to speak with my man. Are my words clear?"

"Yes, of course."

He watched her walk away and was relieved she heeded his command because he had no idea who this man was. Memories of the past flooded him, but he knew the Gordon was dead. What concerned him more was the fact that every time one weed was cut down, two more rose up to take its place.

Fagan walked hurriedly and approached Ruairi's study. The door was closed, and he knocked once. "Ruairi…"

"*Cò leis sibh?*" *Who are you with?*

"I am alone," said Fagan.

"Come."

Fagan opened the door and shut it behind him. He'd lost count of the endless times he'd met with Ruairi behind the closed doors of this room.

Celebrations, mourning, battle plans, and getting into their cups—there wasn't much they hadn't already done. Although there was nothing unusual about Ruairi sitting behind his desk, Ravenna sat in the chair across from her husband with a troubled expression on her face.

"I need to talk with ye. Grace said there was a man in—"

"I know. Ravenna told me."

"Please tell me you didn't tell my sister the man was not a Sutherland guard."

Fagan sat in the chair beside Ravenna. "Of course nae. I'm nae daft."

"Grace didnae give my wife any description of the man. Did she say anything else to ye?"

"Other than the fact that we Highlanders look all alike... She said the man had a large scar over his left eye. Nay one comes to mind, but I told her that I knew him so she doesnae worry upon it."

Ruairi rubbed his chin, and his eyes darted back and forth between Fagan and Ravenna. "Do ye think she's certain of what she saw?"

"Yes, my sister does not lie."

"I didnae say that she does, but I need to be certain of what or who she saw. God's teeth. Who the hell would encroach on my lands again?" His lips thinned with irritation.

By the way Ruairi asked the question, Fagan didn't think his friend had expected a response. "Do ye want me to increase the guard along the border?"

"Aye. Advise the men about what little we know and have them keep a watchful eye. I'm also going to send a missive to Ian. After our brush with the Gordon, I will nae leave anything to chance."

"Fagan, please don't mention any of this to my sisters, Grace in particular. For some reason, she's bound and determined to take my place and work for the king. Up until now, she's been quite harmless in her pursuit, albeit somewhat annoying. If she discovers the guard was not one of ours, I'm afraid she'll do something rash and search for the man herself. That kind of thinking is dangerous. You can understand why I can't let her believe she's capable of undertaking such a task."

Fagan knew his mouth was tight and grim. At first, he might have been taken aback by Ravenna's words, but he knew now that Grace would be foolhardy enough to pursue something like that. He couldn't imagine her being a spy for the English. Her actions were reckless, careless, and she'd surely get herself killed. "When was the idea planted that she wanted to be a spy for the Crown?"

Ravenna sighed. "Shortly after she found out I served the king. I thought perhaps her innocent questions were only a passing fancy, but now that I've seen how eager she is to learn, it worries me. Uncle Walter and I have tried to deter her, but—"

"I wouldnae worry overmuch. I donna think she would ever close her mouth long enough to accomplish the task. Furthermore, she's to be wed. What does her betrothed think?"

"Daniel doesn't know. She wanted to keep it a secret from him. The same as I did from my sisters."

"Aye, that would be a fine marriage filled with

naught but lies and distrust between them." When
Ruairi lifted a brow, Fagan added, "I will nae say
anything about the man."

"'Tis but another day in the Highlands, lass. I
donna want ye to think about this. Fagan and my
men will find out if anything is afoot." Ruairi's eyes
gave Ravenna a firm warning. "But ye arenae to
do anything. Ye are nay longer a spy. Ye've retired
from service, remember? Ye are now my wife,
Lady Sutherland."

Fagan stood. "I'll leave ye and speak to the men."

❧

When Grace spotted the guards, she stepped back,
placing her rump against the stone wall in the bailey.
Perhaps she was thinking about this the wrong way. If
she was going to search for the guard who was in the
woods, she should follow Ravenna's advice. Her sister
had always told her to blend into her surroundings,
and Grace was the sister-in-law of the laird. No one
would think it odd that she was in the bailey. Besides,
it wasn't as if she needed to follow the man. She only
needed to find him.

Even though Fagan said he knew the mute guard,
Grace had a strong yearning to perfect her spying
skills. What better opportunity than now? More to
the point, since Ravenna was hesitant to assist her in
this endeavor, always being the protective sister and
all, Grace would make certain her sister guided her—
willingly or not.

She stepped away from the wall and made her
way across the bailey to where Ruairi and Fagan had

practiced swordplay earlier in the day. She glanced up
and watched the men walk along the walls. None of
their faces looked even vaguely familiar. Maybe she
wasn't handling this the right way either. To see the
men, she had to stretch her neck to look up high on
the walls. That had to be more difficult than being
able to look down at them. She smiled when another
idea struck her.

Grace reached the parapet door and closed it behind
her. She climbed the steps and lifted the latch on the
door at the top of the stairs. The cool breeze greeted
her, and she walked to the edge of the wall. This looked
like the perfect spot. From here, she could see the men
walking along the walls much more clearly than if she
was standing on the ground below. She didn't feel like
she was breaking her neck to do it either

When Fagan approached a group of his men, she
faltered in her purpose. Although these Highland men
looked the same with their kilts and long broadswords,
somehow she always knew when Ruairi's captain was
among them. She placed her hand on the cool stone
and watched the way Fagan tilted his head. She noted
his daunting stance and how he folded his arms over
his broad chest. She remembered being held in those
same arms yesterday.

"Stop it, Grace," she said aloud. "Daniel. You must
think of Daniel."

Needing to suppress her sinful thoughts, she looked
out at the vast ocean, stretching as far as her eyes could
see. The amber hues of the sun reflected off the water.
She turned to her left, appreciating the trees that were
different shades of green, and of course, the beautiful

mossy field that lay ahead. Before she knew it, her eyes betrayed her again by returning to Fagan. He turned and lifted his face into the sun, or perhaps he looked directly at her. She wasn't sure. She stepped away from the wall and paused. After a brief moment, she moved back into place and stole a quick glance.

He was gone.

That suited her mood fine. If she was to be a spy for the king, she couldn't very well be distracted by a certain someone or dwell upon something that could never be. For heaven's sake, they'd only shared one kiss. She needed to stay true to her purpose.

Grace's eyes darted back and forth between the men. Maybe the guard she sought was making sure Ruairi's lands were safe because she didn't see him anywhere. She supposed she'd have to try something else. As soon as she turned on her heel, she was greeted by a wall of a man.

"What are ye doing?" Fagan looked suspicious about her motives.

"I came up here for a breath of fresh air. What are you doing here?" She returned the same look he had given her.

"I saw ye watching me." He folded his arms over his chest and gave her a roguish grin.

"Don't be ridiculous. I wasn't watching you. I was..."

"Ye were what?"

When she hesitated and couldn't look him in the eye, he lifted her chin with his fingers. The touch of his hand was almost unbearable in its tenderness, and her body tingled from the contact. He stared back, waiting in silence as she blinked, feeling light-headed. His gaze traveled over her face and searched her eyes. Near-kisses wouldn't cause her to swoon. She refused.

"Mister Mur—" Her voice softened. "Fagan…"

When she said his name, some kind of unidentifiable emotion crossed his face. His lips slowly descended to meet hers. Heaven help her. She felt her knees weaken. There was a dreamy familiarity to his kiss, something she couldn't quite explain. They were from two different worlds, but she couldn't deny the emotions he stirred within her. It was as if Fagan had a key and had found a way to unlock her heart. It felt as if their souls had known each other in some past life, but she knew that was impossible.

Carried away by her own response, Grace failed to notice that he had wound a hand into her hair to deepen the kiss. He pressed her up against the wall and his heavy body covered hers. He molded her to himself, his arms wrapping around her like a vise. Her breasts flattened against his chest, and she shuddered with desire. When he wedged his thigh between her legs, she gently leaned back and placed her head on the cool stone wall, breathless.

"Fagan, please stop." She placed her hands on his chest, and he leaned his forehead against hers.

"I donna know why ye make me lose all sense of reason." His breath fanned her face. "I had absolutely nay intention of kissing ye again."

"And I could say the same to you. I don't understand. Why does this keep happening to us?"

He let out a low, hearty chuckle. "I donna know, lass."

"I know you don't like me very much."

He pulled back, and his smile turned into another chuckle. "Now I wouldnae say that. Donna get me wrong. Ye have a way about ye that drives me completely mad, and your sharp tongue grates on my nerves, but...'tis apparent that I hold something for ye because I havenae yet run my sword through ye."

She huffed and pushed him away from her, not that she could move him more than an inch. "How very kind of you, Mister Murray."

He moved closer, holding her in place, and his eyes became softer as he brushed the backs of his fingers against her cheek. "Donna start, Grace. Ye called me Fagan. I heard it from your lips. I will hear it from now on. I know this is foolish. Ruairi and Ravenna would have my head, but I can't seem to stop myself. At least all I have stolen is a wee kiss or two from ye."

For some ridiculous reason "heart" came to her mind, but all she allowed to surface was the one thought that mattered most. "I'm betrothed to Daniel."

❧

Fagan knew he had lost all sense of reason some time ago. How could one woman—an English woman moreover—make all his chivalrous behavior fly out the window and not look back? He wasn't thinking clearly, but when Grace kindly reminded him that she was betrothed, reality crept back in—not necessarily sanity, but the truth penetrated him like a steely blade. Yet he couldn't dismiss that little voice inside his head and had to ask the question that weighed on his mind.

"Do ye love him?"

He wasn't sure why that inner voice prodded him to ask, but for some reason he wanted to hear her answer. He needed to know the truth. Perhaps if he did, he'd stop acting like a besotted fool.

Grace stepped around him. "You have no right to ask me that."

"Why?"

"Why does it matter? Whether yes or no, it doesn't change the fact that there is nothing— nor will there ever be something—between us. I'll be taking my leave in a few weeks, returning to England, and you said so yourself…it's more than likely best if we don't speak of this again."

When she threw his own words back at him, he felt guilty. The kiss meant something. He just wasn't sure what. He raked his fingers through his hair. "I donna know—"

"I see you have men on the walls. Are there also guards who ride around Ruairi's lands to make certain they're safe?"

Fagan was taken aback by the abrupt change of subject. "Aye, why?" When she looked like she was deep in thought, he added, "Ye donna have to worry about the guard in the forest. I talked to him."

She looked at him in surprise. "You did? When?"

"Only a moment ago, on the wall."

"The man in the forest was there on the wall?" When she gestured with her hand to his men below, he shifted his weight and glanced down.

"Aye."

For a long moment, Grace looked back at him.

# *Eight*

FOR THE PAST TWO DAYS, FAGAN HAD MANAGED TO
avoid her completely. Not that Grace blamed him.
She knew he wasn't trying to be hurtful, and it was
best that he kept his distance for both their sakes.
Maybe they wouldn't be tempted to do something else
they shouldn't be doing. Of course, that didn't stop
her from reliving private memories of the man. What
irritated her even more was that Daniel had never
come to mind, again. Even throwing her dagger at the
target in the field didn't help to clear her head.

Grace released the blade, and it whipped through
the air, landing at the base of the tree with a
thump. "Damn."

"You need to keep trying," said Ravenna.

"I know, but I have yet to even hit the target. It's
been two days."

Ravenna pulled Grace's dagger from the ground
and wiped the dirt from the blade. "I didn't master this
overnight either. It takes a lot of practice."

When her sister handed her back her weapon,
Grace nodded. "May I ask you something?" She didn't

miss the uncomfortable look that crossed Ravenna's face. "Don't worry. I wasn't going to ask you anything else about mastering spy craft."

"I'm relieved to hear it."

Grace looked down at her dagger, carefully guarding her expression. "Why did your husband increase the guard?"

"What do you mean?"

"Come now, Ravenna. You can't tell me you haven't noticed Ruairi's men lingering around us, even more so when we leave the gates. They weren't this close to us before."

"Ruairi doesn't consult with me on these matters. My husband is laird and I trust that he handles his duties the way he sees fit. Who am I to question his—"

"Do you take me for that much of a fool? Fagan told me he spoke to his man about being in the forest."

Ravenna smiled easily. "Yes, he told me the same. You shouldn't be worried because—"

"Oh, I'm not worried. I'm only wondering why Fagan found it necessary to lie to me, and now I can't help but ask why you do the same. I thought you were done spinning tales, Sister. You'd led me to believe there were no more secrets between us."

"Grace…"

"Don't attempt to patronize me like that. The next words that come from your mouth had better be the truth because those are the only words I will accept."

Ravenna let out a heavy sigh, then her voice went up a notch. "You want the truth? I'll give it to you. No one has any idea who that man was in the woods. Ruairi went through this before with Laird Gordon.

I've learned nothing good ever comes from such things—slaughtered cattle, stolen coin, clan battles. Who's to say what comes next? I'm the one who told Fagan and Ruairi not to tell you."

"Why?"

There was a heavy silence.

"You have no idea what you're doing, what you're asking, and no matter what you say, you are still young and innocent in the ways of the world."

Grace started to walk away from her sister's rant, but Ravenna held her firmly in place.

"Don't you dare walk away from me. You're the one who demanded the truth. Well, the *truth* is that you have no inkling what it's like to be a spy. It's certainly not the glorious work you make it out to be." Ravenna paused a moment and smiled in exasperation. "And you need to realize there is absolutely no celebrity to be had in this. I barely see the king, because the assignments from the Privy Council are given to me by Uncle Walter. I give all my findings to him, and he tells me if the king is pleased or not."

"I never know where I'm going to end up next. Everything is unpredictable, and failure is not an option. I must do whatever is needed to obtain the information I was sent to retrieve. No matter what the cost. Did you hear me? I almost lost the love of my life because I had to betray him. Wake up, Grace! I've been in the Devil's Tavern as a serving girl, walked along the London docks as a prostitute in the darkened hours of the night, and been a mistress to many men."

Ravenna continued. "I placed myself in harm's way more times than I can count, and frankly, I'm lucky to still be alive. You don't know what you're asking me to teach you. I became a spy because I never thought I'd have a husband or a family of my own. I was trained for years by Father, Uncle Walter, and their men. You cannot expect to claim that you're suddenly going to be a spy and that is that." Ravenna closed her eyes and threw her hands in the air. "It's all fun and games until you get hurt, and it's inevitable. You. Will. Be. Hurt."

"But isn't that my decision to make?"

Ravenna scowled. "Did you hear nothing I've said? You have people that love you. You're betrothed to Daniel. Ask yourself if you're willing to give all that up, because that's what you'll have to do. You will be expected to lie with other men when you have no choice, and then you will be returning home to share the same bed as your husband. Is that what you want? Is that fair to Daniel? Are you willing to throw away the love of your life and lay down your life for king and country?"

Grace looked down and ran her fingers along the edge of her blade. She lowered her voice, speaking softly. "Many of the married ladies we know are not a love match."

Her sister studied her intently. "I thought I would've changed your mind when I mentioned that you could lose your life, but I never thought…er, I didn't realize… You don't love Daniel."

Grace could neither confirm nor deny it because for the first time in her life, she had no idea how she felt about anything.

∽

Fagan rode back from the border with five of his men. They'd found no further signs of anyone trying to encroach on Sutherland lands. Of course he and his men could do nothing but keep a sharp eye and continue to stand guard. As he made his way across the open field to the castle, he spotted swishing skirts. The lass who wore the blue day dress made his heart skip a beat.

He gestured for his men to ride ahead as he slowed his mount. For a foolish moment, he forgot where he was and time stood still. He gazed in awe at a flawless painting of a bonny lass in a mossy-green field on a midsummer day. When he heard a curse fall from said temptress's mouth, his woolgathering abruptly came to an end.

Grace's hands were clenched stiffly at her sides. He didn't think she even noticed him as she stormed toward him across the field. But then she glowered at him and turned in the opposite direction. He supposed she definitely saw him now.

Fagan called after her, but she paid him no heed, as he knew she would. When he said her name once more and she didn't stop, he reined in his horse in front of her and blocked her path. She had nowhere to go. Instead of looking up at him or cursing him, she only lowered her head. Following Ravenna and Ruairi's advice, he kept his mouth shut and waited for Grace to say something.

While his horse pawed at the ground, unhappy under restraint, the lass still didn't move. When he refused to budge, Grace finally glanced up at him and her eyes welled with tears. Suddenly, he felt as though he'd been punched in the gut. Without saying a word, he bent slightly forward and held out his hand.

She paused, looked at his extended arm, and then took it. Placing her foot on top of his in the stirrup, she swung up behind him. When he kicked his mount and took off at a gallop, she wrapped her arms around his waist. The faster he rode, the tighter she squeezed. At first, he wasn't sure where he was headed, but then he made up his mind to take her to the beach. He slowed his horse when they reached the sandy path. He didn't think it was his imagination, but as they descended the hill, he felt her head lie gently on his back.

Fagan stopped his mount and swung his leg over the front of the saddle. He grabbed Grace's waist and lowered her to the ground. She immediately averted her eyes from him. While he tethered his horse, she moved to the edge of the water. Wanting to give her a moment alone, he fumbled through his sack, pulled out a blanket, and took his time spreading it out on the sand.

When he'd finished with his task and had held back for as long as he could, he approached her, his steps slowing as he wondered what was wrong. He never saw this side of her and wasn't sure what to do or say. She was always fiery and ready to give her opinion, not restrained. Her azure skirts billowed in the wind, and her brown hair was tousled. The sound of the rolling waves always soothed his soul, and he hoped they would do the same for Grace.

He stood beside her and took a deep breath. "Beautiful, is it nae?"

Tears still trembled on her eyelashes. "Yes." She

gazed out at the sea and spoke in a solemn tone. "You don't have to stand here with me."

"'Tis my pleasure, lass."

"I'm afraid I'm not very good company at the moment."

"Ye told me before. Ye're nae here for my amusement." When she let out a gentle laugh, he placed his arm around her shoulders. "Ye donna have to speak if ye donna want to, but let me offer ye comfort. Let me hold ye."

She nestled her head against his chest. "We both know this is wrong. I don't know why I should let you."

God help him because neither did he.

&

Ravenna's words played over in Grace's mind like a pecking bird that refused to cease. Furthermore, from what her sister had just told her, Ravenna should be the last person giving advice. For God's sake, the woman had pretended to be a prostitute and was a mistress. Grace wondered what Ruairi thought of that particular declaration, and then she realized it didn't matter because the man loved her sister for the person she was. Maybe that's what love was all about.

As Grace stood on the beach with Fagan's arm wrapped around her, she felt even worse than before. She pulled away from him, and he lowered his arm.

"I don't know what the hell I'm doing," she said, wiping her fallen tears.

He turned, pulling her along behind him and

leading her over to a blanket that he had spread out on the sand. "Sit down, Grace."

She was so tired of arguing with everyone that she granted him this one small boon. She lowered herself to the ground and straightened her skirts as he sat on the blanket beside her. When there was a moment of awkward silence, she asked, "Aren't you going to say something?"

He gave her a gentle smile. "When ye're ready, ye will talk to me."

And that was all he said. No more, no less.

She looked out at the rolling waves and spoke in a solemn tone. "Ravenna and I had words."

Out of the corner of her eye, she saw him look at her. "Ruairi and I have words all the time. 'Tis what family does. Do ye want to tell me about it? I cannae say that I can give ye any words of wisdom, but I know what 'tis like to have an annoying brother."

"I know this may not make any sense to you." She gave him a sheepish smile, and he gestured for her to continue. "My father always favored Ravenna. I thought it was because she was the eldest, but now I realize he was readying her for something more, something greater. When our parents died, Ravenna would disappear for hours on end. Hours turned into nights, nights into days. I even caught her one night dressed as a harlot."

"Of course I questioned her, thinking she was somebody's secret mistress or was selling herself. I might've even believed Uncle Walter was stealing our coin and Ravenna was only trying to replenish the coffers. Frankly, I don't really know what I thought, but my sister was always there for us. I wanted to be there for her."

"I'm sorry, lass. I donna understand."

"I always thought my sister would remain unwed. If my father were still alive, I knew he would've been disappointed that his favorite daughter had never married. So I went to court and did my part. I wanted to marry a man of title and make my family, my father, finally proud. But things have changed."

"Why? There's still plenty of time to do those things."

"Ironically, now that I know my sister was a spy for the Crown, I find myself willing to do anything to be her." Fagan was about to speak when she held up her hand to silence him. "Ravenna has sacrificed so much for our family, and now she is truly happy with Ruairi. She has found her peace. I want to follow in her footsteps as a spy, but she says I'm still young and innocent in the ways of the world."

"Ye are."

"Pardon me?" She was about to stand when Fagan grasped her wrist to stay her.

"The farthest ye've ever traveled was from Edinburgh to the Highlands. At nay fault of your own, ye donna know much about people or politics, lass, and both can be verra dangerous."

"Fagan, I'm eighteen years old and suddenly find myself questioning my path. I thought I needed to marry someone like Daniel to make me whole, if that makes any sense. Now I'm not sure if I want to spend the rest of my days in ballrooms talking to the ladies about the latest fashions. I want my life to have meaning. I want to have a purpose, and I find it very difficult to believe that God placed me here only to be a dutiful wife. I should've known you wouldn't understand."

"Och, I understand better than ye think I do. I am nae titled. I have nay lands, nay wife—then again, what could I possibly even have to offer her? I am the captain of the Sutherland guard. I am responsible for the protection of the castle, Ruairi, and our clan. I would give my life for my duty. So aye, I understand. Ye are a bonny lass, a lady. Marry your English lord and have a family. I am certain that was what your father intended for ye."

When she dismissed his words, he added, "Grace, the life ye think ye want to live is verra dangerous. Ye have everything any woman would want or desire to have. The path ye choose to take is your own, but I think ye should take time to think this through." He tapped her on the shoulder in a playful gesture. "When ye think about my words, I know ye will see reason."

"Are you patronizing me, Mister Murray?"

"Nay, *bhana-phrionnsa*. I say the same to ye as I would say to Ruairi. Ye need to think. Donna rush into something because ye believe ye can or should. Ye donna want to find yourself in a situation ye cannae walk away from. Ye're a smart lass. Ye know I speak the truth."

Maybe Fagan did have a point. All she'd ever really desired was adventure and excitement. Until she was certain what she wanted her life to entail, she shouldn't make any rash decisions. That's when she reached the conclusion that she'd lost her mind because she was about to do something she'd never thought she'd do.

She nodded in agreement with Fagan. When a glint of humor finally returned in her expression, he saw it too.

"And donna be so angry with Ravenna. She's your sister. She's only looking out for ye. I often tell Ruairi that sometimes I am the only one who knows what's best for him. He doesnae like it, but he listens. Ye donna want to be your own enemy, if that makes any sense to ye."

Grace gazed out at the ocean. For a moment, the sound of the waves could have lulled her to sleep. She felt as if the weight on her shoulders wasn't as heavy as it had been before. She stuck her fingers into the sand and pulled out a shell to study it. "You do realize that I am an English lady who has taken the advice of a Scottish captain. Whatever is this world coming to?"

*"Gach aon's le chèile an aghaidh an domhain."*

"Pardon?"

"Everyone together against the world." He stood and pulled her to her feet. His thumb gently caressed her cheek. "Are ye all right now?"

"Yes, thank you. I really do feel better."

"I'm glad to hear it."

Pounding hooves sounded from the top of the hill. They spotted two riders as they galloped their horses close to the path to the beach. The men did not wear the Sutherland tartan, nor did they see that Fagan and Grace stood on the sand below. At least Grace was able to notice that much. When everything fell silent, Fagan placed a firm hand on her arm.

"I want ye to stay here. Do ye understand?"

She nodded.

Grace watched him charge toward his mount. He quickly released the tethered reins and swung his leg over his horse. The man didn't even use the stirrups. Within seconds, he was over the hill and gone. She wasn't sure who those men were and realized that she shouldn't be standing here in open view. She bent to gather the blanket when she heard the whinny of a horse. When she stood, she held the blanket in front of her in a protective embrace.

The man's chestnut-colored horse pawed the sand. He sat atop his mount, wearing the same black tunic and dark-colored kilt that he had worn before. And of course that same bloody sword was still sheathed at his waist. She noted his long, black hair, set face, clamped mouth, and dark eyes—which were fixed on her.

"What do you want?" she asked him, not expecting an answer.

"Ye." His voice was emotionless and it chilled her.

Her pulse began to beat erratically at the threatening tone in his deep voice. She felt as if a hand had closed around her throat. She needed to do something fast, but if she tried to escape up the sandy path, she might lose her footing. She struggled to accept the fact that there was no other alternative but the beach. So be it. She wouldn't give in without a fight. She was a Walsingham.

Grace dropped the blanket and dashed along the shore. As the sound of clomping hooves came close behind, she realized she wasn't putting up much of a fight. The man was on horseback, and she was on foot. Instinctively, she did the only other thing she could think of that might aid her. She turned into the water.

As she swam out into the cool depths of the ocean, she tried not to think about her skirts weighing her down or how her breath hitched at the sudden change in temperature. When her arms grew tired, only then did she turn around and realize the man was gone. She looked to her left and then to the right.

"Grace!" Fagan galloped down the beach and called to her.

She clumsily paddled back to shore, and when she could finally touch the bottom, she waved her arms over her head. "Fagan!"

He arrived by her side at the same moment she came out of the water. She was so exhausted that she dropped to her knees on the sand, gasping for breath. Fagan knelt in front of her. He brushed the hair away from her face, and her eyes met his. The strange surge of affection she felt coming from him frightened her.

"Are ye all right?"

She nodded, and his expression changed to one of relief.

"I told ye to wait for me on the beach. Ye picked one hell of a time to go for a swim, *bhana-phrionnsa*." He held out his hand and pulled her to her feet.

She knew he was making light of the situation and not teasing her maliciously. "Who were those men?"

"The only matter of importance is your safety. Let me get ye back to the castle."

"Fagan…" Her feet were firmly planted and she refused to budge.

He stretched his neck from side to side, and then his eyes darkened. "They were damn mercenaries."

# *Nine*

When Fagan and Grace entered the great hall, Kat's eyes widened. "Grace, why are you all wet?"

Torquil stood by the girl's side, studying Fagan from head to toe. *"Dé do naidheachd?"* What's your news? "Ye're nae wet. Did ye throw Grace into the sea? I donna think Da would approve of that."

"Did I… What? Nay, I didnae throw Grace into the water. Where is your father?"

Torquil shrugged.

Fagan placed his arm around Grace's waist in an instinctive gesture of comfort and led her to the stairs. "Why donna ye change your wet clothes? I'll find Ruairi and Ravenna, and then I'll meet ye in Ruairi's study."

She nodded and lifted her wet skirts as she climbed the steps. The idea had crossed his mind to shield her from the truth, but Grace needed to stop living in a fantasy world. Ravenna was right. Her sister was young and innocent to the ways of the world. He also couldn't deny that he'd decided to be honest about the men at the beach in the hope that he'd curtail any more of Grace's asinine ideas about working for the Crown.

"What's wrong with Grace? Why is she all wet?" asked Kat.

To Fagan's surprise, Torquil took the girl by the hand. "Come, Kat. Let's go to the kitchens." The boy started to walk away and then looked back. "Do ye want me to find Da and Ravenna for ye?"

"If ye see them, send them to your father's study."

As Fagan entered the bailey, a familiar curse cut through the air. Ravenna walked toward him hurriedly, glancing uneasily over her shoulder. The reason for her distress was clear—again.

Angus followed her.

No wonder Ruairi had a strong urge to throttle his wife on occasion. Fagan also had a difficult time understanding why the lass had such a foolish fear of the wolf. Angus never hurt anyone. More to the point, Ravenna was more dangerous than the animal. When her eyes met Fagan's, her voice was both soft and alarmed.

"Help…"

He waved his hand in a dismissive gesture. "Angus! *'Se peasan a th'annad. Dèan às!*" You're a pest. Be gone!

"Thank you for that."

"Where is Ruairi?"

"I haven't seen him since I returned from shooting targets with Grace."

"Can ye find him and bring him to his study? We need to talk."

"Of course. Is everything all right? Oh, please don't tell me my sister did something. She was rather angry at me."

He found himself quickly coming to Grace's defense. "Nay, 'tis naught like that." He looked around the bailey and hesitated. "I saw Kat and Torquil in the great hall. Have ye seen Elizabeth?"

"I wasn't looking for her, but she's usually in the library. I'll go and find Ruairi for you."

"And I'll make certain Elizabeth is in the library." As he turned to walk away, Ravenna reached out a hand to stay him.

"Should I be concerned?"

He smiled. "Nay, 'tis but another day in the Highlands."

She lifted a brow and spoke dryly. "You always have a way of making me feel so much better, Fagan."

❧

Grace changed her wet clothes and tried to comb the sand out of her gritty hair. Ravenna was right. The only world Grace knew was her simple life of having dinner with Uncle Walter and his family, living in the manor house, and now and then being able to attend court, which was only recently. And to think the man with the scarred face was a bloody mercenary. Heaven help her. She'd been careless in assuming the man was one of Ruairi's guards when she'd seen him in the trees. She didn't want to dwell on the fact that she and Ravenna could've been hurt by her own foolhardy behavior.

After Grace was presentable, she made her way to Ruairi's study. She didn't need to knock because the door was open, and Ravenna, Ruairi, and Fagan were already seated. When she entered, Fagan immediately rose and approached her.

"Are ye all right?"

She nodded in response and turned with a start when Ravenna touched her arm. The troubled look on her sister's face told her that Ravenna was aware of the encounter on the beach—well, that and the fact that Ravenna embraced her.

"I'm so relieved you're all right. Come and sit, and tell us what happened."

Grace sat in the chair with her fingers tensed on her lap. Ravenna and Fagan took their seats flanking her, while Ruairi sat in the chair behind his large wooden desk. Grace couldn't help but feel like she was in the middle of an inquisition.

"Start at the beginning. Why were ye at the beach?" asked Ruairi.

She became increasingly uneasy under her brother-in-law's scrutiny and awkwardly cleared her throat. She was caught by surprise when Fagan spoke for her.

"Lady Grace wanted to see the beach again and I escorted her."

She'd have to remember to thank him later for not mentioning the little quarrel she'd had with Ravenna that had made her weepy and irrational. "Yes, I had asked Fagan to take me."

"Tell us what happened, Grace," said Ruairi.

She stole a quick glance at Fagan, and he gave her an encouraging nod. "As Fagan and I stood on the beach, we saw two riders galloping on the path above us. Fagan rode after them, and I stayed where I was on the beach."

Ravenna's voice went up a notch. "You left her?"

Grace turned to Ravenna. "It wasn't like that.

There were only two men, and we didn't think they took notice of us standing on the beach below. I knew Fagan needed to find out who they were. I urged him to go while I waited for his return."

"But there were more than two men," Ravenna clarified.

Grace detected an odd tone in her sister's voice. She turned to face Ravenna. "You can't place blame on Fagan since neither one of us knew of the other man."

"Please continue," Ruairi cut in.

"There isn't much else to say. The same man that I saw in the woods found me on the beach. He sat on his mount and stared at me. He didn't move. I thought about running up the path, but then I figured my skirts and the sand would weigh me down. Deciding my only option was the beach, I ran along the edge of the water. I heard hoofbeats behind me and decided that I had no choice but to try to flee into the water."

"That was quick thinking," said Ravenna.

Grace nodded. "I swam out into the sea as far as I could, and only when my arms and legs were tired did I dare turn around. When I finally had the courage to look, the man was gone, and Fagan was calling me from the shore. Why would mercenaries be on your lands, Ruairi?"

"I donna know, lass. That's what I intend to find out."

❧

Fagan's mind raced. Ever since he and Grace had left the beach, the scene played in his mind over and over again, refusing to cease. He tried to remember all the details, but it was difficult to remove his emotions from his recounting. How could he? He'd left Grace. She could've been hurt. He didn't need Ravenna to remind him of his poor judgment.

When Ravenna and Grace left the study, Ruairi placed two tankards on the desk and filled them with ale.

"'Tisnae your fault. Grace wasnae harmed."

Fagan rolled his neck from side to side. "I should've been more cautious. She was all right, aye, but I shouldnae have taken the chance. She could've been hurt or worse."

"But she wasnae. Ye know as well as I do that ye cannae think that way. If ye start to question your actions every time something is afoot—"

"I know, but somehow that revelation doesnae make me feel any better." Fagan grabbed a tankard and was taking a drink of ale when the door opened.

Ravenna closed the latch behind her. "Grace will be all right. She's going to rest for a bit." She walked across the room and sat in the chair beside Fagan. Lifting a brow, she leaned her arm on the desk, tapping her fingernails in an annoying gesture.

"I see the look in your eyes, Wife. I told ye that I donna want ye involved."

"And I heard you the first three times, Husband. You are aware the man tried to harm my sister. You should be thankful I'm not out there hunting him myself. Instead, I'm sitting here talking to you like a good wife. Now…do you think the mercenaries have anything to do with Laird Gordon or the Earl of Orkney's son, Robert Stewart?"

Fagan chuckled when Ruairi sighed, and in return, his liege gave him a hostile glare. Fagan was always amused when his friend realized his wife wasn't going to relent on something.

"I donna know. Redshanks," said Ruairi.

"Pardon?"

"Is that nae what the English call mercenaries from the Western Isles? They wear their kilts and wade bare-legged through the rivers in the coldest weather. The men are often MacLeods or Campbells, among others, and armed with bows and two-handed claymores. These men are dangerous, offering their services and providing loyalty to only those who pay the highest amount. In the past, they've kept to the borderlands or traveled to Ireland, but something has drawn them here to the Highlands. I donna know why they're on my lands or what the hell they want. Until I know what that reason is"—Ruairi continued to speak calmly—"nay one is to leave the gates without an armed escort. Do ye understand, Ravenna? There is nay room for debate on this."

"Yes, of course."

"I'll increase the men at the border and make certain nay one comes in or out without us knowing it," said Fagan.

"Aye. I'm also going to send another missive to the Munro to keep him alert. If this is some type of revenge for Gordon or Stewart, Ian should be aware. My dungeon is ready and waiting for one of those bastards to set foot on my lands again."

Grace awoke with a start. She sat up on the bed and the room was dark. She couldn't believe she'd fallen asleep so early, but after all the excitement she'd had, she shouldn't have been too surprised by her weariness.

She lit the bedside candle and illuminated her bedchamber. As she brushed back the fallen hair from her eyes, she realized she still wore her day dress. She rose from the bed and looked out the small window. Blackness greeted her, and she knew it was the dead of night. Her stomach promptly reminded her that the last time she'd eaten something was in the morning to break her fast.

Grace donned her silk slippers and walked out into the hall. Everything was silent, and only one torch lit the wall. She managed to find her way down the stairs and into the great hall where a dark shadow greeted her with a wagging tail.

"I see it's only the two of us, Angus. Do you want to walk with me to the kitchens?"

The wolf followed her, and she made her way into another shadowy room. She reached to her left and hit her hand on the wall.

"Of course this couldn't be easy." She lifted her other arm to the right, and something dropped to the floor. "Just my luck." She felt Angus brush her leg as the wolf sniffed around whatever it was she'd dropped to the ground. She bent over and placed her hand on the back of the animal.

"Angus, why can't you be a good boy and pick up whatever fell? I can't see a darned thing."

The only response was a wagging tail that thumped hard against the wall. Grace tapped her fingers around the cool stone floor until she felt the candle that had fallen and brushed a boot. She jumped and fell backward on her rump.

And then she froze.

That's when a warm chuckle greeted her. The man lit the candle and the flame flickered in his eyes, which were amused but beautiful nonetheless.

"Fagan…"

He placed the candle down on a nearby table. "And just what are ye doing wandering around the castle in the middle of the night, lass? Out of the way, Angus."

"I'd slept much longer than I had intended. I'm famished."

Fagan lowered his hand and pulled her to her feet. "Sit down at the table, and we'll get ye something to eat then."

Grace pulled out the wooden bench and sat at the kitchen table. "What are you doing up so late? Or perhaps I should ask why so early."

Fagan walked over to the pantry and lifted the curtain. "I couldnae sleep and I heard ye talking to Angus." For a moment, he disappeared into the room, and then he reemerged with a loaf of bread in hand. "This was all I could find."

"Bless you, Fagan."

He placed the bread on the table, and Grace tore a piece off the end. She was so hungry that she didn't even notice he had poured her a cup of mulled wine. He pulled out the bench and sat across from her.

As she looked up, she noticed the cup and took a drink. "Thank you." Briefly, she closed her eyes as she satisfied her thirst, but then she opened them when she felt a nudge under her arm. Angus looked at her imploringly.

"Angus, ye're badly behaved."

"It's all right." She took a piece of bread and tossed it to the wolf. The animal devoured the food with his massive jaws in seconds. When Angus gave her another pitiful look, she shooed him away. "Now that's enough. Off with you."

Fagan chuckled. "Ye know? I could tell him the same, and he only stares at me like I'm daft." He hesitated, and a worried expression crossed his brow. "I should have ne'er left ye alone. It was my duty to protect ye."

She waved him off. "Fagan, I spoke the truth in Ruairi's study. You couldn't have known about the man. It's not your fault." When he glanced away from her, she reached out and touched his hand. "It's not your fault," she repeated.

"Are ye all right?"

She rolled her eyes and took another bite of bread. Wiping the crumbs away from her lips, she smiled. "You shouldn't feel any guilt over this. I wasn't harmed. Besides, I'm a Walsingham. Of course I'm all right."

"Aye. How could I forget?"

She took another sip of wine and studied him over the rim. She never thought the two of them would be sitting here now, peaceful, talking over candlelight. Grace had to admit that she found some comfort in being open with Fagan. Not only that, but she found the steely captain was becoming much more…tolerable. Frankly, he wasn't nearly as exhausting as he had been before. Perhaps her feelings had changed for him because they no longer sparred with each other, at least not in a hateful way.

She tried to remember the last time she'd truly enjoyed herself with a man, realizing she'd never talked to Daniel this way. She didn't believe in tales of chivalric love, but she briefly wondered if the kisses she'd shared with Fagan were some of those stolen moments that the bards often talked about.

❧

"Ye look like ye're deep in thought."

Grace blinked, and Fagan didn't miss the slight shake of her head. "Pardon? Oh yes. I suppose my mind was elsewhere."

He gave her a roguish grin. "I certainly hope 'tisnae my company that ye wish to avoid."

"No. I'm sorry. It's just been a long day, and I'm weary."

He lifted a brow. "Weary? Ye slept most of the day away." She opened her mouth to say something, but when she realized he was only jesting with her, she graced him with a smile.

"Do you think my sisters are safe here?"

Fagan hesitated. The woman didn't ask about her own safety, only that of her sisters. He paused a moment longer because he didn't understand where the conversation was heading. He needed to weigh his answer before he responded.

"Are you going to answer me or sit there like a dolt?"

He leaned his arm on the table. "I heard ye. And

aye, I know your sisters will be safe here. The castle is impenetrable." Fagan wouldn't mention the fact that the Sutherland guards had managed to hold the Gordons at bay at the border. She might think they warred with the neighboring clans all the time—well, not too often.

"Grace, ye donna need to worry. We will protect ye and your sisters. Why do ye think Ruairi entrusted me with your escort back to England? I'll have ye know…they say my prowess on the battlefield is feared by many."

"And who says that?" she asked dryly.

"Men."

She laughed and folded her arms over her chest. "What men?"

"Careful, *bhana-phrionnsa*," he warned. "We've been getting along so well."

"How many of these mercenaries do you think there are?"

"'Tis hard to say, but we've only seen three of them. Perhaps they have a few more, but I donna know."

"What do they usually want, or what could they possibly want?"

Fagan suddenly had a sense that Grace was more concerned about her little adventure than she was letting on. "The men serve whoever pays the highest coin. They'll do whatever they're told and swear nay fealty to any liege. Many of them have traveled to Ireland to fight with the Irish, but some have remained in Scotland."

"You're saying these men do as they're instructed for coin?"

"Aye."

"Then why would someone pay them to take me?"

❧

Fagan waited for Ruairi and Ravenna next to the tree line in the field. The grass was wet with the early-morning dew, and the orange and yellow hues of the sun rose just over the horizon. That little voice inside Fagan's head had a hard time understanding something. Why didn't Grace tell anyone that the scarred bastard had actually spoken to her? God, he knew why. She didn't think it was important enough to mention. Yes, she'd make one hell of a spy for the Crown for sure.

He thought it best to meet outside the castle walls because he didn't want Grace stumbling on them by mistake, and he wasn't in the mood to tell her what they were doing gathered without her. Fagan leaned against the tree, watching Angus as the wolf stalked some small animal out in the field. Without warning, Angus turned and made a mad dash into the tree line, sticks and branches snapping under the wolf's massive paws. At least the wolf disappeared before Ravenna spotted him, because she and Ruairi had just come through the gates.

As they walked side by side, Ruairi reached out and took Ravenna's hand in a gentle gesture. Fagan still had some difficulty watching the man he had known for years, the strong Highland laird and warrior, showing a moment of vulnerability with a woman. Ruairi was undoubtedly besotted with his wife.

"*Madainn mhath,*" said Ruairi. *Good morning.*

"Aye. I hope so."

"What's the matter?" asked Ravenna. "We received word that you wanted to meet us here this morn."

"My path crossed Grace's last eve in the kitchens. I found out that she neglected to mention a wee detail about the man on the beach."

"And what's that?" asked Ravenna.

"She had words with him. She asked him what he wanted, and he said 'ye.' That's when she decided to run."

"But that could mean anything. She was a woman alone on the beach. Perhaps he only meant to frighten her."

Fagan raked his fingers through his hair. "Aye, but what if—"

"—the two other men who led Fagan away from Grace were only a distraction from their real purpose," said Ruairi, finishing Fagan's thoughts.

Ravenna waved Ruairi off, and her voice went up a notch. "That's completely absurd. Who would want to make off with Grace?"

"Aye, her sharp tongue would surely deter any man, and she'd most certainly drive the poor bastard mad," said Fagan. "But what if that was the bastard's true purpose and Grace was the target?"

Ravenna's eyes narrowed, and she pursed her lips. "First of all, you may think you're amusing, but let me assure you that you're not." She rubbed her hand over her brow. "I understand why you would both draw that conclusion, but you know my sister has nothing to do with the Crown. For heaven's sake, she's only been to court twice, and the only peer of the realm that she consorts with is Daniel."

"And donna forget ye and Lord Mildmay," said Fagan.

"No one knows of my and Uncle Walter's connections to the Crown."

"Are ye certain of that, lass?" asked Ruairi.

Ravenna started to pace. "But that makes no sense. For the sake of argument, why wouldn't the men come after me or Uncle Walter? Why would they want Grace? Perhaps it was only a strange coincidence that she was on the beach at that time and crossed paths with the man."

"Mayhap," said Ruairi.

Fagan knew by the look on Ruairi's face that his friend only said the words to appease his wife. But more to the point, Ravenna didn't know that Fagan had seen that same expression for years. Ruairi had his doubts and so did Fagan.

"Donna worry, Wife. We'll make certain Grace is safe. Fagan will provide your sister with an escort anytime she leaves the castle."

"That's wonderful, but who is going to protect Fagan from Grace?"

# Ten

FOR THE PAST TWO WEEKS, GRACE HAD BARELY BEEN able to breathe. Fagan followed her everywhere. She couldn't even go to the garden without the man hovering over her shoulder. She knew what he was doing. He had refused to let her out of his sight ever since that scarred vagrant had chased her on the beach. She'd lost count of how many times she'd told the daft man he was not to blame.

Grace sought solace in the library, the only place she knew Fagan avoided like the plague. Heaven forbid the man should pick up a book. He might catch something. She and Elizabeth sat in the two chairs in front of the stone fireplace with their noses buried in books. Grace should've known the quiet minute was exactly that. The peaceful moment was broken when papers shuffled behind them. As Kat cleaned up her drawings, she let out a heavy sigh.

"I'm weary of this. I'm going to find Torquil."

"No," said Elizabeth and Grace at the same time. Grace stood and replaced her book on the shelf.

"And why not?" Kat glanced at Grace, pursing her

lips in defiance. Then Grace walked over to the table and started to clear away the mess that her sister had tried unsuccessfully to clean up. "I asked you a question, Grace, and I know you heard me. Why not?"

As Kat pretended not to understand Grace's scolding look, Grace continued with her task while not paying her sister any heed. There were some days when her sisters drove her completely mad, and she hoped this wasn't another one of them. Grace could feel Kat's eyes on her and knew it was only a matter of time before her wily sister prodded again.

"If you refuse to tell me why I can't take my leave to find Torquil, I'm just going to go."

Grace faced her sister and took a deep breath. She placed her hands on Kat's shoulders and looked up at the ceiling. She was trying to be patient and understanding, especially since what she really wanted to say was "because I said." But she knew those words would only cause further argument.

"You can't be chasing that boy all the time. He's at the age where he doesn't want to share his company with a girl. He doesn't want you following him. You've both been getting along quite well, but I wouldn't push him too far if I were you. Don't you think he has friends that he wants to be with on occasion?"

"But I *am* his friend."

"Yes, but you need friends of your own and have to find something to do other than occupying your time with Torquil."

"But we haven't been quarreling. We've been playing with Angus, running in the fields, and we've stopped practicing our swordplay. Torquil doesn't mind my company. I think he enjoys it."

Elizabeth stood. "How about we go to the stables? You can see the animals."

Kat shrugged. "All right. I do like petting the horses."

For the first time since Grace could remember, she was grateful for Elizabeth's intervention. They walked through the halls, and Kat ran ahead of them and out into the bailey. When the warm rays touched Grace's cheeks, she lifted her face to the sun. She knew it wouldn't be long before the blue skies were gray and the winter solstice would once again rear its ugly head. She shivered just thinking about the cold weather.

Kat made her way over to John, the stable hand, who was brushing one of the horses. He was an older gentleman with graying hair and always had a warm, tender kind of smile. He looked up and his expression brightened when he saw Kat.

"Good morn. 'Tis a lovely day, lassie. Are ye and your sisters wanting to go for a ride?"

"No. I only wanted to pet the horses. May I brush him for you, John?"

"Och, nae this one, lassie. An Diobhail is too much horse for ye."

"He's Fagan's mount, is he not?" asked Grace.

"Aye, m'lady." John dropped the brush and turned to Kat. "Wait here, lassie. I have a mount just for ye." He disappeared into the stable and returned a few moments later with the same quiet mare that Kat had ridden to the beach. He tied off the animal away from An Diobhail, picked up the brush, and led Kat and Elizabeth over to the horse. As John showed her sisters the proper way to brush the horse, a warm voice spoke by Grace's ear.

"Ye wouldnae be taking An Diobhail for a ride now, would ye?"

"Of course not. Kat wanted to brush him."

"Do your best with him, Lady Katherine. He's a fine horse."

"I will, Fagan."

Grace lifted a brow. "I was wondering where you've been. You haven't been stalking me today."

His eyes darkened. "Miss me, Grace?"

She didn't want to answer his question for more reasons than she could count and was thankful when Elizabeth interrupted the conversation at the perfect time. Her sister was proving herself very useful today.

"Perhaps we can all go for a ride. I—" Elizabeth stopped in mid-sentence, and a soft gasp escaped her.

When the sound of pounding hooves entered the bailey, Grace and Fagan turned around. Fagan shook his head, and Grace spoke under her breath.

"Bloody hell."

"Aye."

Ruairi's redheaded neighbor stood disheveled in the bailey with a score of men.

❧

"Ian, 'tis good to see ye." His long, red hair was blown awry, and his tunic was half pulled out of his kilt. Munro had been known to frighten men on the battlefield by his fierce looks alone. What Elizabeth saw in this man was beyond Fagan's comprehension.

"Where is your laird? Do ye think ye can pull him

away from his bonny bride long enough to speak with me?"

Fagan was about to respond, but Elizabeth walked up beside him. Her voice was light and airy.

"Laird Munro, how wonderful to see you again. Did you have a pleasant journey?"

"And 'tis a pleasure to see ye as well, Lady Elizabeth. Aye, 'tis a fine day. Our journey was marked with nay noteworthy incidents, which is how I like it." When his smile matched hers in liveliness, Fagan heard a loud sigh and assumed the sound came from Grace.

"Grace, why donna ye see to your sisters? I'll take Ian to Ruairi's study."

Somehow he knew by the look on Grace's face that she was going to do everything in her power to make certain Elizabeth was cured of this ailment she had for Ian, one way or another. While she took care of Elizabeth, perhaps Grace could do something to help treat him too, Fagan thought. They entered the great hall just as Ruairi placed his boot on the foot of the stairs.

"Ruairi," said Fagan.

Ruairi turned, and his eyes lit up in surprise. "Ian, what the hell are ye doing here?"

"'Tis good to see ye. I hope I'm nae keeping ye away from anything of importance." Ian gave Ruairi a knowing grin. "Speaking of which, where is your bonny lass?"

"She's with Torquil."

"Aye, well, I can enjoy the company of kin when we've finished having a wee chat."

As soon as the men set foot inside Ruairi's study,

Fagan closed the door, and Ruairi pulled out the ale. He placed three tankards on his desk and filled them.

"I received your missives."

Ruairi handed each of them a tankard and sat in the chair behind his desk. "Aye. Damn mercenaries. The bastard who chased Grace on the beach told the lass he wanted her, but we donna know if his words were only to frighten her or if he had another purpose in mind." He tapped his finger on the rim of his cup. "Have ye seen these men?"

Ian took a drink and placed his tankard down on the desk. "'Tis why I am here. After I received word from ye, I placed more of my guard at the border. Ye can ne'er be too cautious. My men saw five of these bastards for hire making their way south, and my men tracked them to the English border. I'm nae sure what they wanted, but I say let the bloody English have at them."

Uncertainty crept into Ruairi's expression. "We must nae overlook the fact that these mercenaries always have a purpose and might've been sent by Robert Stewart in retaliation for the Gordon and Orkney, but 'tis my hope this is the end of it."

Fagan cleared his throat. "I donna know if ye both are in agreement with this, but I donna believe Stewart's hand can reach this far into the Highlands while he's imprisoned. And even if he could, our numbers are too great."

"I agree with ye, but I'm nae yet lowering my guard. I suggest ye do the same, Ian," said Ruairi.

Munro took another drink and sighed. "I grow tired of men like Stewart, and why cannae the bloody

English leave us be? *Tha mi duilich.* I didnae mean your wife and her sisters." *I'm sorry.*

Ruairi waved him off. "One would think that since Ravenna is now my wife, and Lord Mildmay has the king's ear, this would all be behind us. Naught is for certain anymore. At least your men saw the bastards cross the border." He gave Fagan a quick nod. "And ye should now have a clear path to escort Grace home within a sennight. Mayhap take a few more of your best men with ye to be safe."

Ian's eyes widened, and then he threw back his head and let out great peals of laughter. Fagan didn't notice that he had clenched his mouth tighter in response to Ian's merriment. He was glad his friend found Ruairi's words so amusing.

"What are ye laughing at, ye bastard?"

Ian took another drink from his tankard and then choked out his words. "And who is going to protect Fagan from Lady Grace?"

"My wife asked me the same."

Fagan shook his head with disgust. *"Thoir an aire.* I should run ye both through for opening your mouths again." *Be careful.*

"Och, donna be cross with us. Ye know 'tisnae too often we find a Highlander, let alone a Highland captain, being bested by a lass, and an English lass at that. As of late, we need to have a good laugh, eh?" Ian gave Fagan a mock salute.

"I'm happy that I could provide ye both with enjoyment, but *tha sin gu leòr." That is enough.* He leaned toward Ian, placing his elbows on his thighs. "And while we're on the subject of the lasses, let me be the first to offer ye a piece of advice. If ye donna want to find *your* eye blackened, I suggest ye stay far away from Lady Elizabeth."

"Fagan," warned Ruairi.

"My apologies. Was I nae to open my mouth, my laird?"

"Lady Elizabeth? Why would I stay away from her? What are ye talking about?"

Fagan sat back in the chair and lifted a brow. He couldn't help but turn up his smile a notch. He found even more pleasure when his laird sighed and cast a look of death upon him. Fagan knew that Ruairi would make him suffer for his words, but for now, he'd sit back and revel in the moment.

"I wasnae going to say anything, but my wife told me that Elizabeth seems to have taken a sudden fancy to ye."

Ian placed his hand over his heart, and his voice went up a notch. "Me? What in the hell would she want with the likes of me? Ye do know that lasses run at the sight of me." He hesitated. "Ye are both jesting with me."

"I wish we were," said Ruairi.

"How can that be? The only words I've ever spoken to her were in kind. She's a young lass. Why wouldnae she fancy someone her own age?"

Ruairi had a serious look on his face. "I donna know."

"Mayhap she misses her father, eh?" Fagan bit down on his lower lip to stifle the laughter that wanted to escape his mouth.

A grim expression crossed Ian's face, and he shifted

in the chair. "Let me make something clear to the both of ye." He pointed to Ruairi. "Ye have Ravenna." He threw his hand in the direction of Fagan. "And there isnae a more suited pair on this green earth who deserve each other more than ye and Lady Grace do." He stuck his thumb to his chest. "But I donna want, nor do I need, a lass, let alone an *English* lass who fancies me."

Ruairi tilted his head to the side. "Ye know? I said the same words before I wed my wife. Donna ye remember?"

Ian's eyes narrowed. "Donna make me wipe that smirk from your face, Sutherland. I donna want ye two meddling in my life. I'm sure Lady Elizabeth is a fine lassie, but clearly she has nay sense if she wants anything to do with the likes of me. Ye need to keep your brood here under your roof because I sure as hell donna want them crossing the border to my lands. Do ye understand? I have enough troubles with the Highland lairds. Who in their right mind would want to add English lasses in the mix?"

Fagan slapped Ian on the shoulder. "Grace and I have tried to deter Elizabeth, and 'tis more than likely a passing fancy. Donna worry upon it. She's only fifteen and has plenty of time to come to her senses. But whatever ye do, for God's sake, try nae to encourage the lass."

"Ye donna need to lecture me on how to deter the lasses." Ian gave a quick nod to Ruairi. "Mayhap ye should come to see me from now on. It seems like I take a chance every time I set foot on Sutherland lands. I'm afraid ye've been invaded by the English, my friend."

Ruairi casually rested his arm on the desk, and a devil-ish look came into his eyes. "I just had a thought. Grace will be taking her leave with Fagan. Mayhap if ye take Elizabeth out of my hands, I'll only have my wife and wee Katherine under roof. Ye know ye could be willing to help out a friend for as much as I've helped ye."

Ian took another drink of ale. "Aye, there is nay denying that ye've helped me with the crops and supplied me with men in the past on more than one occasion, but have ye nae learned anything? Women are like damn midges, naught but pests, and I'm afraid ye and your lands are sorely infested."

After having to watch Elizabeth as she sat on the edge of her seat, hanging on every word Laird Munro said, Grace had had more than enough. She lingered longer than she should have in the hallway to the bedcham-bers only to make certain her besotted sister sought her bed and didn't do something foolish. When noth-ing out of the ordinary occurred, Grace said a silent prayer of thanks and relieved herself of guard duty. She walked to the parapet, needing to clear her head. The longer she stayed in Scotland, the more her thoughts became muddled, especially about her future.

The flickering torchlight cast the Sutherland guard in shadows as the men walked along the wall. There was no light of the moon or any stars lighting the night sky. Other than the dim light of the torch behind her, darkness enveloped her, and Grace was content being alone. When a scraping noise came from behind her, she turned.

Fagan closed the parapet door and was adjusting the hilt of his sword in his scabbard. He grinned. "I thought I'd find ye here."

"Why? Miss me, Fagan?"

"Did Ravenna talk to ye?"

"About what?" As he stood beside her on the parapet, she found herself inching away from him. His nearness made her senses spin.

"Ian's visit."

"No, she didn't. Was everything all right?"

He looked out into the darkness. "Ruairi had sent Ian a missive about the mercenaries, and just to be cautious, Ian had increased his guard. Munro men followed the vagrants as they made their way across the English border."

Grace released the breath she didn't know she was holding. "They're gone."

"Aye."

"That's a relief. That man with the scarred face was a little frightening."

"Aye, well, Munro looks just as fierce. 'Tis too bad Elizabeth doesnae feel that way. Did ye see her fawning all over the man during the meal?"

"Yes, please don't remind me. I don't know what she sees in him."

"Well, I donna think ye need to worry about Ian returning her…whatever this is." Fagan gestured with his hand, and then Grace looked back out over the darkened bailey. He elbowed her in the arm in a playful manner. "Truth be told, I think ye lasses frighten him."

"We should. All you men should remember that

it doesn't take that much strength to blacken a man's eye."

"Careful, *bhana-phrionnsa*."

With an odd twinge of disappointment, she spoke quietly. "I suppose since the mercenaries have left Scotland, you'll now be able to escort me home."

"Aye. We leave within a sennight."

Grace nodded, and there was a heavy silence between them.

"To be truthful, I donna quite know what to say."

She flattened her hands against the stone wall for support because no words came to her mind either. Fagan placed his hand under her chin, turning her to face him. He touched her jaw with a gentle, caring gesture, and for a moment, time stood still. She lifted her hand and clutched his against her cheek.

"My words fail me as well."

He gave her a gentle smile. "They say there is a first time for everything." Hastily, she pulled her hand away. "I'm only jesting with ye, Grace."

"I know. I've really loved the time that I've spent with my sisters, and I think they'll be fine here in the Highlands. But please promise me that you'll look after them. You know they mean everything to me."

"Ye have my word. I'll watch after them as if they were my own."

"Thank you."

"Ye donna need to thank me, lass." He lowered his gaze as if he was collecting his thoughts.

"What is it?"

His eyes met hers. "I was going to apologize to ye for stealing a wee kiss or two, but if I speak the truth,

I'm truly nae sorry. Och, aye, I know it was wrong, but I tend to lose all sense of reason around ye. I cannae offer up one single excuse for my actions."

"I can't say that I'm any better, you know. I'll be returning to England and marrying Daniel. Yet as I stand here before you, I cannot get you out of my mind, Fagan Murray. What I feel is not fair to Daniel—not to mention that Ravenna and Ruairi would kill us both if they knew what we've done." She shook her head. "I don't know what else to say on the matter other than I'm so confused."

"Mayhap there is naught else to say between us." He pulled her into the circle of his arms, and she rested her head on his muscled chest. She breathed in his spicy scent as he smoothed her hair, placing his chin on the top of her head. "Your confusion is matched, lass. My mind tells me one thing, but my heart says another. *Chan eil mi riamh cho toilichte 's a tha mi an diugh.*" He thought briefly about not translating his words, but he was no coward. He whispered, "I was never so happy as I am this day."

# *Eleven*

GRACE TOOK ONE LAST LOOK AT HER BEDCHAMBER AND closed the door. In that moment, she knew her life would never be the same; the next time she visited her sisters, she would no longer be a Walsingham. She stood in the hall with her hand on the latch of the door and her head bowed. For a moment, she was afraid to let go.

"Do you have everything? If you forget something, I can always bring it to you when I see you," said Ravenna.

Grace dropped her arm and pasted a bright smile on her face. "I don't think I've left anything behind." A certain Highland captain came to mind, but she quickly banished the thought.

"I'm going to miss you. We're all going to miss you. Are you certain you're going to be all right at the manor house alone? Perhaps I could ask Uncle Walter to have someone else look in on you as well."

Grace waved her sister off. "There's no need for that. I'm not the family spy for the Crown."

"I'm sorry that your time here was more eventful than expected."

Grace offered her sister a forgiving smile. "You couldn't have known about those men. I'm fine. Truly."

"I've been thinking a lot lately about the conversation we had in the field."

"Don't worry. I'll keep practicing my aim. I remember your instructions."

"Not about that. I want to share something with you that Uncle Walter once told me: You don't choose who to love. Love finds you. I suppose what I'm trying to say is that you cannot, and most certainly should not, force your feelings for Daniel. I only want you to be happy, and you don't have to marry him if you don't want to. The banns haven't even been posted yet."

Grace spoke in a solemn tone. "I know our father wanted the best for us. He groomed you, Ravenna, to take his place as one of the realm's most valuable spies. To be honest, I still haven't decided what to do with the knowledge you've given me about spy craft, nor is my mind made up as to whether or not I'll be having *that* particular conversation with Uncle Walter when I return. But I do know that our mother and father wanted Elizabeth, Katherine, and me to wed well. You've already chosen your path, and I'm trying to stay on mine."

When a concerned look crossed Ravenna's face, Grace added, "I see the love you share with Ruairi, Sister. Perhaps one day I will be blessed with the same. Daniel and I could grow to love each other."

There was a heavy silence.

"I can see it in your eyes," Ravenna said. "You're

troubled, and you without a doubt have something on your mind. Is it Daniel? Are you confused about whether or not you should say your vows?"

"May I ask something of you?"

"You may ask me anything, as long as your question doesn't have anything to do with working for the Crown."

Grace puckered her lips with annoyance. "I assure you my question has nothing to do with king and country." She met her sister's eyes. "How did you know that you were in love with Ruairi?"

Ravenna's mouth dropped open. "Umm…"

"Since I've never been in love, I'm just curious how you knew Ruairi was the man that you were destined to share your life with. How did you *know*? You don't have to answer if you don't want to."

"It's not that I don't want to answer you. I'm only surprised by your question. Let me see. When did I know that I loved Ruairi?" Ravenna bit her lower lip. "I guess when I realized that I cared for the man more than I wanted to spy on him. Once I allowed the barriers to fall between us, I no longer saw him as a Scottish laird, the enemy. Being English or Scottish didn't matter. I cared for a man, and he cared for a woman. I saw the goodness in him. He was kind to his people and to his son. I suppose I always knew."

Ravenna's eyes glazed over as if she were in a trance, and she continued. "I've learned that the heart does not lie. The thought of never being with him or having him in my life again shattered me. Not a day went by that I didn't think of his smile or remember his laugh, his touch, and how that alluring Scottish accent always made my knees tremble." She shook her head. "I'm sorry. Did that answer your question?"

Grace cleared her throat. "Yes, that was more than enough."

They walked to the bailey where the waiting horses and the carriage were ready to depart. As Elizabeth and Kat stood in the courtyard, Grace felt a sharp stab in her heart. She needed to be strong, to keep her chin up for her sisters. But when Kat ran toward her and threw her arms around Grace's midriff, that little gesture was almost Grace's undoing. She choked back a sob.

"I'll miss you! Who's going to keep Torquil and me out of trouble? Are you sure you can't stay? Ruairi has room for us all." Kat pulled back and glanced at Ravenna's husband. "Isn't that right, Ruairi? Tell Grace there's enough room for us all. Tell her she can stay."

When the man's eyes widened in panic, Grace tried to stay the giggle that wanted to escape her.

"Aye, Lady Grace is welcome to stay."

Grace approached him and patted him on the arm. "That must have hurt quite a bit, Laird Sutherland, but rest assured, I'll be taking my leave to England and leave you all in peace." As a look of relief passed over his face, Grace leaned in close. "But I will say this… I am leaving Elizabeth and Kat in your care and under your protection. If you do *anything* to place them in harm's way, I will kill you. And just so we're clear, you've wed my sister. If you do *anything* to hurt Ravenna…"

"Come now, *bhana-phrionnsa*. Ye didnae just threaten my laird, did ye?" asked Fagan.

Ruairi gave Grace a slight pat on her shoulder. "Ye will be sorely missed, Grace, but ye best be on your way. Be safe, lass." He turned, and Grace didn't see him roll his eyes at Ravenna.

"I'll miss you, but we'll see you again for your wedding. You're going to be the most beautiful bride. Daniel will not be able to take his eyes from you." Elizabeth wrapped her arms around Grace.

When Grace lifted her eyes, Fagan lowered his to the ground. They both knew the day of reckoning could not be postponed forever. There was no sense in denying the inevitable. The man she'd sparred with and at first despised was her escort back to England. In a strange twist of fate, the Highland captain she had grown to care for was returning her home, delivering her straight into the waiting arms of her betrothed.

Grace bid her final farewell, and Ravenna accompanied her to the waiting carriage. The driver stepped down and opened the door, but before Grace took his hand, she turned and embraced her sister again.

"I wish you the very best," said Grace.

Ravenna pulled back and placed her hand on Grace's shoulder. "I know you're not fond of the Highlands, but thank you for coming here and sharing my wedding day. And don't worry about the girls. I'll take good care of them. We'll see you in the spring for your wedding." She lowered her voice in a conspiratorial whisper. "But I will support whatever decision you make. You're my sister." When Grace didn't respond, Ravenna smiled. "Do tell Uncle

Walter and Daniel that I wish them well. Safe travels to you all."

Grace nodded and stepped up into the carriage. The driver closed the door, and she settled back against the seat. As she rode out the gates accompanied by ten Highland warriors on horseback, she turned and waved, leaving billowing trails of dust in her wake and the only family she knew behind.

Fagan rode in silence. He wasn't in the mood to talk to his men, and he sure as hell didn't want to think about escorting Grace back to England. At times, the lass drove him completely mad—she had blackened his eye after all. But when she lowered her defenses and he caught a glimmer of what lay beneath the surface, Grace was the kind of woman who comforted his tired soul…and challenged him at every turn.

The sound of clomping hoofbeats brought him back from his woolgathering. Fagan and four of his men led while five guarded the rear. Not long after they left the gates, Fagan realized that he didn't want to be the one trailing behind Grace's carriage. He knew his logic made no sense, but he didn't want to watch her leave. He couldn't. As long as she remained behind him, he wouldn't have to erase the memory of seeing her go.

Only when the threat of darkness fell upon them did Fagan gesture the party from the dirt path and into a clearing. They'd stopped twice along the way, and Fagan had managed to avoid the lass because his words failed him. He tethered his horse to a tree and approached the carriage as Grace stepped down.

"I hope your ride isnae too uncomfortable. We'll stop here for the eve and give the horses a chance to rest."

"I'm all right, but I do need to take a walk. Pray excuse me." Grace stepped around him, and he grabbed her elbow.

"I'll accompany ye."

She lifted a brow. "I assure you this is one task that I'm perfectly capable of performing on my own, Mister Murray."

"Aye, donna wander too far into the trees." Fagan watched her walk away, and a hand came down on his shoulder.

"Do ye think the mercenaries will return?"

Calum, Fagan's second in command, gazed around the clearing, his hand on the hilt of his sword. His red hair was almost the same color as Ian's, but the man wasn't as fierce looking as the Munro. Then again, Fagan didn't meet many men who mirrored Ian's wild appearance. His friend gave new meaning to the term "wild Scots" for sure.

"I donna believe so, but we cannae be certain. Make sure the men stay on alert. We will make camp here for the eve."

"Aye, captain."

Fagan rarely had to tell his men what to do because each of them knew his purpose well. The horses had already been unfastened from the carriage and the animals were grazing. One of his men started a fire as some of the others scouted the perimeter, making certain their camp was a safe place to bed down for the eve.

The heavy thicket surrounding the clearing would provide enough of a blanket to shield them from any possible attack. If any threat did come upon them, Fagan and his men would have enough time to draw their swords to fend off the enemy. A familiar voice cursing through the trees only further confirmed Fagan's thoughts.

He walked through the tall, green grass and came to a dead halt when he reached the edge of the clearing. "Problem, *bhana-phrionnsa*?"

Grace's voice was hoarse with frustration. "My dress is tangled. Every time I move forward, my skirts pull out behind me. I don't want to rip them."

He unsheathed his sword. "Donna move."

She gasped. "What are you doing? You're not going to cut my dress, are you?"

"Trust me."

Fagan swung at the nettles, thistles, and branches, clearing a path so that he could get to her. As he cut his way toward her, she leaned her head back, as if to prevent him from removing it.

"I certainly hope you know what you're doing."

"I know how to wield my own sword, lass." When he finally stood within a hairbreadth from her lips, he gave her a roguish grin. "And ye'll have to take my word that I wield it verra well."

❧

Grace couldn't move. Not only was her dress tangled in the brush, but Fagan's body was so close that if she moved even an inch forward her lips would be locked with his. She knew she was in trouble when she couldn't think of a cold retort, and then she silently cursed her body when she took a sharp intake of breath.

His eyes froze on her lips. "'Tisnae verra often I find ye at a loss for words." He rested one of his hands at her waist and leaned around behind her. Any words that came to mind were long gone. "Now hold still." He gave her skirts a firm tug.

"Be careful."

He spoke through clenched teeth. "If ye feel ye can do any better, I'll let ye have at it." He gave her dress another pull, and curse words were thrown like stones. "'Tis really stuck in the brush."

"Well, try not to tear it."

"There." He stood, and his eyes met hers. He brought his hand to his lips and sucked the blood from the small scratch on his thumb. "Ye are finally free."

Grace had a sudden feeling that the man meant in a literal sense, especially when he abruptly turned on his heel and walked back into the clearing without her. She lifted her skirts, managing to walk out of the brush relatively unscathed. Fagan was carrying a bundle from the carriage and placed it down on the other side of the fire.

"What are you doing?"

He knelt on the ground and pulled out a blanket. "I'm making a tent for ye. Ye will sleep on this side of the fire. If anyone stumbles upon us, they will have to go through me and my men first. As ye know, they cannae escape through the brush behind ye."

"I don't think the weather is going to turn. I can sleep on a blanket near the fire." Fagan continued with his purpose. "If anyone does come, I don't want to be trapped in a tent. I can reach my dagger much faster if I'm not climbing out of there."

"Aye, well, donna forget I've seen ye wield that blade. Furthermore, if ye decided to use your dagger as a weapon, I wouldnae only be concerned for your safety, but I would also fear for the safety of my men." When he looked up and gave her a boyish grin, she couldn't help but smile.

She shrugged with indifference and then mirrored his tone, mocking his accent. "Aye, well, donna forget that I've bested ye before. I know how to defend myself." When he didn't respond, Grace knelt on the ground. "May I help you with that?"

"Aye." He held out his hand. "Let me see your dagger, and be sure nae to cut yourself, *bhana-phrionnsa*."

"Oh, you do make me laugh, Mister Murray." She pulled out her blade from under her skirts and handed it to him.

"Thank ye." He drove a stake into the ground with the hilt of her dagger, and then he handed it back to her with a smile. "That is the closest I ever want to get to that blade."

"Come now, Fagan. Don't tell me you're jealous because you can't throw a dagger like me or my sister."

"I donna think many men could best Ravenna, lass, but I do agree with ye. Ye're verra dangerous with a blade."

As she sheathed her weapon back under her skirts, she knew Fagan jested with her. "I know my aim isn't too accurate, but Ravenna says the only way for me to get better is to practice."

"Aye, and ye do need *a lot* of practice, lass." When she slapped him on the arm, he didn't even flinch. Instead, he held up his hands in mock defense. "Donna be cross with me because I speak the truth."

"Yes, well, I've learned that sometimes the truth hurts."

"In all seriousness, donna give up. I've ne'er known ye to yield to anything. Ye are rather persistent, if nae a wee bit stubborn at times."

"I could very well say the same of you."

"I am nae denying it." He stood and pulled her to her feet, gesturing to the tent. "'Tisnae much, but it will provide ye shelter if ye're chilled."

"It's perfect. Thank you."

"Do ye want something to eat? I have some dried beef and oatcakes."

She walked over to the carriage. "Ravenna had the cook pack a basket for all of us. Can you help me reach it?"

"Aye, where is it?"

She pointed to the basket on the back of the carriage. "There."

Fagan lifted his arm and reached for the food. The muscles underneath his tunic tightened, and Grace tore her gaze away from him. She'd spent so many hours trying to learn him by heart but knew she needed to shut out any awareness of him. When she couldn't resist another peek, she chastised herself for her foolish behavior.

At that moment, she realized the fates were laughing at her expense. The man was bent over, removing food from the basket. For God's sake, she heard herself swallow. Fagan's kilt rode low on his lean hips and his buttocks stuck out in front of her. She was a lady. She shouldn't be having such sinful thoughts about a man. That revelation quickly fled as Fagan leaned over even farther to reach something on the bottom of the basket.

Not being able to watch him any longer, Grace moved to his side. "Why don't you let me do that? You can gather your men to eat."

He stood to his full height. "All right."

Praise the saints, the man agreed. She didn't think she could bear watching his firm buttocks bobbing up and down anymore.

She finally sat with Fagan and a handful of his men around the fire. The setting sun was now replaced with the light of the moon. The land was quiet around them, even more so since none of the men conversed. The only sound came from the logs that crackled in the fire. Fagan stood and placed another piece of wood on the burning embers as she watched the flames rise and fall.

He sat on the other side of the fire, away from her. She tried to relax, but he held her eyes and she couldn't look away. He stared back in silence. Hugging her legs to her chest, she lowered her forehead to her knees. She sat in the same position for some time, and when she lifted her head, he was gone.

Grace stood and brushed down her skirts. She'd make one more visit into the trees before she sought her bed. She had just taken a step away from the fire when someone spoke.

"Lady Walsingham, do ye want to take a torch with ye?"

She turned, and the red-haired man pulled himself to his feet. "Calum, is it not?"

"Aye, m'lady."

"No, thank you. I'll only be a moment."

She retraced her steps into the brush. Fagan had cut down enough of those prickly plants that she should be able to relieve herself without injury. She'd made certain that she didn't wander too far into the woods and turned to make sure she didn't step too far away from the fire. She ran her boot over the ground to try to crush anything that stuck up from it. She couldn't imagine her nether regions coming into contact with those sharp thorns. After taking care of her personal needs, she stood and straightened her skirts.

A branch snapped behind her, and she jumped.

"Who is there?" The only response was another snapping branch a lot closer than the last one. "Fagan, if you're trying to frighten me, I will pull out my dagger. I don't think you want me to use it."

When no one answered, she stood perfectly still. She dared not breathe. If that dastardly man thought to catch her unaware, she'd be more than happy to blacken his other eye. She didn't find this amusing in the least.

As a scraping sound came from a nearby tree, all sorts of images came to mind, and all of them were far from pleasant. Perhaps someone was sharpening their blade to use it against her. Then again, she'd also heard tales of supernatural occurrences in Scotland. Perhaps the sound she heard wasn't a person at all. When a specter suddenly came to mind, she knew she'd lost all sense of reason. She rubbed her boot along the ground and felt for a rock. She picked up the stone and tossed it toward the sound that she'd heard.

Branches and twigs snapped. Someone or something scrambled in the woods. Not being able to see the forceful sounds that echoed in the darkness, she shivered from a sudden chill.

Something moved out of the corner of her eye.

A large, menacing figure loomed toward her, and she froze. Her breath hitched in her lungs as she felt her heart pounding through her chest. She began to shake as fearful images built in her mind. When a chill, black silence enveloped her once again, she clenched her hand until her nail bit into her palm.

The darkened figure crept closer, and she forced herself to straighten her spine. That's when Grace reached the conclusion that she'd do the only thing she could think of to save her life.

She screamed.

# Twelve

FAGAN HAD TO REMOVE HIMSELF FROM GRACE'S presence. When he realized he wanted nothing more than to touch her soft flesh and kiss her sweet lips, he decided to share his company with his mount and some whisky instead. He patted An Diobhail on the neck and took a much-needed swig, and then he took another. Ruairi had known that Fagan would need something strong to survive Grace's company the entire way to England. His friend had been kind enough to make certain Fagan was supplied with plenty of drink for his travels.

As the fiery liquid soothed his nerves, Fagan made his way over to his men to make sure they stayed at their post, even though he knew they did. He had to keep busy because every time he looked at Grace, he felt like he was punched in the gut. A shrill scream shot through the darkness, and he ran into the clearing.

Fagan and Calum clamored into the forest with swords drawn. Grace didn't move as they ran to her side. Calum held up a torch, moving from left to right, then stilled as an enormous red stag stood no more than a few yards away. How the noise or Grace's scream didn't frighten off the animal was a mystery, but when a branch snapped under Calum's foot, the deer leaped off into the trees.

*"Gabhail aigir na frìthe?"* asked Fagan. *Taking joy in the deer forest?*

Grace clenched her teeth tightly, and that's when Fagan gestured for Calum to depart, but not before Fagan grabbed the torch. The lass continued to glare at him, frowning. She pointed her finger at his chest exactly like the first time they'd met.

"I don't even have to know what those words mean, but I'm sure they were not kind. So before you say another word, I thought the animal was one of the men from the beach. I am perfectly aware the vagrants left Scotland, but that was the first thought that came to mind." She continued to speak in a clipped tone. "I'm weary. I've had enough excitement for one evening, and I don't want to hear anything further."

He lifted a brow as she walked back to the clearing with long, purposeful strides. Following her, he placed the torch back into the flames as Grace sat on a blanket in front of the fire. She made every effort not to look at him, but that little nagging voice inside him refused to be stilled. The temptation was too great not to say anything. He found the perfect opportunity when she was about to crawl into the tent.

"Grace…" When he said her name, she turned and looked at him as if she dared him to say a single word. Deciding not to start another argument, he honestly tried to stay his tongue. But at the last moment, he found he couldn't resist. "Sleep well, my *dear.*"

"Arse."

When Grace cursed him in the same tone as a Scottish warrior on the battlefield, he couldn't stay his smile. The lass had spirit. He supposed that's what he admired about her. As she snarled at him and entered the tent, he briefly wondered if she'd be lonely in there all by herself. That's when he hastily resumed his purpose.

The whisky would be his only bed partner this eve, as it had been for a fortnight.

❧

And she thought sleeping in the same bed with Elizabeth and Kat was uncomfortable. All that was missing were flailing arms and legs kicking her in the gut. Although she tried to adjust her position many times, the ground was hard beneath her. She might as well have been sleeping on rocks. Maybe she was. All she did was toss and turn. To add to that misery was the fact that she felt like a bloody fool.

She always prided herself on not being a fragile flower, but now she had made an idiot of herself in front of the men. Could there be anything more mortifying than that? At least she'd stood her ground with the animal. She could very well have just cowered like Ravenna did every time she laid eyes on poor Angus.

Grace turned over onto her back and blew the hair away from her lips. Inside the tent was brutal torture. She was so hot. There was no circulation, and she felt as if she was suffocating. She wished Fagan would've let her sleep under the stars next to the fire, but she understood. She was traveling with ten men after all.

She kicked the blanket off her legs and spoke between clenched teeth.

"I can't stand this anymore," she muttered.

She made her way clumsily out of the tent and stood. Immediately greeted by a brush of cool air on her cheeks, she closed her eyes, letting the soothing breeze wash over her. A few of the men slept around the fire, but her eyes were drawn to only one.

Fagan's strong back faced her. Even through the dim light of the fire, she could see how broad the man's shoulders were. She couldn't say she was surprised by the brazenness of her open admiration, but she needed to continue to fight this confusing need to be close to him. But as quickly as that logic came, it went. Although she knew her behavior was wrong, her gaze still roved and lazily appraised him.

"Out looking for deer, *bhana-phrionnsa*?"

Grace grabbed the blanket out of her tent and spread it on the ground. "I can't sleep," she whispered.

"At least close your eyes. The sun will rise in a few hours."

When he turned over, she mentally sighed. How could she possibly sleep with the man facing her? She wasn't in the mood for games so she did the only thing that came to mind. She turned her back on him and closed her eyes.

Of course morning arrived faster than she would've liked because the next she knew, she heard Fagan's voice through the haze.

"Are ye going to sleep the day away?"

Grace had a difficult time opening her eyes, but when she'd finally managed what should've been the simplest of tasks, Fagan was already putting out the embers of the fire with a bucket of water. The sun was up and apparently so was she. She pulled herself to her feet, her back cracking in protest.

Fagan chuckled. "It will nae be long. Ye'll be back in your own bed before ye know it."

"I count the days."

She folded the blanket as the men cleared the camp. While the horses were being readied, she decided to make her escape into the trees. As soon as she turned her back, Fagan spoke.

"Be sure to call upon me if ye need anything. Mayhap if we're lucky, we'll be able to have something good for sup this eve."

She heard one of the men laugh in response and presumed the sound came from Calum. If this was any inkling of how the day was going to be, she'd already had more than enough. She turned around and balled her fists at her side.

"Fagan…" When his eyes met hers, she pointed to her eye. "One more word, I dare you." He nodded and looked away. She was certain the deer mishap would not be mentioned again, especially since Fagan's pride was now at stake.

When Grace returned, the men were ready to depart. The driver held out his hand to assist her into the carriage, and she gazed around for a certain Highland captain. She didn't see him, and she had to admit that she was disappointed. She stepped up into the carriage to find an oatcake placed on the seat. Although the man wasted no time to get on his way, at least he remembered to leave her something to break her fast.

Before long, she once again found herself settling back and looking out at the Scottish landscape. The mountains were vast, the land so green, and the sky was a beautiful blue. Heather carpeted the fields, and her mind suddenly burned with the memory of her first kiss with Fagan. She would never forget a single detail. How he held her, kissed her, and touched her. Pensively, she looked out at the clusters of pine trees and the small stream that snaked next to the trail, but she didn't see any of the sights before her. She realized for the first time in her life that her future looked vague and shadowy.

❧

The skies blackened and rain pelted him in the face. Fagan lowered his head, and stinging drops in his eyes and on his cheeks prevented him from lifting it. He should've known better than to stop so early to sup. They ought to have traveled a bit farther. Perhaps then they wouldn't have been caught in the storm. He turned his mount around and reined in beside the carriage. Thunder crashed, and his mount shied.

"We cannae ride in this weather! We'll make our way to a crofter's hut beyond that pass!"

The heavy rain temporarily blinded him, and he couldn't see inside the carriage. He had to assume Grace nodded or was in agreement with his words. The trail was becoming too muddy for them to try to hasten their pace. He rode up to Calum, trying to shield his eyes along the way.

"We'll ride ahead to the crofter's hut in the glen. If I'm nae mistaken, I think the barn is still there." There was a loud clap of thunder, and lightning split a nearby tree right down the middle. An Diobhail became skittish, and Fagan patted the horse on the neck.

When they finally reached the top of the glade, the barn was a welcome sight. As long as everyone had a roof over their heads, God had granted them a boon. Fagan looked over his shoulder. The horses were struggling, slipping in the mud. The heavy weight of the carriage didn't help matters. The coach would never clear the crest.

The men dismounted and smacked their horses on the rump. Fagan wasn't surprised when the mounts did not linger and trotted down the path to the field below. He gestured for the coachman to stop, and Fagan and Calum flanked the horses.

Grace shouted. "Do you want me to get out?"

"Nay! Ye stay where ye are."

Another clap of thunder echoed through the glen, and the carriage horses became agitated, jostling in their harnesses. Fagan and Calum grabbed the horses' bridles and spoke in a soothing tone. Slowly, they coaxed the animals forward, but every time the horses stepped, they lost their footing.

"There is too much mud. I didnae want to do this, but I donna think we have a choice. We need to unload the carriage." Fagan nodded to the driver. "Ye keep the horses steady."

Fagan and Calum stepped around the coach and untied the two packhorses that trailed behind. The remainder of Fagan's men were starting to remove the trunks from the carriage when Grace called out.

"Are you certain you don't want me to get out? I will."

"I'm nae quite ready for that yet, lass. Ye stay where ye are. Let us try this first."

They unloaded everything they could from the coach and placed the bundles in a pile beside the trail. They'd have to come back for them later. Fagan and Calum walked to the front of the carriage, once again flanking the horses. After some gentle persuasion and a few more tries, the animals finally cleared the crest, and the carriage slowly descended into the valley below.

When they reached the glen, Fagan walked over to the carriage and knocked on the door. "Remain here until I come for ye."

At least Grace was dry.

The men had already gathered a few horses in the barn. Since there wasn't enough room for more than three animals, some of the mounts had to stand out in the rain. For a few moments, Fagan stood under the shelter of the barn watching the storm, which did not appear to be letting up any time soon. But when he didn't hear another rumble of thunder, he led some horses into the trees and tied them off. At least he could give the mounts some sort of protection from the elements.

His feet, as well as the rest of him, were drenched as he approached the carriage and opened the door. Hastily, he brushed back the hair that dripped in his face.

"Ye're going to have to make a run for it."

Grace gave him a compassionate smile. "You're soaked."

"Aye. 'Tis what happens when ye're caught in the

rain. Are ye going to sit there and watch me drown, or are ye going to come out?"

She leaned forward on the edge of the seat. "I don't think I have much of a choice."

He extended his hand and helped her down, and she made a mad dash into the crofter's hut. The room was small, but at least it would keep Grace dry. He walked around, which took no time at all, and found kindling in the corner. Other than the old table and a chair that lacked stability, there was a pallet in the corner. This would have to suffice.

"My apologies that the accommodations arenae what ye're accustomed to, but 'tis dry. I'll make a fire for ye."

She gave him a warm smile. "Please don't worry about me. I'm fine. Will your men all fit in the barn? You're all drenched."

"My men have slept in worse." When she shook off the rain from her skirts, he laughed. "Ye're barely wet."

"Yes, I must thank you for—"

Before she could finish her words, he shook like a dog and sprayed her with water.

"Thank you for that."

"'Tis my pleasure, lass."

⚜

Fagan picked up a few pieces of kindling and stacked them to start a fire in the hut. His tunic clung to him like a second skin. Every muscle could be made out with little left to the imagination, and his long hair was draped to the side over his shoulder. Fagan Murray was a fine specimen of a man, and Grace didn't even realize that she'd licked her lips at the sight before her.

"Truly, that can wait. Why don't you put on some dry clothes? You don't want to catch something."

"Nae until the fire is lit for ye."

God how she prayed the darned thing wouldn't start. She could stare at that lovely view all night long. As soon as the idea popped into her mind, the kindle sparked. She suppressed a sigh.

"Thank you, but I could have waited until you were dry. What about my trunk and the other things you unloaded from the carriage?"

Fagan stood and brushed his hands together. "They can sit where they are until the morrow. Nay one will be traveling this eve, especially in this weather. Your trunk will be fine where 'tis, unless ye had something ye need now."

She waved him off. "No, of course not."

He looked back at the pallet in the corner. "I have another blanket in my bag. I donna think 'tis wet. I'll bring it to ye. Give me but a moment. I want to see to the horses. Some of them werenae too fond of the thunder and lightning. An Diobhail was a wee bit skittish."

"I've been meaning to ask you something. An Diob—"

When she struggled with the name of Fagan's mount, he said, "An Diobhail."

"Yes. What does it mean?"

He chuckled in response. "Do ye really want to know?"

"I wouldn't ask if I didn't."

A flash of humor crossed his face. "The Devil."

Her eyes widened. "The Devil?"

"Aye, he was naught but a wee bastard when he was a colt. One day he was limping around in the field so I examined his foot. As I was pulling out a stone, he turned his head back and bit me in the arse. He's had the name ever since, and I think it suits him quite nicely. Donna ye think?"

Grace couldn't control her burst of laughter and held her hand over her chest. "Oh, I'm sorry, but that is almost as good as me punching you in the eye. Perhaps your horse and I would get along famously."

He pulled his tunic away from his skin. "Aye, well, I'm glad ye find the tale so amusing, but I need to see to the horses and change these wet clothes." He turned and grabbed the latch of the door, pausing. "Care to join me?"

Since the man didn't specify which task he had wanted her to join, she could only assume that he'd returned to his roguish ways. Before she lost her wits, she spoke in a dry tone. "I'd rather muck out stalls in the barn."

"As ye will…"

When he closed the door, she gazed around her shelter. At least she'd be dry. The pallet in the corner certainly couldn't be any worse than her insufferable time in the tent. She pulled what was left of a chair over in front of the fire. Placing her hand on the seat, she pushed on it, needing to be certain the old wood would support her. She placed her rump gently on the chair and gradually sat back.

At least the smoke was masking the musty odor

in the room. She'd been surprised when Fagan had wanted to stop so early to sup, and her belly rumbled now in response. After what the men had been through, she couldn't very well ask them to retrieve the bundle of food that had been left on the top of the hill. She'd just have to keep her mind occupied with something else.

Grace placed her elbow on her knee and rested her chin in the palm of her hand. This was going to be a long night. She wasn't even weary. Her eyes went back and forth between studying the flames and looking at the dirt floor. When she couldn't stand the restlessness any longer, she stood and stretched her back. That's when she heard a scratching noise coming from the corner.

Taking four carefully placed steps, she stopped when she reached the pallet. She stood like a statue. She didn't think the sound came from a crackling in the fire. She thought again about the noise she'd heard, which she believed was more of a scraping sound. Patiently, she waited. What else did she have to do?

Nothing stirred.

She nudged the pallet with her boot, and there was no movement. Perhaps she had imagined it. She took her seat again and threw another piece of wood into the fire. She'd be sure not to stir up the heat too much because she had no intention of repeating the unbearable temperature that she'd had in the tent.

There. She definitely heard that scratching noise again. Grace walked over to the pallet and kicked it with her boot. Nothing. She would go mad if she kept hearing that sound all night. Lifting the edge of the pallet, she pulled it away from the wall.

She gasped.

A large, wiry rat moved its way along the edge, and she squeaked louder than that abhorrent creature. Why God had created such abominations was beyond her comprehension. She hated rats as much as Ravenna despised dogs and Angus.

When the rat moved another inch toward her, Grace began to shake as fearful images built in her mind. All she could think of was that creature crawling under her skirts. She dropped the pallet and made a mad dash to the chair. Stepping up onto the seat, she didn't have time to worry if it would crash under her feet.

In her frenzy to escape, she lost sight of the rat. How could she be so careless? Her eyes darted back and forth, searching. She had to calm her racing heart, willing herself not to scream. She'd already been made the fool with the deer. If Fagan had to come in and kill a rat for her, she'd be made to endure his endless taunting.

She glanced over at the table, which might as well have been a million miles away. Her feet would have to touch the ground again. But what other choice did she have? There was a worn tankard right in the middle of the table. She looked at the floor, and when she didn't see anything, she leaped from the chair. Hastily, she grabbed the tankard and returned to her perch.

Grace wasn't certain what she was going to do, but maybe she could capture the rat in the tankard and throw it out the door. When she spotted the creature in the middle of the floor, her body moved into action before her mind. She threw the tankard at the rat but missed, and the tankard thumped hard against the wall. All she had managed to do was make the vermin change direction. But at least the dreaded thing was now heading toward the door.

She didn't have enough courage to place a toe on the floor again to open the door. That's when she realized there was only one thing left to do. She bunched up her skirts and pulled out her dagger that was strapped to her thigh. She could do this. Ravenna had taught her well. Grace only needed to remember her sister's instructions.

Moving her hand, Grace slid the dagger in place, moving the blunt edge of the blade into the crease of her hand. Putting her weight on her right leg, she kept her left leg slightly forward, trying not to fall from the chair. Her arm was perpendicular to the ground. Remembering to keep her movement fluid, she realized this was her moment of glory. She could do this by herself and didn't need a man to protect her.

Grace lifted the dagger and hurled it at the target.

Fagan opened the door, but it was too late. His eyes widened when the blade lodged in the frame, mere inches from his head, as the rat ran out the door.

# Thirteen

FAGAN CONTINUED TO GAZE IN WONDER AT THE BLADE that was at eye level and still shaking from the impact. He couldn't believe how the woman's aim could be that bad. Perhaps Grace should stick to using her fists because she was spot-on there. Then again, maybe she was using his head as a target. He pulled out the dagger and shook his head when he saw Grace was standing on the edge of the unsound chair. He moved abruptly toward her.

*"Tha thu gus mo liathadh."* You're driving me gray. He grabbed her arm to assist her. *"Feuch nach tuit thu."* See you don't fall. She stepped down from the chair and held out her hand for the dagger. When he placed the hilt gently on her palm, he spoke with a heavy amount of sarcasm. *"Na leòin thu fhéin."* Don't hurt yourself.

"You do know that if you want me to understand you, you actually need to stop speaking Gaelic."

"Aye." He closed the door. "I know that I'm going to regret asking this, but what in the hell are ye doing?"

She turned away from him and shivered. "I saw a rat, a rat of immense proportions. I. Don't. Like. Rats."

"Why didnae ye call me? I would've killed it for ye."

Grace picked up a tankard that was on the floor against the wall and placed it on the table. "Because after the disaster with the deer, I didn't think my pride could handle jesting about a rat."

"Well, I'm here now. I'll find it and get it out for ye."

"You already did. When you opened the door, the vermin ran out."

He chuckled. "And ye tried to kill the wee bastard by throwing your dagger at it? Did ye ever think ye might have been more successful had ye just opened the door and let it out?"

She held up her hand to stay him and spoke in a warning tone. "Fagan, I'm in no mood for—"

"All right, all right. I'll ne'er pretend to understand why lasses have such foolish fears over naught. Between Ravenna with Angus and now ye with the rat… I think ye women should be worried about things of far more importance, rather than spending your time fretting over things that will nae cause ye harm." He shrugged with indifference. "Mayhap I should be saying a prayer of thanks. At least I have yet to hear ye complain about the weather, the journey, your hair, or your dress."

Grace lifted a brow. "Is this truly the discussion you want to have with me right now?"

"Nay, I was only making conversation. I brought

ye a blanket." He held out the cover in front of him more as a peace offering.

She took the blanket and placed it on the table. "Thank you, but I don't think I'll be sleeping anytime soon."

"Ye said so yourself. The rat went out the door. There is naught more to fear."

Grace walked over and stirred the fire.

"My men and I are sleeping in the barn. Donna hesitate to call upon me for any reason, even for a rat. Do ye need anything else before I take my leave?"

She took a step toward him and placed her hand on his arm. "Please don't go. Will you stay with me for just a little while longer?"

He knew this was a bad idea. He kept telling himself to walk out the door. Now. Turn. Go. What the hell was he doing? What was he waiting for? God, she was still waiting for him to answer, and he stood there like an idiot. He surprised himself when his eyes lowered and froze on her lips.

"How could I refuse such a request?"

Grace was relieved that Fagan had agreed to stay. That way she didn't have to confess that she was nervous about the rat. If the vermin returned or if, God forbid, another one should come upon her, Fagan would be there to ward off the intruders. Perhaps she could talk him into leaving his sword with her for the night. His weapon was certainly longer than hers. More than likely, she could send the rat to its maker without even getting too close.

"Are ye hungry? I have something to drink and dried beef in my satchel in the barn. At least I believe the beef is still dry."

Thunder clapped overhead, and she jumped. Fagan had changed his wet clothes. She wouldn't send him back out there, especially not for her. "I'm fine."

"Lass, ye donna speak the truth verra well. 'Twas but a simple question I asked of ye." He shook his head. "I'll be right back." He grabbed the latch on the door, and she touched his shoulder.

"You're dry now. You don't have to go out there for me. You and your men have done enough."

"I'm nae going out in the rain for ye. I'm going for me. I could use a drink, and I could eat. And truth be told, so could ye."

The door closed, and Grace shrugged. There was no sense talking to someone who wouldn't listen to reason. A sudden heavy rain pelted the thatch roof. When water started to drip on the table, she briefly closed her eyes. She'd rather drown in the crofter's hut, as long as the rat didn't return. The door swung open, and Fagan secured it with the latch.

"'Tis really coming down out there."

"So I see. You're drenched again, Mister Murray. Sit down by the fire." Grace grabbed the blanket from the table and shook it out. When she turned, Fagan stood by the flames. "Please sit in the chair. I'll pull the pallet over and sit on the floor." He sat down carefully, and she wrapped the blanket around his shoulders.

He pulled the cover off his large frame. "Nay. I'm all wet. Ye'll need this to sleep this eve."

"Then take off your tunic and cover yourself with the blanket."

He lifted a brow and gave her a roguish grin. "But *all* my clothes are wet."

"And that will never happen."

Fagan said something under his breath that she knew she didn't want to hear, and then he took a swig of something. He lifted his hand and grabbed the back of his tunic, pulling it over his head one-handed. When his eyes met hers, she didn't realize that she needed to lift her fallen jaw. His bare chest glistened in the firelight, and every line of his body was defined. She imagined her fingers exploring every single crevice of his hard flesh.

"Are ye going to stand there and stare at me, or are ye going to take my tunic and hang it by the fire?"

She pursed her lips. "Actually, I was going to just stand here and stare at you, but I suppose I could hang up your tunic." He gave her the garment and she placed it near the fire on a nail in the wall.

When she turned back around, he had covered himself with the blanket. She couldn't say she was pleased that he was now hidden from view, but at least he had some sense because she certainly did not. She dragged the pallet across the floor and sat down beside him.

"Are the horses all right?"

"Aye, I placed a few of them under the trees to give them a wee bit of shelter."

"Is the barn dry for your men?"

He handed her something to drink. "There are a few leaks in the roof, but we'll survive."

She brought the wine sack to her lips and swallowed twice before she realized that her throat burned. She became plagued with a coughing fit and brought her hand to her lips. "What is that?"

"'Tis what Ruairi and I drink. *Uisge beatha*."

"And what does that mean exactly?"

"Water of life."

Grace turned her head to the side and coughed again. "I don't know about life, but if I take another drink of that, your *water* will surely bring about my death."

"'Tis an acquired taste."

"I should say so. That's dreadful."

"Here." He handed her a piece of dried beef.

"I'll take anything to kill the taste on my tongue." Hastily, she tossed the food into her mouth.

"I donna suppose we ever have to worry about ye getting into your cups then."

"No."

She looked into the flames, trying to slow her racing mind. She was alone with Fagan, and his mere presence made her heart skip. After a heavy silence, he spoke.

"I donna know if I'll be returning to England with Ruairi and Ravenna for your wedding in the spring. I'll likely send Calum in my stead."

She continued to stare into the fire that she didn't see. "Is there a reason, or do you find my company that unbearable?"

He paused. "I find that I enjoy your company too much, lass. 'Tis the problem."

Grace could feel his eyes watching her.

"I am nae daft enough to believe that I could've ever had ye, but I donna think I can watch ye be in the arms of another man, even Lord Casterbrook."

She gazed up at him.

"Ye're unlike any lass I've ever met. Ye challenge me and drive me completely mad. I knew that from the first time I saw ye. I didnae think I would, but I have to admit that I rather like it. If I had something to offer ye, I would fight to make ye mine. But I have naught to give."

She reached out and took his hand. "I don't like when you speak that way. A man is not defined by his wealth or his personal possessions. It is a man's character that makes him who he is. You're a kind and honorable man, even if your bloody mouth annoys me."

He smiled, and she dropped his hand. She bent her knees and hugged them to her chest. "If we're speaking the truth, I have to confess that I haven't decided if there will be a wedding in the spring." When he didn't respond, she continued. "Daniel is a kind man, but I don't know him all that well. The more I think about it, the more I want my marriage to be like Ravenna's." She looked at him and smiled. "Without all the tartans, kilts, and bagpipes, of course."

He rolled his eyes. "Of course, but what do ye mean?"

"Do you see the way my sister and Ruairi look at each other?"

"Aye. 'Tis hard to miss."

"Daniel and I have *never* looked at each other that way. And we certainly don't talk to each other the way…" She lowered her voice to a whisper. "The way that I talk with you."

A muscle ticked in Fagan's jaw and he stood. He grabbed his tunic from the wall, and Grace pulled herself to her feet.

"I must take my leave."

She slid her body between him and the door. "I don't want you to go."

"Lass, if ye donna move away from that door, I cannae be held responsible for my actions. And I donna think ye'll like them."

She lifted her hand to his chest and he stiffened. "Fagan, I don't understand what this is between us—"

"Your hand."

"But I know you feel the same. I'll never share with Daniel what I've already shared with you. If only for one night, I want to know love. I want to feel love. And I want to know it with you. Please stay."

Fagan felt like a stallion cornered by a mare. Grace's brazen words had been spoken and could not be taken back now. She didn't realize the danger she was in by blocking his only means of escape. She was playing with fire. He guided her hand to his kilt, perhaps to shock her back into reality and to show her what she did to him. But when her hand moved on its own accord, stroking, caressing…

"Ye have nay idea what ye're doing."

"Am I doing it wrong?"

"Nay, lass. Ye're doing everything right."

His mouth ravished hers. The time for restraint had

long since passed. He cupped her breast through her dress and then slid the sleeve down over one shoulder so that he could touch her naked flesh. He squeezed her taut nipple, and she tore his mouth from his.

"Fagan, please…"

He wasn't sure if she was begging him to stop or to continue. He lifted her into the cradle of his arms, and when she wrapped hers around his neck, he knew that he had his answer. Gently, he lowered her onto the pallet. He tugged her dress down enough to expose both of her breasts, and he sucked one of her nipples. Hard.

She moaned, even as she clutched his head close for more. He happily obliged her and teased her with his teeth and tongue. He made her gasp, sigh, and yearn. He was determined to make her feel something special that she'd never again feel with another man.

He moved to her other nipple and rolled it between his thumb and forefinger. As she ran her nails over his shoulders, he wanted nothing more than to bury himself in her womanly heat. But he would take it slowly. He wanted to savor everything about Grace.

Lifting his head, he brushed his lips against hers as he spoke. "I have dreamed of this moment, of ye, for many nights. Ye are much sweeter than I ever could've imagined."

His tongue explored the recesses of her mouth, and her dress crept up onto her thighs as she nestled against him. She ran her fingers down the length of his back. His hand caressed her bare leg, moving to her inner thigh, and she shuddered. When he shifted his body to remove her dress, she placed her hand on his chest to stay him.

"Wait. This doesn't seem right."

He had no idea how he was going to stop now, and he needed every ounce of restraint to pull away from her, but he did. He pushed himself to his knees before her. She was so damn beautiful with her lips slightly parted and her hair in total disarray. He tried to imprint the picture in his mind.

"I will be bare before your gaze, but you will not be bare before mine? How is that fair, Mister Murray?"

As if her words set him free, he growled in response and with a flick of his wrist, his kilt fell to a heap on the pallet. When her eyes openly studied him, he hardened even more before her wanton gaze.

"May I touch you?"

"Lass, ye donna have to ask to touch me."

When she hesitated, he took her hand and guided it to himself. Her fingers encircled him, and he showed her how to move to give him pleasure.

"Like that?"

"Aye," he said through gritted teeth.

He tugged her dress off her body, and then he froze. His eyes lazily appraised her, and his fingers lightly trailed over her breasts. "Ye are so verra bonny."

⁓

Fagan gave her a long, passionate kiss, the kind Grace was growing addicted to. She realized that she didn't want to share this feeling with anyone else—ever—only this man before her.

The way he fondled her breasts made her yearn for something just beyond her reach. All she knew was she craved more of his touch. She was fully aware of the hardness that brushed against her belly. But when his hand moved and slid up her inner thigh, she was glad the shadows from the crackling fire hid the flush in her cheeks.

"Fagan!" she cried out as he rubbed her most sensitive spot between her legs. She reached down and stilled his hand.

"Shhh…let me pleasure ye, if only for this night. Och, lass. Ye are so wet for me, so ready."

When his lips touched hers, all sanity fled. The man thrust his finger partially inside her at the same time his tongue entered her mouth. She couldn't catch her breath, couldn't—and didn't want to—stop the rush of heady pleasure.

She gripped his shoulders as he battered her defenses. She felt a vaguely unsatisfied ache down there, something she didn't quite understand. Fagan's caresses were making her mad with need. She wanted more. She needed…him.

"Fagan, please."

He pulled up her legs to straddle his waist, his member resting at the folds of her womanly heat. Gently, he pushed against her, and she thought she'd fall apart.

"Is this what ye want, lass?" His voice was thick and heavy. "Because once ye say 'aye,' there is nay turning back."

She lifted her fingers to his lips, and he kissed them. His eyes darkened with emotion, and a hot ache grew in her throat. "Yes. I want nothing more than to be with you."

He leaned over her and stilled. "This may hurt for

a wee bit, but I give ye my word the pain will lessen. Trust me."

"I do."

He kissed her, and she gasped when he entered her with a single thrust. He held perfectly still and placed his forehead to hers. His body shook, and sweat beaded on his brow.

"Are you all right?"

His eyes widened. "Me? Are ye?"

Grace gazed into his eyes and never wanted to look anywhere else again. She brought his lips to hers and kissed him as if he were her lifeline into this world and the next. Slowly and with unbearable tenderness, he moved inside her. At first, there was a slight discomfort, but then she found herself releasing her body, her mind, and her heart to him.

He reached down and rubbed the sensitive spot between them. She wasn't sure what she was doing but knew that he hadn't yet sought his own pleasure. She ran her fingernails down his back and he groaned.

"Did I hurt you?"

"Och, nay." He lifted his head. "I want to come inside ye." When she shifted and lifted her hips to seek a more comfortable position, he growled. "God…oh, God…aye, lass, aye…"

She could feel something building, thundering toward a peak. Between Fagan's words and the expert touch of his hand, she was coming apart. Their bodies were in exquisite harmony with one another. They were as one. "Fagan…"

"After ye, after ye…"

Waves of ecstasy flowed through her. The pleasure

was pure, and she cried out for release. Passion inched through her veins, and her whole being flooded with desire. She yielded to the searing need that had been building between them. Fagan grunted, and love flowed in her like warm honey.

He gently brushed the hair back from her forehead with his thumb. He captured her eyes with his and caressed her cheek before he rolled onto his side and draped his arm over her. His breathing, as well as hers, was heavy. She nestled her bottom into his groin, rubbing her fingernails over the tiny hairs on his arm. He spoke softly against her ear.

"Are ye all right?"

"Mmm… I think I'm doing rather well."

He kissed her on the top of the head. "I'm glad to hear it."

"And you?"

He nuzzled her neck. "I couldnae be better."

Grace rolled over and faced him. She lifted her hand to his cheek. "I want to remember you like this always."

He kissed the palm of her hand, and then his eyes narrowed. "There is naught to remember about me because ye are now mine."

# Fourteen

FAGAN HELD GRACE IN HIS ARMS UNTIL THE RISING SUN peeked through the slits in the door. He clung to the memory of last eve as if the woman in his embrace had saved him from drowning in a stormy sea. As he lightly fingered her loose tendrils, she nestled her head into his chest. He regarded her with curiosity as his mind was puzzled by new thoughts. Ideas he had never thought possible.

Grace stirred, her usually lively eyes sparkling up at him with weariness. "Mmm… I don't want to rise. You're so warm. Can't we just stay like this all day and shut out the rest of the world?"

"I'm afraid my men wouldnae agree to that. Besides, what if the rat returns? I donna think ye'd want to be lying flat on the pallet if he does."

She swatted at him. "That's why I have you and my dagger to protect me."

"Me, aye. Your dagger, nae so much." When she was about to protest, he silenced her words with his lips. He pulled back and gazed down lazily through half-closed lids. "Are ye all right?"

"I couldn't be better, Mister Murray." She gave him a soft smile.

"Did I hurt ye? I tried to be careful."

She ran her nails lightly over his arm. "At first, it was uncomfortable, but after a while I can honestly say that I enjoyed myself."

"Next time will nae be as unpleasant. I promise ye that."

"Oh, I don't think it's wise for there to be a next time between us. I have to say that's not a very good idea."

He lifted a brow. "What do ye mean?"

Grace raised her hand to his cheek. "For one night, I wanted to know love. I wanted to feel love. And I told you that I wanted to know it with you, being held in your arms. You gave me that."

"And I told ye… I *warned* ye that once ye said 'aye,' there was nay turning back."

She hesitated, blinking in confusion. "I don't understand." She sat up and held the blanket over her chest.

His eyes narrowed. "What is there to understand? I took your innocence."

"You didn't take anything. I *gave* you my innocence."

Fagan rose from the pallet and donned his kilt. "And if ye're with child, 'tis my child."

"Don't be ridiculous. I'm not enceinte."

"And ye say that because ye've had so much experience with this in the past?"

Grace pulled herself to her feet and wrapped the blanket around her. "Is that your concern?" When he didn't respond, she quickly added, "Ravenna told me she'd been with men before Ruairi because of her duties to the Crown. Yet she was never with child."

"Nevertheless, ye show up in the Highlands demanding to speak to your sister who ye thought was with child."

"You know very well that I didn't know Ravenna's purpose."

He pulled his tunic over his head. "I am nae going to quarrel with ye over this." He stepped around her to the pallet, and she turned to face him. "Let me tell ye how this is going to be, and then mayhap ye will nae be so confused. Like it or nae, Lady Grace, ye're mine. Ye gave yourself to me of free will. Lest ye forget ye're the one who stood between me and the door. I am taking ye to England for ye to break off your betrothal with Casterbrook. Once that's settled, ye will return with me to the Highlands." His voice became softer. "I know I donna have much to offer ye, but I give ye all that I have. I give ye me."

She poked him in the chest with her finger, and her voice went up a notch. "No one tells me what I can or cannot do, especially a man, a Highlander, who thinks he knows all and what's best for everyone around him." She spoke through clenched teeth.

"You have this way about you that makes me frustrated because you're so completely headstrong. My apologies if you thought last night bonded us together for all eternity, Mister Murray, but I assure you that was not my intention. You know perfectly well that your laird, as well as my sister, would never approve of this union, ever. And unless *you* intend on telling them about our little indiscretion, as far as I'm concerned, last night never happened."

He gestured down to the pallet, and her eyes widened at the spot of blood.

"There is proof that I took your innocence, *bhana-phrionnsa*. I donna think ye want me to call in my men to bear witness to what happened here between us last eve."

"You wouldn't dare." Her jaw slackened when she realized he was dead serious.

"I am naught like the Englishmen ye favor. I take responsibility for my actions. I ruined ye for any other man. There is nay turning back now. The deed is done. Ye are mine."

❧

Fagan walked out the door, and Grace was thankful he was out of sight. She could have throttled the man. Fury choked her and curses flew from her mouth. She was irked by his unreasonable demands, especially since his chivalrous attitude finally surfaced at a most inopportune moment. Frankly, his unwarranted behavior cast a shadow on the best night of her life. She would never forget the memories of their tender moments together.

But she thought they had had an understanding. Her intent was not to force Fagan to the altar and shackle him into a marriage, of all things. Any man would've been relieved to be released from such a burden—but not him. Then again, she was learning he wasn't like most men. She had a hard time understanding why he would even consider being strapped to an English lady. She knew he put up with her as a courtesy to Ravenna and Ruairi, but he didn't have to take things this far.

Grace quickly dressed and folded the blanket. She needed to find Fagan and talk some sense into him, praying he didn't open his mouth to his men about their encounter. With one last look around the crofter's hut, she rested her eyes on the pallet on the floor. Memories of Fagan and his gentle touch warmed her heart, but when she thought of his demands, the man fired her blood again and not in a good way.

She walked out of her shelter and was greeted by the warm rays of the sun. Everything was calm, and the horses were grazing. No one would ever suspect that a savage storm raged through the glen last night if they hadn't experienced it for themselves. Grace closed the door behind her and hastily increased her pace to find Fagan. She didn't have to look far. He approached her from the woods, leading two mounts.

"Are ye ready? My men are securing the carriage horses now."

"Yes, but we need to talk."

He stopped when he reached her. "What about?" His tone was innocent, but she knew better.

"Don't be coy with me, Mister. You know exactly what I want to discuss." When his expression hardened, Grace softened her voice and reached out and touched his arm. "Fagan, I cannot lie to you. Yes, I wanted to be with you and I did so freely. I meant what I said. I favor the way you and I have grown to talk with each other." She met his eyes and held them.

"If only for a moment, I wanted that special time and

the man to be you. But as I told you, what we shared was only for one night. I didn't expect you to wed me because you took my innocence. I was perfectly aware of the choice I made. You once told me the path I choose to take is my own, but I should take the time to think things through. Can you honestly imagine spending the rest of your life with me? We'd kill each other. Why can't we just go on with our lives? No one knows." She glanced at him for any sign of objection, and he studied her thoughtfully for a moment.

"But I know."

And that was all he said. He walked around her and left her standing alone. She glanced down at the grass with its blanket of morning dew and took a deep breath, praying for patience. She had to get him to see to reason, and she only had the remainder of the trip to England to accomplish the task.

"My lady, we are ready to depart," called Calum.

She lifted her skirts and made her way to the carriage. The men had already gathered her trunks. The bundles they'd left next to the trail from the evening before were also securely fastened to the coach. She took her driver's extended hand as he assisted her into the place where she'd spend the next several hours thinking of a way to change Fagan's mind. She said a silent prayer she could.

❧

*Tha e ceàrr. It's wrong.* Those words plagued his thoughts because Fagan knew in his gut he was right. That's why Grace's words made no sense to him. Contrary to what the woman thought, his decision was not an easy one to make, and it continued to tear him apart.

He considered himself an honorable man. He prided himself on being true and just. Granted, he had bedded his share of willing women, but he'd never been attached to any of them. And on no occasion had he ever taken away the innocence of a lass. Whether the woman was English or a Scot made no difference. His actions would've been the same either way. But Grace was nobility, and he was not. What kind of life could a Highland captain possibly provide for an English lady? He'd go daft trying to sort out the madness.

Once again, he resumed his place and rode in front of the carriage with a handful of his men. He wasn't sure why he stayed there because he could have followed the carriage now. He wasn't saying his farewells, and after Grace broke off her betrothal with Casterbrook, Fagan would be taking her home to Scotland.

"I hope we donna encounter another storm like we did last eve, eh? Praise the saints we had the barn and the crofter's hut in the glen. The horses werenae verra fond of the thunder and lightning. Mayhap next time we will nae be so lucky," said Calum.

"I ne'er mind traveling as long as the storms are kept at bay. But the storm has delayed our journey. We need to push farther while the light lasts. Och, and I want to keep an eye on Big Gray. He was favoring his left leg after pulling the carriage up the hill in the mud. Although he trails behind the coach this day, keep a watch on him. We cannae afford to lose a good horse."

Calum gave a short nod. "Aye."

Fagan continued to push his men throughout the day. They only made two short stops to rest and water the horses. To his relief, he'd managed to take the coward's way out and avoid Grace during those times.

Under the dusk sky, his men wearily bedded down for the night. He started to pitch the tent for Grace when he heard a moan behind him.

"Please, I beg you…"

He turned his head and narrowed his eyes. He refused to listen to her attempts to try to sway his mind at every opportunity. He was about to give her a verbal thrashing when her words surprised him.

"If I become chilled, I'll cover myself with a blanket. I cannot sleep in that tent again with its stifling heat. If you're worried about your men, I'm sure you'll sleep with one eye open to protect me."

He hesitated. "Are ye certain? I donna mind making ye shelter."

She gestured to the sky. "The sun was shining all day and no clouds are in sight. You can start to see the stars. The weather is not suddenly going to turn."

He stood. "If ye're sure. *Fuirich air falbh on teine.*" When she lifted a brow, he translated for her: "Donna get too close to the fire."

Grace lowered her voice. "I won't make that mistake again. I don't want to get burned."

❧

*Men.* And Grace thought her sisters were difficult to understand. She'd spent the entire day confined in the carriage trying to think of a way to convince Fagan to come back to reality. She had failed when she simply tried to talk sense to him. She should've known the easiest way wouldn't work with Fagan. Unknowingly, he gave her no choice but to move on to her next idea. She was determined to show him what life would be like with her by his side—day after day, night after night.

She sat on the blanket before the fire, and an innocent expression crossed her face. "Fagan?" When he glanced up from the flames, she tried to stay her smile. "I'm hungry. Could I possibly have something to eat?"

"Ye just ate."

"I know, but do be a dear and grab me something from the basket, would you?"

He reluctantly rose and walked to the carriage as she tried to think of another way to annoy him. When he approached her with a handful of dried beef, she smiled her thanks. He walked around the fire and lowered himself to the ground.

She once again met his gaze over the flames. "You know? I'm not really all that hungry. I think I've changed my mind. I don't want to waste the food. Could you take this back and fetch me some water instead?" She placed her hand to her throat. "I find I'm a little parched from the journey."

His eyes narrowed, and he pulled himself to his feet. He stepped around the pit of the fire and held out his hand. "Is there anything else I can get for ye while I'm up, *bhana-phrionnsa?*"

She lowered her voice, and a smile played the corner of her lips. "As I said, the water will be fine, but I'll be sure to tell you if there is anything else you can do for me."

"How daft do ye think I am? Ye may think of me as some dumb Scot who isnae educated like the men of your country. And even though your actions make it clear that ye are far above my station, I will nae be made the fool in front of my men. If ye want something, get off your English arse and get it yourself."

When Fagan turned, she reached out and grabbed his kilt. "Wait! That was not what I meant. I don't think that way at all. I was only trying to—" She couldn't finish her words because he gave her another icy glare and stormed off into the trees.

Grace closed her eyes and cursed her stupidity. She hadn't meant to insult him. As she remembered the look on his face, she cringed. She'd hurt him. All she wanted to do was make him realize that he could be marrying one of those haughty English ladies whose behavior was absurd. During her brief time at court, she'd seen some women whose demeanor was a definite embarrassment to the fairer sex. Her only intent was for Fagan to know that she could drive him completely mad if they were bound as man and wife. And she'd failed miserably.

She waited for him to return, but the night wore on. She lay down on her blanket and closed her eyes but couldn't sleep. The fire crackled and popped, and a cool breeze blew through her tendrils. At least she was not subjected to the heat in the insufferable tent.

Once again, Grace found herself wide awake and gazing at Fagan's empty blanket. Sleep would not come until this madness was resolved. She rose and stepped gingerly around the seven sleeping men. Since most of the men slumbered, that meant three of them were somewhere on guard, including the one she needed to talk some sense into.

The horses were tethered at the tree line, but all she could make out were shadowy shapes. Realizing this was another of her ridiculous ideas, she turned around to go back to her blanket.

"What are ye doing, Grace?"

She jumped and placed her hand over her heart. "Fagan? Where are you?"

"Over here." She heard a shuffling noise and then made out his frame as he rose to his feet and leaned against a tree. "Ye shouldnae be wandering around in the dark. My men are standing guard and could have mistaken ye as a threat."

She made her way toward him and stopped. "I couldn't sleep."

"So ye came out here, mayhap to get me to fetch something else for ye?" His voice was laced with sarcasm.

"I only wanted you to see what you'd be getting yourself into by marrying me. You'd be spending the rest of your life bound to me. I'd drive you mad."

He chuckled. "As opposed to ye nae already driving me mad?"

She folded her arms over her chest. "Then why go through with this idea that you must wed me? Ruairi will be cross with you, and Ravenna will be furious with me."

"I'm nae going to discuss this with ye again. I took your in—"

Grace spoke through clenched teeth. "If you say that one more time, I'm going to—"

He pulled her close, and the caress of his lips on her mouth and against her neck set her aflame. Why did his kisses have to be so darned persuasive? When he nibbled at her earlobe, she let out soft mewling sounds that she didn't even know she made.

She felt her knees weaken, and as if he sensed she was about to fall, he tightened his grip around her. He had a way of shattering the hard shell that encircled her, and her skin continued to prickle with the heat of his touch. When he drew her even closer and she felt his hardness, she pulled away.

"We have to stop this. Now." She pushed herself away from him. "We cannot do this."

"We already did." Fagan's sultry voice made her shiver in the night air.

"You cannot be my husband. You can't. This is completely absurd. I should've never let you kiss me the first time, but yet we keep finding ourselves in these moments together."

"Mayhap the fates are trying to tell us something, eh?"

"Fagan, please, I beg you to see reason."

"Ye cannae say that I didn't warn ye. I gave ye several chances to deny me, but ye didnae. There is nay sense fighting the inevitable. Ye are now more or less my wife. All that is missing is the formality of the vows, lass. Best ye accept that."

Grace's annoyance increased when she found that her hands were shaking. She couldn't see his eyes, but she let bitterness spill over into her voice.

"I want you to tell me that you would still want to wed me if we did not share a bed." When he hesitated, her temper flared. "Of course you wouldn't. Now you want to be honorable when you were nothing but a nightmare to begin with. I don't think I'll ever understand you."

"Well, ye'll have the rest of your life to figure me out, *bhana-phrionnsa*." The man had no idea that his righteous behavior was going to bring about his death.

She threw words at him like stones. "Let me make something perfectly clear. I am not... I *will* not marry you. Whatever you say or claim, I will deny. I refuse to spend the rest of my life in the Highlands, especially as your wife. You are completely mad." She was so angry that she couldn't stop the next words before they flew from her mouth. "I am a lady of title and birth. You are nothing but a lowly Scottish captain, not even fit to be a pig farmer."

She stormed away from him, until a firm hand grabbed her arm. "You're hurting me."

Fagan spoke between clenched teeth. "Damn it, Grace! Donna push me because I promise ye that ye'll nae like the man I will become."

# Fifteen

As Fagan trailed back to camp in the wake of the fiery dragon, Grace sought her blanket and turned her back on him in a huff. At least they weren't yet wed. She would've kicked him out of their bed for sure. As he lay on his blanket, the woman's words pounded in his brain. *Pig farmer?* Her venomous declaration stung and it was too late to take back now, not that she'd be willing to retract anything she'd said.

He gathered his bedding at first light, before the blazing sun rose on the horizon. He glanced at Grace, who was sleeping peacefully. Instantly irritated, he shot her a cold look of disdain. He didn't want to see her. He didn't want to hear her, and he sure as hell didn't want to talk to her. She'd said all there was to say last night—or should he say, only a few short hours ago. At least Princess Grace was able to rest with a clear conscience and hadn't tossed and turned all night as he had.

While his men cleared the camp, Fagan found himself once again in a foul mood because of a Walsingham woman. Memories of Grace's soft kisses didn't even calm him because all he could think about was her sharp tongue. He shook his head and didn't even realize he was doing it. He knew one thing for certain. Lord Francis Walsingham, Grace's father, should've placed the lass over bended knee more often than he had. Perhaps then she wouldn't be as prickly as she was now.

They rode at a hard pace for a few hours before Fagan decided to stop and rest the horses at a loch. The sky was a rich blue. Mossy, green mountains stretched into the heavens, and the clear water of the loch rippled in the gentle wind. Scotland was beautiful. No one could ever deny that, not even the English.

Fagan took off his boots and tunic, tossing them onto the grassy shore. At first, he cringed as tiny pebbles stabbed the bottoms of his bare feet, but as he waded past his knees into the cool loch, the ground beneath him softened. More to the point, the sharp pain in his feet didn't compare to the dagger Grace had thrust into his heart.

The water was colder than he had anticipated, but he needed something to cool his ire. He dove in and held his breath as long as he could. When he surfaced, warm air brushed against his skin. He combed through his hair with his fingers, smoothing it over his shoulder. As he made his way back to shore, Grace stood on the bank with an unreadable expression on her face. He prayed the daft beauty had enough sense to stay away from him, but as she approached him, he knew she was asking for nothing but trouble.

❦

Grace had finally fallen asleep in the carriage when she was jostled awake. She hadn't slept all eve. She knew her angry retort had hardened Fagan against her. She didn't want to hurt him, but he needed to give up this notion that she was his solely because they shared a bed—well, a pallet—for one night.

She took a moment to compose herself. Deciding to give Fagan some room to breathe was likely a wise decision. She climbed out of the carriage and stepped down onto the grass. After ambling away from the men and into the brush to see to her personal needs, she walked back toward the water. All was quiet, calm. She closed her eyes and basked in the solace that enveloped her.

With the warm breeze blowing through her hair and the sound of water lapping against the bank, she sighed. Something rustled in the branches not far from where she was standing, and she opened her eyes to find a little bird staring back at her.

A small dunlin was perched on a tree branch with top feathers the color of rust and a rounded, black belly patch underneath its small body. For some reason, she knew these birds could be found near the sea. She also knew the birds preferred estuaries to seek out insects— the kind that flew and the ones that generally had six legs and crawled. She crinkled up her nose in disgust and made herself think of something else.

*Like the bare-chested man who was walking out of the water.*

Fagan was wet from head to toe. His hair was straight, reaching the middle of his upper arm. His broad chest glistened in the sun. Her gaze lowered. A thin line of hair traveled from his navel down to the dripping kilt that rode low on his lean hips. Praise the saints. Did she actually hear herself swallow?

The Highland Adonis reached the shore. As he was bending over and picking up his tunic and boots, it was pure torture to watch the muscles that rippled across his back in a dazzling display of manliness. But then he rose to his full height and shot her a cold look, and each of them assessed the other's anger.

"By the expression on your face, I must look damn good for being lower than a pig farmer. Wouldnae ye say?" He thundered past her, and she could feel his hostility toward her.

"Wait!" She wasn't surprised when he didn't stop, and she had to increase her gait to keep up with him.

Raising his hand in the air as a firm warning, he kept moving farther away from her. "Donna come closer. I donna want to talk. I donna want to see or hear ye. We are done talking." His voice rang with command.

"Does that mean you've come to your senses?"

He stopped dead in his tracks and whirled around on her. "Nay, it means ye'd better come to yours. Since ye seem to be taking the time to figure out ways to annoy me, why donna ye spend your time more wisely and find out how ye're going to be a dutiful, *obedient* wife when we are wed."

The man turned his back on her, and that's when Grace's temper flared. Her voice went up a notch. "What did you say?" When he didn't respond, she ran to catch up to him. She firmly placed her feet in front of the large wall that was Fagan.

He briefly closed his eyes and then glared at her. "If ye donna want me to throw ye over my shoulder and smack your wily arse like some insolent lassie in front of my men, I suggest ye clear my path."

Shock yielded to fury. "You wouldn't dare."

"Lest ye forget. I am but a lowly captain of the Sutherland guard, but I will do whatever needs to be done."

When he stepped around her, she thought it best to leave him alone. She also believed it was in her best interest not to wait around to find out if he would follow through on his threat. Needing to give Fagan more time to cool off, Grace walked back and stood at the water's edge. Suddenly realizing she'd give anything for a bath right now, she sat on the grass and removed her boots. Her feet were much cooler as the air brushed against them. Standing, she brushed down her skirts to remove the grass and then lifted them, wading into the water.

"Grace…"

She glanced over her shoulder to see Fagan standing on the bank. She lifted a brow and spoke with an air of indifference. "I thought you weren't speaking to me."

"My men are with me. If ye wish to bathe or wash up, now is the time."

She nodded and watched his broad back as he walked into the clearing. No matter how much she wanted a bath, she couldn't bring herself to remove her clothing with ten men standing nearby. With her luck, one of them would stumble across her and she'd never live through the humiliation.

Bunching her skirts up to the side, she moved farther into the water. Tiny rocks poked into the soles of her feet and slowed her pace. She stopped when the water reached mid-thigh because that was as far as her skirts would allow her to go without becoming wet. As she stood in the lake, feeling fresh and recharged, she cast another quick glance over her shoulder. No one was in sight. Hastily, she lifted her skirts higher around her waist and walked deeper into the water before anyone saw her bare bottom. Her body was still tender from her time with Fagan, and the soothing coolness of the lake was just what she needed.

A skipping stone danced across the water and sprayed droplets into her face. She stumbled, fumbling for her skirts, and almost dropped them into the lake. She turned around in a huff to see Fagan trying to mask a smile.

"We are about ready to depart."

"All right." She paused, and the man didn't move. "Are you going to stand there, or are you going to let me come out?"

"Aye. I'm going to stand here and watch ye come out."

"Fagan…"

"Ye donna have anything new to show me that I havenae seen before."

Grace was in no mood to argue. She took a step forward, and Fagan held a gleam of something in his eyes that irked her. When certain parts of her skin started to show, she dropped her skirts in the lake and walked out of the water in a huff. She refused to give the beastly man the satisfaction.

"Are ye going to ride in wet skirts?"

She picked up her boots from the grass and bristled

past him to the carriage. "Come now, Mister Murray. I'm no fragile flower. Your men are ready to ride, are they not?"

❧

Fagan had changed into a dry kilt and couldn't believe the stubborn lass was riding in the carriage in a wet dress just to spite him. At least the top half of her wasn't soaked. What was he going to do with Lady Grace? She'd definitely keep him on his toes, not to mention the fact that he'd have to sleep with one eye open.

Calum reined in beside him. "The lady doesnae seem to think verra highly of ye, eh?"

"Aye, well, she has her reasons." Fagan kept his expression composed.

"Will the lass be returning with us to Scotland?" When Fagan lifted a brow, Calum added, "I heard ye say as much to her."

"Aye, 'tis part of why she'd like to remove my head."

"Must we even travel to England then, captain? Cannae we return home?"

"There are things I must attend to in England. Our stay will nae be long. I promise ye that." Fagan's mind started to wander off when, without warning, eight men clamored out of the trees with swords drawn. At the same time, four riders approached on horseback from the path ahead.

Fagan and Calum unsheathed their weapons, but before they could even make contact with a single blade, sounds of metal on metal rang through the air behind the carriage. Men bellowed, and the echo of death sent a shiver down Fagan's spine, especially because he wasn't sure if the fallen men were his.

He kept a tight rein on An Diobhail. Using the breadth of his horse to his advantage, Fagan urged his mount forward. An Diobhail pounded one of the men in the shoulder with a heavy thump, making the man unsteady on his feet. The colors of the man's plaid were black and blue, the tartan of the bloody Campbells. The same color Fagan would bestow on his enemy if he didn't kill the bastard first.

Fagan and Calum continued to thrust and parry with the four men on horseback. Three of Fagan's men were engaged in battle on foot, but he didn't have time to turn around and see what was happening behind him. He had to trust that Grace knew to stay in the carriage.

He heard a grunt and turned as one of his men fell to the ground in a pool of blood. He pushed An Diobhail closer to the enemy and impaled the bastard on his sword. At the same time, Calum groaned as he received a slice to the upper arm. When Fagan turned his mount to aid Calum, his throat ached with defeat.

A man stood to the side of the carriage with a blade pressed to Grace's throat. The bastard had long, black hair and wore the bloody Campbell plaid and a dark tunic. He had a large scar over his left eye that traveled down the length of his jaw. At that moment, Fagan realized he was looking at the same man who had given chase to Grace on the beach—one of the mercenaries.

"Fagan…"

He didn't miss the unsteadiness in Grace's voice,

but he refused to take his eyes from his enemy. "Let her go."

The man laughed. "Let her go? She's who we came for."

Calum sat on the ground, holding his arm, which bled like a river. Another one of Fagan's guards lay slain in the grass and two others on the path. He looked back at the man with a steely gaze. "Where are the rest of my men?"

The man nodded over his shoulder toward the back of the carriage. "Dead."

"What do ye want?"

"I already told ye what I want."

Fagan's eyes narrowed. "Ye're nae leaving here with her."

The man's voice hardened ruthlessly. "I am nae leaving here without her."

"Ye need to listen to me verra carefully. I am the captain of the Sutherland guard, and I have the entire force of the clan at my back. Ye have killed my men and your death is inevitable. Leave now, and let the lass go. Mayhap ye—"

*"Na can an còrr! Tha sin gu leòr!" Say no more! That is enough!*

Grace's eyes widened, and that was the last Fagan remembered before he embraced the darkness.

❧

Grace screamed when Fagan fell to the ground with a thump. He didn't move, and blood spilled through his hair from his wound. Her heart shattered at the sight before her. Without hesitation, the same bloody coward who'd knocked Fagan over the back of the head had the audacity to grab An Diobhail's reins. The man strutted toward her with a sly grin and the horse in tow as if he'd won Fagan's mount as some great prize. Grace wanted nothing more than to kill the bastard herself.

The incorrigible man at her back removed the blade that rested against her throat, but not before nicking a piece of her soft flesh. He replaced his weapon with a sack over her head. He lifted her onto a horse, and she knew the mount was An Diobhail. She felt as though a hand had closed around her throat. Discreetly, she reached down her right leg and made certain her skirts covered the dagger that was still strapped to her thigh.

"Give me your hands." As he bound her wrists, he added, "I give ye fair warning nae to be foolish. If ye try to escape or scream like that again, I will nae be so kind. Do ye understand?"

"I must know if the captain is all right." A hand slapped her hard on her left thigh, and she cried out. When An Diobhail shied, the bridle jingled, and a loud crack came down somewhere near the horse's head. Not only did these Scottish hounds kill Sutherland men and hit Fagan over the head, but now they resorted to hurting an animal. She shouldn't have been surprised. The devil had a special place for men like this.

"Nay, he's nae all right. He's dead, and ye will be too if ye donna shut your mouth, ye English cunt."

Fear and anger knotted inside her. She breathed in quick, shallow gasps as her mind swirled. Fagan had been struck over the head—the same as Kat had fallen and hit her head. Fagan was only injured. He needed to be patched up and most certainly required stitches, but he was not dead. It would take far more than some paid assassin and a bump on the head to send Fagan Murray to his maker. The steely captain would not fall so easily. But when she didn't hear any sound from him, panic was rioting within her. She clenched her hand until her nails entered her palm. Hot tears trickled down her cheeks, and she bit her lip to control her sobs.

*Heaven help her.*

What if the man was telling the truth? Fagan's last memory of her was one of pure disgust. A cold knot formed in her stomach. Their relationship could not end like this. It couldn't. She was a lady, and he was a Highland captain. Didn't he know that she had to fight him? It was in her blood. She was English.

How could she have openly admitted that a secret part of her wanted to be with him, desired to be his wife? How could she have been expected to give in so easily and tell the man she loved him? The truth was that she didn't give a damn if he was a lowly captain, but she had to respect her father's wishes and set an example for Elizabeth and Kat. After all, that's why she became betrothed to Daniel in the first place.

When An Diobhail moved forward, she cringed, knowing the animal stepped near Fagan's body. The mere thought tore her apart. Any moment now she had to wake up from this nightmare. Dire thoughts continued to stab away at her, and this time she could no longer help herself. A sob escaped her. She'd had to watch Fagan Murray get pummeled over the head and buckle to the ground before she could admit that she loved him. How could she be so foolish? How could she realize her feelings so late? And now she was made to endure a cruel punishment as the mercenaries forced her to ride Fagan's mount, the last piece of anything she had left of him.

"Please…I beg you not to leave the captain on the path. If he is truly… He deserves to be buried," she cried out. "You can't leave him like this! You can't! I won't leave him!"

One of the men chuckled. "Och, donna worry your bonny head about it. He isnae on the path. I threw him in a ditch."

When the other men laughed in response, Grace wept aloud. She didn't care who heard her. She couldn't wait for the opportunity to place her dagger straight into their blackened hearts.

She knew they followed the path for some time by the sound of hooves pounding the dirt, but when the horses veered off into the trees, she lost all sense of direction. All she could hear were the snaps of branches and twigs rustling beneath… Wait a moment. Was that the sound of the sea in the distance? She tried to pay close attention.

A breeze picked up and she could smell the salt air. Where were they taking her? They rode at least another few hundred yards and stopped. Someone pulled her roughly off the saddle and she was unsteady on her feet. A hand wrapped around the fleshy part of her arm with a grip of steel.

"You're hurting me."

"'Tis the least of your worries. Hurry up." She

stumbled along beside the man and could barely keep up. *"Feuch nach tuit thu. Gabh air do shocair."*

Grace stopped, shaking off his arm. She spoke between clenched teeth. "If you want me to understand what you're saying, you're going to have to stop speaking Gaelic. Perhaps if you take this bag off my head and I could see where I'm—"

"Watch your step and shut your mouth, wench."

"I am a lady, you—"

She didn't finish her words because pain shot up her arm. When she fell to her knees in agony, the ground was hard beneath her. The man lifted her to her feet and then tossed her over his shoulder as if she weighed nothing at all. He carried her for what felt like an eternity and continued speaking to the other men in Gaelic. She no longer felt the warmth of the sun on her back, and the air changed to cool and damp. They made their way toward what sounded like a rattling chain. The squeak of a metal door opened, and Grace was placed back down on her feet. Her wrists were unbound and the sack was pulled off her head.

Torchlight blinded her. She squinted, needing time to adjust to the light. When a firm hand shoved her into a darkened nook and the door slammed behind her, she quickly realized she didn't need time to adapt.

The torch disappeared with the men and so did her sight.

# Sixteen

GRACE STUMBLED BLINDLY INTO THE DARKNESS. SHE held out her arms in front of her and couldn't even see her hands when she waved them mere inches from her face. Shuffling her way across the gritty floor, she reached a wall and rubbed her fingers over the cool stone. She had to be in some type of cave. Of course she was. The bloody mercenaries had housed her in the cliffs near the sea.

She sat down with her back pressed against the wall. Pensively, she looked out into the darkness, as if she had anywhere else to gaze at the moment. Fagan's name echoed in the black stillness of her mind. The dreaded nightmare played over and over, creating an unbearable pain in her head. Even now, she swore she could feel the blade at her throat as she was forced to watch Fagan fall to the ground lifeless—not that she knew for certain he was.

Girding herself with resolve, she decided that until she saw his body, she refused to acknowledge that he was dead. She had to believe he was all right because if she didn't, she'd lose her own will to survive. And she wouldn't give in so easily without a fight, especially to the bloody Scots.

Grace drew a deep breath and forced herself to settle down. She forbade herself to tremble. After all, she was the one who had plagued Ravenna about learning spy craft. More to the point, Grace was a Walsingham. She only wished the actual spy in the family would've instructed her instead of evading her questions. Now she was left with no words of wisdom and forced to follow her own instincts, something that past experience told her could be dangerous.

Although these big brutes had caused her pain, they hadn't made any attempt to kill her—yet. That meant they needed her alive because they wanted something. But what could she possibly possess that these men would want? Until she knew the answer, she'd keep her ears open. Unfortunately, her eyes were wide open, but she couldn't see a darned thing.

She sat on the stone floor of her prison for hours. When she felt as if the walls were closing in on her, she pulled herself to her feet and held out her arms in front of her. She took small steps until she reached the metal door. Running her fingers over the frame, she discovered the door was made of wood and had metal bars at eye level.

"Is anyone there?" When no one responded, she called out again. "Can anyone hear me?"

Grace could barely make out a faint flickering light in the distance, but she didn't think she had imagined it. As she waited behind the first barricade that stood between her and her freedom, the unsavory Scots being the second obstacle, the light grew brighter as the flame reflected from the passage wall. When one of the men approached the door, the torch he held not only illuminated the cavern but also confirmed that she was being held in a small nook in the cliffs.

His black eyes impaled her. "What do ye want?"

She recognized the Scottish cur as the one who had struck Fagan, and it took a tremendous amount of restraint not to reach through the bars and strangle the bastard with her bare hands. She swore she'd have her revenge, but she couldn't afford to make careless mistakes. "I want to speak to the man in charge."

"I'm in charge."

She couldn't help but smirk. "Now I know that isn't true. I demand to speak to your captain."

"Watch your tone, ye English wench. He'll speak to ye when he's good and ready."

"Then perhaps you can give him a message for me." When the vagrant didn't respond, she added, "Please tell your captain that unless he intends on starving me to death or leaving me here to rot in this cold, dark cave by catching the ague, I need food, water, blankets, and a candle." The man turned his back on her, and she called after him. "Can you at least leave the…" He was gone. "Torch."

Grace leaned her back against the door and slid to the ground with a huff. She brushed her hands over her face and smoothed her hair. Once her thoughts strayed from plotting the demise of Fagan's assailant, she tried to think of a way in which to use her dagger and make her escape. Perhaps she'd take the captain hostage, the same as he had done while holding a blade to her throat. She was thankful that she had some wits remaining because she was able to recognize that her idea was absurd. The man was a mountain and she was a valley in comparison.

The bolt slid, and Grace stood. The door swung open, and the same vile man returned. He placed the lit torch in a crack in the wall outside the door and handed her a tankard of water. Then, casting her a scornful look, he tossed some blankets to the ground with indifference. A small piece of bread fell onto the gritty floor and rolled into the corner.

"How kind of you," she said dryly.

He gave her a sinister grin and closed the door behind himself.

"Wait!" She rushed to the bars, trying not to spill the water. "What about the candle?"

The bloody cur had the nerve to smirk. "Be thankful the captain gave ye what he did. Now shut your mouth, wench!" He lifted the torch from the wall and once again disappeared into the dark passage.

She placed her back against the door and took a drink of water. The beastly man couldn't even leave her a candle. On second thought, perhaps it was best she couldn't see the room or the food for fear of what that entailed. When she finished what little she had for a meal, she covered herself with a blanket. She hadn't slept and knew she needed to stay sharp. She'd close her eyes if only for a moment.

Grace fell asleep in blackness and woke up to the same. The misery of her predicament still haunted her, and there was sourness in the pit of her stomach. When she realized she'd wallowed in despair long enough, she permitted her rebellious nature to surface. She'd been confined long enough. She wasn't certain, but this had to be a new day. And she was determined to get answers.

She made her way to the door and hesitated. When she didn't hear anything, she called out. "Hello! Is anyone there? Can you hear me?" When no one responded, she bellowed, rattling the bars on the door. Nothing or no one stirred, but she would continue to scream until someone came.

Several moments passed. Filled with disgust, she turned away from the door. She reached around on the gritty floor, somehow managing to wrap her fingers around her tankard. She'd get the bloody captain's attention one way or another. She banged the metal cup against the bars on the door, the sound reverberating throughout the cave. She pounded, screamed, kicked, and banged some more. Finally, a light appeared at the end of the passage and started moving toward her. As the light came closer, one very angry, scarred captain thundered toward her.

He held up the torch to the bars. "What the hell do ye want? Unless ye want me to come in there and beat ye for your insolence, shut the hell up."

Grace stood to her full height, but her stance wasn't as daunting as she had hoped it would be. "Why do you hold me? Do you seek ransom?"

"Ransom? I assure ye that we are all verra well paid."

"Please…" She glanced around her nook. "I'm not going anywhere. Tell me what you want. Perhaps I can help you."

"Ye already have."

"I don't understand."

"I donna care. This is your last warning. Keep your mouth shut."

She tried to speak in a calming tone. "I know you want something from me, because I'm still alive, but you can't keep me locked up in here without food or water. If you want me to stay hale, I'll need those things." When she saw the steely look in his eyes, she added, "Please, captain. I'm sure you'll recover whatever it is you seek. I'm still your prisoner, locked within the stone walls. You're in command."

He nodded in response and turned his back on her. "And a candle."

He took a few steps away from her before he muttered, "Shut your mouth, and I'll think about it."

That conversation went better than she had anticipated. At least the man didn't harm her, and she'd be provided food and water. Now she just had to find out what these men were after. Tired of sitting forever in the dark, she stood by the door and waited for someone to return. What she wouldn't give to have light!

Being in the dark enclosure made Grace lose all sense of time, but once again, light was shining through the bars. The seedy captain opened the door and placed the torch in the stone wall. He entered with bread, cheese, and water in hand and gazed around her cell, his eyes resting on the blankets on the floor. When his expression wasn't as angry as before, she said a silent prayer of thanks that he finally recognized her conditions were far from acceptable. After he placed the food on her blanket and the jug of water on the floor, he took a frank and admiring look at her. She cast her eyes downward.

"Thank you for the food and water."

"Take off your dress."

Grace was too startled by his words to offer any kind of objection and was shocked when his eyes suddenly twinkled in amusement. She stared at him, tongue-tied. Her sister had given her fair warning that if Grace wanted to serve the Crown, she'd have to lie with men to obtain the information she was sent to retrieve—all for the sake of king and country. But there was no way, as long as Grace lived and breathed, that she would ever... She could not even begin to imagine that bloody Highlander's hands on her—or worse.

A shiver ran down her spine.

"Mayhap ye didnae hear me, eh? I said... Take. Off. Your. Dress."

"Oh, I heard you just fine." Her eyes narrowed. "If you think for one moment that I will permit you to touch me... I'd sooner die than have your hands on me."

The man lifted his arm, smacking her hard across the face with the back of his hand. She saw stars and they weren't from the sky. The pain in her jaw almost knocked her unconscious, but she fought to remain coherent.

"I ne'er said my *hands* would be touching ye."

She brought her fingers to her cheek. She knew what he meant and choked back a sob when she thought of Fagan. Let the bastard try and touch her again. She'd pull out her blade and cut off his manhood before he even realized he was no longer a man.

Heaven help her. She had to think. If she attempted to use her only weapon now and he took it, she'd lessen her chance of escape. She needed to wait for the perfect time and use the element of surprise. But if he forced her into something she was not willing to do, she'd be left with no choice.

"Did ye think I wouldnae want something in return for the food and water? I am nae that generous."

Her temper flared, and she spoke between clenched teeth. "You can beat me until my very last breath, but I will never—"

He stepped around her, eyeing her as if she was his next meal. "And what makes ye think, ye English cunt, that I need your consent to take what is already mine? Ye are my prisoner, my lady. Kneel before me."

When she stood her ground, refusing to budge, he pinched the top of her shoulder. Pain shot through her neck and shoulder, bringing her to her knees before him. He lifted his kilt, and his disgusting manhood jutted out in front of her eyes. Fagan was the only man she'd ever seen. And Fagan was twice the man in every sense of the word.

The captain leaned toward her. "Take me into your mou—"

Grace threw back her head and let out great peals of laughter. She needed to tread carefully. A few "ladies" at court had said that men compared the size of their manhood with one another. She hadn't been exactly sure what that meant at the time, but presently, this was the only idea that came to mind.

Stealing another quick glance at his man parts, she chuckled. "That's all you have to offer? I've seen a bigger cock on a newborn babe!"

He shifted his weight. "Stop laughing."

Not only didn't she stop, but she continued, louder. She may have even pointed. "I cannot believe you threatened me with *that*."

He dropped his kilt and covered himself, but was not soon enough. Stepping around her, he kicked the jug into the wall. Water spilled to the ground—her water. He took the food from the blanket, turned on his heel, and strode through the door. The lock jiggled, and he lifted the torch from the wall.

"Donna test me. There are other ways to make a lass heel."

She'd gone and done it now. Even though she prevented the man from taking her body against her will—at least for now—she'd lost her supply of food and water. This was the first time Grace thought perhaps she'd been wrong all along in believing that she could master spy craft. Worse yet, she had a hard time admitting that maybe Ravenna was right.

ఆశ

Another Scottish dog dared to enter her private hell, placing food on her blanket and another jug of water on the floor. Dirt and filth matted his long, red hair and his tunic was torn. He wore a plaid of the same colors as the bloody captain, and she realized they were all made from the same cloth.

Grace dropped to her knees and didn't even wait

to pour the water into a cup. She drank straight from the jug, and he chuckled. The cool liquid soothed her throat and she couldn't get enough.

"Do ye want me to bring ye more?"

"Yes, please." She coughed and then gulped more water, wiping her chin with the back of her hand. She grabbed a chunk of bread and a piece of cheese. "And more food if you can spare it."

"More food? I've ne'er seen a lass eat as much as a man."

"Then perhaps you shouldn't neglect giving her food and water. How long has it been?"

"Two and a half days. And ye should try nae talking to the captain with such a sharp tongue. He did this to teach ye a lesson. Did ye learn it?"

She nodded.

"Good. I'll bring ye more food and water." He closed the door behind him and left the torch in the wall outside the door. While she quenched her thirst and appetite, she felt drained, hollow, and lifeless. Her heart was aching for Fagan, and her stomach pained her from hunger. She hastily broke what was left of the bread and cheese in half, hiding the pieces within the folds of her blanket. She wouldn't risk losing anything that would aid in her survival again.

Before she knew it, the man with the red hair returned with another jug of water and more bread. "This will have to do." His eyes widened at the sight of the empty blanket. "Ye ate all that already?"

"You didn't give me anything for two and a half days. I'm surprised your captain even let you bring me more."

"He's nae here, but I wouldnae test him anymore if I were ye. Ye donna want to make matters worse. He said as long as ye behave, ye can have something to eat and drink."

"How kind of him." She glanced up at the man. "There were other men in my party. When you brought me here, did any of my traveling companions survive?" Grace tried to kill the sob that lingered in her throat.

He shrugged with indifference. "I donna know. I wasnae there. We're paid verra well for our troubles. If the captain was told nae to take any other prisoners, he wouldnae."

"How much longer will I be here?"

"As long as it takes to release the Earl of Orkney from his prison."

She lifted a brow. "The Earl of Orkney? I can't say that we're acquainted. What does this man have to do with me exactly?" When he didn't respond, she added, "I'm locked behind a closed door with no means of escape. What harm could there be in telling me your purpose? Perhaps I can help you find whatever it is you seek and put an end to all this madness."

He rubbed his chin with his fingers. "Donna mistake my intent as a kindness to ye. I am only following the orders of my captain." He paused as she waited for him to continue. "A servant from Orkney had evidence against the earl, information which could still cost the earl his head if 'tis placed in the wrong hands. The woman is nay longer of this world." He smirked. "But before she died, she gave a testament to an English spy who travels to Edinburgh to present this evidence to the king."

An innocent expression crossed her face. "I told you. I don't know this man. I've only been to Edinburgh a few times at court and recently attended my sister's wedding in the Highlands. I haven't been out of England long enough to know anything about this man or evidence that someone has against him. And I certainly don't know an English spy. For heaven's sake, I live in a manor house in—"

He gave her a chilling smile. "We know where ye live and who ye are. That's why we have ye with us. Word has been sent to the English spy that we *will* kill ye if the evidence is delivered to the king. There is naught ye can do but sit, wait, and pray. Once we kill the spy, ye can take your leave of this place."

The door closed, and she shuddered. An inner torment began to gnaw at her. Grace wasn't daft. The men wouldn't let her go. She knew too much. These men were going to kill the English spy, but which one? A cold shiver spread over her because she knew her family held many secrets.

Between Uncle Walter and Ravenna, Grace wasn't sure what they had done or who was in danger.

# Seventeen

Grace was losing her mind. Time was becoming a big blur as one day ran into the next. She needed to find a way to make her escape before Uncle Walter or Ravenna came for her. She had to warn them. She was terrified for her family. The poor excuse for a captain hadn't been to see her since she'd humiliated him and his lack of manhood, rightfully so. That's what he deserved for behaving as a beast. She couldn't stand the sight of any man who claimed a woman's body by brutal force. The captain had no respect for the fairer sex, and she considered it abhorrent the way he kept her penned up like a dog all the time. For heaven's sake, she was starting to become like an animal, eating and drinking on the floor like Angus.

"Hello! Can someone please help me?" Grace stood by the door, resting her cheek against the cool metal bars.

The red-haired man walked through the passage and held up the torch to the door. "I just gave ye food and water. What the hell could ye possibly want now?"

Her voice was unsteady, weak. "Please… I don't feel well." She moved away from the door and hunched over in the corner with one palm resting on the stone wall. Her other hand held her stomach, and she moaned for added impact.

"What's the matter with ye?"

"I don't know how many days have passed, but I think my woman's time is coming due."

The man swore under his breath and wiped his brow. "Och, just my luck. What do ye need?"

"I haven't seen the light of day, and my stomach pains me. It's cool and damp within the walls. Perhaps some warm air will do me some good."

"I'm nae letting ye out of there, ye daft wench. The captain would have my head."

"And he also left you in charge, did he not? What if your captain returns to find me deathly ill because you did not see to my welfare? I told you that I'm not feeling well. If you won't allow me to get some air, then perhaps you can come in and assist me during my woman's time."

He paused, and then his response held a note of impatience. "I'll be back."

Thankfully, he didn't see the smile that crossed her face when she stood. These Scottish mercenaries might be superior in battle, but underneath that steely exterior was still a simple man who wanted no part of a woman at the slightest mention of monthly courses. When he didn't return, she thought briefly that the guard might have taken the coward's way out and disappeared, but then he opened the door.

"I give ye fair warning… Ye will listen to my

command. If ye make any attempt to escape, I will kill ye, and I will nae hesitate. Do ye understand?"

Grace smoothed her skirts. "Yes, of course." She walked out the door, and he gestured her forward. She silently measured the number of steps that she took from the door along the straight path of the passageway. When the stone walls veered off to the left, she started to count over again, stopping when the cave widened into a larger natural room.

Two men sat at an old wooden table and glanced up as she walked past them. Their snakelike eyes studied her intently. She must be quite the sight with her dirty dress and tangled hair. Then she realized she looked the same as they did. She gazed into that looking glass, studying herself with displeasure, and her mouth spread into a thin-lipped smile. She wasn't surprised when the men paid her no heed and continued to speak with each other in Gaelic.

"Wait," said the man who escorted her. He extinguished the torch and nodded to his cohorts. As she started to make her way through a narrow passage, she suddenly stood immobile, blinded by sunlight. She lifted her hand to shield her eyes and felt a nudge on her shoulder.

"Ye said ye needed air. Get on with it, or I can always take ye back to your hole."

"Give me a moment. I cannot see," she chided him.

"God's teeth." He gave her a less-than-friendly shove out onto the cliffs.

Light-colored rocks reflected the brightness of the sun, stabbing her eyes with shooting pain. She shut her eyelids and tried to open them slowly several times.

She barely caught sight of the man's massive frame as he sat perched on a rock, watching her like a hawk. The way he gawked at her, studying her every move, made her wonder if she could get him close enough to merely push him over the edge. She only stopped pondering the scheme when she was able to lower the hand that shaded her eyes.

Grayish-white cliffs were all around her, and the smell of salt water engulfed her senses. She glanced over the guard's shoulder for a sign of escape, any sign of a path that led to freedom.

*Nothing.*

Not wanting to make the man suspicious of her, Grace gazed down into the sea. Wave after white wave pounded into the jagged rocks. Surprisingly, there was no sandy beach as there had been at her brother-in-law's home.

"Donna even think about it. There isnac anywhere to run."

"I don't think I'll be jumping to my death anytime soon, but thank you for your concern."

"Watch your tongue, lass. I told ye this before. I can always take ye back and leave ye in the dark."

"How long have I been here?" she asked, raising her voice above the roar of the water.

He shrugged. "A sennight."

"A sennight?" She couldn't believe she'd been confined for that long. She knew Uncle Walter would need longer than seven days to reach her, but the journey would only take Ravenna a few days. Not wanting to show her concern and give the guard anymore ammunition to use against her, Grace closed her eyes. Clenching her stomach, she feigned a sharp pain.

"Oh, I feel as though I'm going to be sick. Is there perhaps a place above the rocks where I can seek some privacy in the trees?" When he didn't respond, she opened her eyes to find him gesturing to the crag.

"Choose a rock. There are many from which to choose."

"You cannot be serious."

"I am nae letting ye out of my sight."

She shrugged with indifference and turned around. "All I was asking for was a moment alone to see to my personal needs, but I give you fair warning that if I did get my woman's time, you will have to seek me a few supplies." She fumbled to lift her skirts and took her time doing it.

"Is there ever going to be a time when ye're nae a pain in the arse?"

She dropped her skirts and paused, making certain to remove her smile before she turned to face him. "No, but you should've taken that into consideration when you decided to hold me against my will and treat me no better than an animal." She closed the distance between them. "Let's go then, shall we?"

"I give ye fair warning that—"

"Yes, I know. You'll kill me if I try to escape. A moment of privacy, that's all I ask." She pointed behind him. "Is the path that way?"

"Aye, but nay tricks." He rested his hand on the hilt of his sword, as if she needed a subtle warning, and he followed her up the rocks. *Feuch nach tuit thu.*

"Pardon? You do realize that I'm English. I don't speak a word of Gaelic."

His tone was impatient. "See ye donna fall."

"You have no trouble warning me that you'll kill me if I try to escape, but you're telling me to be careful so that I don't fall and injure myself? I'll never pretend to understand men."

"If I hear that sharp tongue of yours one more time, I'm going to cut it out and hand it to ye."

When she hesitated, looking over her shoulder, he almost bumped into her. "I have to say, you must really know how to woo the ladies."

He pushed her forward. "Behave."

They walked a path that was not easily seen, one rock looking like the next. If there were any visible markers, she didn't see them. When they reached the top of the ridge, a thick line of trees was in front of her. She didn't have much of a choice. That would have to do. She said a silent prayer that she had mustered the courage to follow through with her scheme.

"If you'd be kind enough to wait here, I'll walk into that grass over there in between the trees. Would that be all right with you?"

He waved his hand in a dismissive gesture. "Aye, but donna attempt to—"

She walked away from him. "Oh, I know, or you'll kill me."

Grace made her way into the tree line, lifting her skirts to avoid getting tangled in the brush. She was flanked by waist high golden grass. Both the nearby tree trunk and the tall grasses provided enough cover to shield her. She fumbled underneath her skirts, and when she felt the hilt of the blade in her hand, she unsheathed her weapon.

In all her years, she never tried to maim another person, because there hadn't been a single instance in which she'd feared for her life or that of her family. But the man left her with no other alternative. She needed to injure him, slow him down, and then she'd be able to make her escape. She refused to be bargained over by the mercenaries to draw Uncle Walter or Ravenna near, only to have the men kill a member of her family.

At that moment, Grace knew she was making the ultimate sacrifice because if she was caught, the guard wouldn't hesitate. He'd end her life without even thinking twice. To her surprise, the decision was less complicated than she'd thought. The choice was her family's safety or leaving this man whole to kill another innocent victim.

The time was now or never, and failure was not an option.

Once Grace and her dagger were in position, she paid attention to every detail. When she thought she was ready, she pulled back her arm and found herself pummeled to the ground with a heavy thump.

*"Na dean sin."* Don't do that. Fagan held Grace tight by his side on the ground, and when she met his eyes, she gasped, pulling his head closer and smacking her lips to his.

"I knew you were alive!"

The lass continued to plant kisses over his cheeks,

his eyes, and his head. His face was wet with her tears, and he was never so happy to see her well. For days, he'd been mad with worry.

"Shhh… I'm relieved to see ye too, but we donna want to alert the guard."

"My lady!"

She stiffened beneath him. "I'm feeling a little better! I just need but a few more moments! Thank you!"

Fagan gazed down at her and smiled. "I donna even want to know."

She brought her hand to his cheek. "At times I feared the worst, but I prayed for your safety every day. How did you survive?"

"I was knocked out. The bastards thought I was dead and left Calum there to bleed to death. When I woke up, Calum told me what had happened. I was able to patch him up and the next day sent him off to seek Ruairi and men in arms."

"Oh, Fagan. There is so much that I want—need—to tell you."

"Whatever 'tis ye have to tell me can wait." He reached over in the grass and handed her the dagger. "Place this back under your skirts now. They havenae harmed ye, have they?"

"Nothing that I wasn't able to handle. How do we get out of here?"

He brushed back the loose tendrils that had fallen into her face. "Ye have to trust me. Ye need to return with the guard until Ruairi brings more men—"

She shook her head. "I cannot. Please don't make me go back in there. Listen to me. These men hold me because a servant on Orkney had some type of evidence about the Earl of Orkney. The mercenaries have since killed the servant, but the woman was able to give this information to Uncle Walter or Ravenna before she died. That's why they hold me. They're going to kill my uncle or my sister before either one of them is able to deliver the information to the king in Edinburgh. The problem is… I don't know which one of them has the evidence. I must come with you. If I'm not held prisoner, I can't be used to bargain against them."

Grace's eyes widened as Fagan felt the tip of the blade at his back.

"That's verra true, my lady. 'Tis good that we still have ye then, aye? Get up verra slowly and drop your sword to the ground."

Fagan let out a heavy sigh, and then he lifted himself from Grace. "Let the lass go and take me in her stead."

The red-haired man laughed. "I donna think so. I will nae tell ye again to drop your sword to the ground, and while ye're at it, ye can throw away the blade ye carry in your boot."

As Fagan removed the sword from his scabbard, he hesitated. Grace sat in the grass, and he cast a determined look at her. She knew not to move. Without giving the bastard behind him any warning, Fagan spun around as steel met steel. He thrust and parried with the mercenary with every intention of removing the bastard's head from his shoulders. At least that was what he'd hoped.

Out of the corner of his eye he spotted two armed guards making haste toward Grace. The lass had her back toward the men and didn't even know they were coming. He wouldn't chance her being harmed or take a risk that she might do something rash. He had to protect her—even if that meant protecting her from herself—so he did the only thing that came to mind. He held up his arms and yielded, dropping his sword to the ground.

Grace sprung to her feet and stood between Fagan and the guard. "Please don't kill him."

Fagan placed his hands on her shoulders and tried to move her to the side, but she wouldn't budge. "Grace…"

"What kind of man are ye that ye hide behind the skirts of a lass, eh?" The men threw back their heads and roared with laughter. "Mayhap he's nae a man at all? Tell me… Does the lass hold your bollocks for ye as well?"

"He's more of a man than any of you ever will be!"

One of the guards removed Fagan's blade from his boot. When Grace lowered her arm and her fingers trailed down her thigh, Fagan stilled her hand. Now was not the time to lose their only weapon.

The guard grabbed Grace forcefully by the arm. "Come. Ye should be happy that ye have a companion to share the darkness with now—well, until the captain returns and decides what to do with our new guest. Back in the dark ye go with nay food and water for your insolence."

"Go to hell," she spat.

The guard's eyes darkened. "Donna say I didnae warn ye."

❧

Grace found herself once again embraced by Hades with the hounds of hell guarding the entrance and exit of the bloody gates. But in this instance, Fagan was by her side. Together they'd figure out a way to end this madness. If anyone could discover a way out, she had to have faith it would be him. They sat against the stone wall, and he wrapped his arm around her. She laid her head on his chest and sighed.

"I'm so sorry. I wasn't thinking. When you dropped your sword… I just didn't want to lose you. You must think of me as a fool."

He kissed the top of her head. "I donna, but ye need to control your anger around these men. They are hired for a reason, and if ye nay longer suit their purpose, they donna need ye. 'Tis better to say naught. I donna want to see ye hurt."

"I don't think you can see me at all."

"There is truth in that. Are ye really all right, Grace?"

She paused. "Now that you're here, I'm much better. I was sick with worry about you." She gently rubbed his arm. "What are we going to do about Ravenna and Uncle Walter?"

"Ruairi should be here soon. As long as the weather holds and it doesnae rain, he should be able to track us here. He's nae the best tracker, but I've been leaving signs around for the past few days that I know even he could follow."

There was a heavy silence.

"Do you know anything about this Earl of Orkney?"

"The king imprisoned the earl, his own cousin Patrick Stewart, because the earl resisted his laws on Iona. The lands of Orkney were then forfeited to the realm. Ye know how I told ye the Gordon was

Ruairi's father-in-law?" He hesitated. "Lass, I cannae see ye nod. Ye would have to say aye or nay."

"I wasn't thinking. Yes, I remember."

"Gordon joined Patrick Stewart's son, Robert, to gather arms against the realm. They had intended to seize the Palace of Birsay, and then Kirkwall Castle and St. Magnus Cathedral, but your sister stopped them."

"Ravenna?"

"Aye, she sent word to the king. I donna know what evidence this servant has or had, but this is the first I've heard about it."

"From what the guard told me, I know these men will not stop until the Earl of Orkney is freed."

"I donna think the king would ever release Stewart. Mayhap the evidence of the servant was enough for the king to finally take his head, but I donna know for certain." Fagan rubbed his hand over her shoulder. "So now that ye've had ample time to think about your choices, are ye going to give up learning about spy craft and leave it to the actual spies? I'm certain Lord Mildmay and Ravenna would be relieved to hear it from ye when ye see them."

"Do you want to know something?" When he didn't answer, she added, "Fagan, I cannot see you nod. You would have to say yes or no."

He chuckled.

"In truth, I've had a lot of time to think about a great many things, especially between us. Oh, how I've regretted the hurtful words that I said to you. I wish I could take them back. But you have to know that I didn't mean them, any of them. I only wanted you to see reason. I'm English; you're not.

Nevertheless, my mind, my *heart*, couldn't imagine losing you. I couldn't bear the anguish of never seeing you again, never having you in my life. That fear alone was nearly my undoing." She rubbed her fingers over his chest and was for once thankful for the darkness.

"I know you're a man with pride and honor, but I pray that you feel something deeper for me. I don't want the only reason you want to wed me to be because you took my virtue. I know this makes no sense, because my mind tells me to run, and my heart tells me to stay. But I promised God that if he returned you to me, I'd be honest with you. There is something that I've been meaning to tell you for quite some time. I can't imagine my life without you in it. Yes, I will marry you. As long as we're together, that's all that matters. I love you, Fagan."

He gave her a quick pat on the head. "I know."

# Eighteen

WHEN GRACE SAT UP ABRUPTLY, FAGAN TRIED TO STAY
a chuckle. He knew the lass had fought her feelings
toward him at every turn. Granted, the words she said
were true. He was a man filled with pride and honor,
but that was part of the reason why he was so persistent about their future. The woman was so caught up
in the fact they were enemies that she'd never lifted
the veil to see what was in front of her eyes. She
finally admitted her true feelings for him only when
she thought he was dead. The amusing part of that was
he didn't blame her.

For days, he'd driven himself mad with worry. The
thought of Grace being held captive by barbarian mercenaries was pure torture. She was a beautiful woman,
and he knew these types of men took anything for
their pleasure. The idea that any other man would lay
his hands on her tore at his insides. That's the moment
when the clouds parted and he realized that his feelings
for the lass went far deeper than one night of passion.

Even though he knew it was in his best interest
to tell Grace how he felt, he wasn't ready. He didn't

want to have this conversation here in the dark, being held prisoner by a bunch of mercenaries. But from the silence that encircled him, he knew he might not have a choice.

"*I know*? That's all you're going to say to me after I gave you my heart? Now I really am the fool."

"Grace..." He reached out, fumbling to take her hand. "Ye are an intelligent lass. Deep in your heart ye've always known how I felt about ye. I donna want to start our future in this place. I want to gaze into your eyes and see your bonny face when I tell ye that ye've made me the happiest man alive." He pulled her into the circle of his arms and held her there.

She sighed. "Oh, Fagan. We are quite the pair, you and I. Do tell me you have an idea of how to get us out of here. We need to escape before Ravenna or Uncle Walter arrives."

"The more I think on the matter, the more I believe that we donna need to worry about Ravenna. Ruairi would ne'er let her come. And besides, Calum should have reached Sutherland lands before the mercenaries sent their message. Ruairi is already on his way."

"But you know my sister. What if she received the message after Ruairi departed? There wouldn't be time for her to contact Uncle Walter for help. Do you think she'd sit idle when mercenaries have made a threat on my life?"

"I heard Ravenna with my own ears. She gave her word to Ruairi that she's retired from serving the Crown. She is now the dutiful wife of the Sutherland laird."

"Dutiful wife? You do know my sister is a

Walsingham? If she thought one of her sisters was in danger, I'm confident that she'd travel on her own, even if that meant defying her husband. I don't think we should sit around and wait for Ruairi and his men. If there is something we can do, any chance we can escape, we need to do it. The captain is away and I don't know when he'll be back. But I do know there are fewer men standing guard now than before, and I'm fairly certain there are only three of them. Do you think you can handle them if they're separated?"

"I donna question my prowess on the battlefield, lass. I give pause because I donna want to see ye hurt. One wrong move, Grace, and these men will nae hesitate to kill ye. Ye cannae do something rash. Your actions—and I must say your sharp tongue—could make matters worse."

Her voice went up a notch. "You know me."

Fagan hesitated. "That's exactly my point."

"I admit that sometimes I might act out of anger or pride—"

"Might? Ye know that ye do."

"But Fagan—"

"I need to think. I am nae yet ready to place my future wife in peril."

He felt a poke in his chest and assumed it was her finger. "You listen to me. If you have any intention of being my husband, then you need to understand something. I will do anything for my own blood, as I would do for you. No one threatens my family."

"Are ye sure ye donna have any Scots blood in ye, lass? I find it hard to believe all that fire within ye belongs to the English."

Grace dismissed his words and continued. "I am not willing to risk my sister or my uncle's life by not even trying to escape because you fear I might be placed in harm's way. Besides, Ruairi is your liege. He would kill you if anything happened to my sister, his wife."

"And I would ne'er forgive myself if anything happened to ye."

"Then instead of thinking of all the reasons why we shouldn't attempt to do anything, let's work together and come up with an idea to save my family."

*"A bheil fhios agad?"*

"Fagan, at least be man enough to insult me in English."

"Do ye know?"

"Do I know what?"

"That ye sound exactly like Ruairi." He chuckled. "God help me. I will nae only wed the woman I…er, care for, but I'll be marrying my best friend."

"And I think, Mister Murray, every marriage should be so lucky."

⌘

"Wake up!"

Drifting back and forth between sleep and consciousness, Grace wasn't sure if she was dreaming or if Fagan was calling to her. She fought to open her eyes. For a moment, she forgot where she was. "Where are you?"

"Shhh… I'm standing by the door. The light comes closer. Do ye know what to do?"

She stood and stretched her aching back. "Yes," she whispered.

"Nay matter what happens, ye stay back."

"I understood that the first five times you told me."

"Then remember it again."

It was a pity there wasn't any light. The man could've seen her rolling her eyes at him. She stood against the wall as the torch was placed in the crack outside the door. When the lock jingled, the guard walked in and hesitated. Fagan tackled the man, pummeling him into the stone wall.

Two fists came down on Fagan's back with a heavy thwack and he grunted. He pulled away from the guard and returned an elbow in the man's face, but something wasn't right. Grace inched closer to the light.

Her heart sank.

The guard wasn't one of the three men who had been watching her. This was the bloody captain, the scarred man. Heaven help them. The leader and his men had returned. She wasn't sure if Fagan noticed who the miscreant was. Although she'd promised to stay back and not intervene, words escaped her.

"Fagan, it's the captain!"

If he didn't bring the scarred vagrant to his knees now and the man called out, there would be no escape. The captain balled his fist into Fagan's gut. If that wasn't bad enough, then he lifted his leg and gave Fagan a swift kick out the door.

Fagan landed hard on his back and then flew to his feet. He shoved the captain back against the door as it closed with a bang. Grace pushed, and the latch must have closed. The darned thing locked, and she was trapped inside alone.

The torchlight on the wall was flickering, and large

shadows contorted in strange images on the wall. The
captain reached down and pulled out a dagger from
his boot. With a sudden forward movement, the blade
scraped Fagan's arm. She tried not to make any noise,
fearing she'd distract Fagan from his purpose.

"I should've made certain ye were dead myself."

Fagan stepped back, missing another swing of the
blade. "Aye, ye should have."

"I will nae make that mistake again."

"Aye, well, ye can try."

The captain swung his weapon again, and Fagan
ducked in the nick of time. He quickly stood, ram-
ming his fist into the man's face. She heard a crack
and blood dripped down the captain's nose. Grace
could not tear her eyes away from the men. She was
even afraid to blink. Lifting her skirts, she unsheathed
her dagger. She was thinking that perhaps she could
toss the blade to Fagan through the bars, but then he
disarmed the man. She breathed a sigh of relief when
the captain's dagger fell to the ground.

Without warning, the captain dropped to the floor
and wrapped his legs around Fagan's, bringing Fagan
to the ground with a heavy thump. Fagan sat up, and
the man's arms encircled him, holding Fagan against
his chest in a firm grip. The man choked Fagan with
one arm while extending his other arm to reach for
the dagger.

Fagan fought to set himself free as Grace panted in
terror. This could not be happening. The hilt of the
dagger was now at the captain's fingertips. Fagan kicked
and struggled against the restraining arm at his throat.

In a split second, Fagan's eyes met hers. As if she had

some strange hint of foresight, she was suddenly fully aware of everything around her. She couldn't quite explain the feeling, but something passed between them and a sense of dread washed over her. His eyes sent her a private message as if he was saying good-bye or he was sorry, maybe both.

Without a doubt, this had to be one of the moments that Fagan talked about because Grace no longer thought rationally. She permitted her anger to rise, fear for his safety guiding her. Her heart was hammering, her breathing ragged. How could she be expected to stand, helpless, and watch the man she loved die—again? Oh, no. Fagan would not die like this. They would be wed, have children of their own, grandchildren even, before she'd ever allow him to depart from this world.

She leaned her body against the door and stretched her hand through the bars. Gripping the dagger, she knew she didn't have ample time to study the target. Fagan's life depended on her aim. The captain's fingers wrapped around the hilt of the blade, and Grace released hers into the air.

Fagan cried out in agony.

❦

*"A mhic an Diobhail!"* O son of the Devil!

"I'm sorry!"

The captain was about to impale Fagan with his dagger when Fagan pulled Grace's blade out of his own thigh. Using all his strength, he drove the pointy end straight into the bastard's black heart and gave it a twist.

Heavy footsteps echoed in the corridor, and Fagan realized that he had failed Grace. Five paid killers rushed into the cavern with wide eyes and glowered at him. He was certain it didn't help matters that he was covered in blood, their captain's and his own. As the red-haired man stepped forward and glanced at his fallen comrade, there was a raging storm in his eyes. Fagan knew that expression all too well. The man turned and met Fagan's eyes, already killing him with his steely gaze.

The red-haired guard gestured to his men. "I am in command now. See to the captain, and I will see to this bastard."

"Aye, captain."

Two men lifted the scarred man's body and carried the corpse out of the cave. As two other guards grabbed Fagan under the arms, pulling him roughly to his feet, he closed his eyes to mask the pain.

"Leave him alone!"

"Shut your mouth, ye English wench. And donna worry about him because I'll be back for ye next."

"Fagan…"

He turned his head and winked at Grace. "Nay worries, lass. We're just going to have a wee chat."

The men led Fagan into the larger cave. As soon as they dropped him to the ground, another guard clamored into the room from the narrow passageway. He was just as big and ugly as the others and gazed around at his cohorts.

"Where is the captain?"

"Dead, thanks to this arse," said the red-haired guard. "I am now in command."

"Our tracker has sent word that the spy travels with four men." To Fagan's surprise, the man spoke without hesitation or questioning the authority of the new captain. He supposed these men thought coin was coin. It didn't matter who was in charge as long as they were paid.

"Aye." The fiery dragon looked down at Fagan and his eyes darkened. "Lucky for ye that I donna have time for ye right now, but I shall take great pleasure in killing ye both, slowly, for the death of our captain." He gave his men a gesture of dismissal, and the same two guards escorted Fagan back to Grace.

They opened the door and shoved him inside. When he fell to the ground, Grace flew to his side. The door closed, and once again they were embraced by darkness.

"Fagan, are you all right?" She gulped hard and smoothed back his hair with a trembling hand. He realized his face was wet from tears that were not his own.

"Lass, ye're leaking on me."

Sobs shook her, and she spoke in a weak whisper. "Please forgive me. Dear God. That look on your face will be lodged in my memory for all eternity. Oh God. Please be all right. Please tell me you're all right. Are you all right?"

"Am I all right? Ye. Stabbed. Me. Did I nae tell ye to stay back? Thank God I was granted a boon and your aim isnae as good as your sister's. Ye could've hit me in the heart or something far worse."

"I know. I'm so sorry. You're a handsome man and I'd like to keep you that way."

"I wasnae speaking of my face, lass. I was talking about the part of me that makes me a man."

There was heavy silence.

"I know ye're distraught, but ye need to calm yourself. What's done is done. Now I need to take care of this wound before it festers. Can ye help me sit up?" he asked through gritted teeth. When Grace placed her hands underneath his shoulders and lifted, he cried out. *"Gabh air do shocair."* Take it easy.

"Did I hurt you?"

"Nay, I'm fine. Do ye have anything in here that I can use to bind my leg?"

"Only the blankets in the corner, and I wouldn't give one of those rags to Angus. You can use a piece of my shift." After a moment, she grunted. "I can't tear it, and I can't see a darned thing. Oh, Fagan. I was wrong. We shouldn't have tried to escape. I've only made matters worse. You're injured, and now Ravenna and Uncle Walter are in danger because of me."

"Bring your skirts closer and lift them so I only tear the shift. I could make a binding even in the dark. I've certainly made enough of them during my lifetime. And I donna want to hear ye talk that way. The Grace I know would ne'er give up. She's the most stubborn wench I've ever known."

"What are we going to do?"

"When the men took me away, one of the guards said the spy was traveling with four men." He moaned when he tied off the binding. "I think 'tis Lord Mildmay because Ruairi wouldnae allow Ravenna to come, especially only accompanied by four men. Your uncle has been working for the king for years. I'm certain he's been placed in more dire situations than this. He'll know what to do, and I'm sure he has prepared his men. I have nay doubt he knows that these men arenae to be trusted. He'll be ready."

Fagan lowered his painful leg to the floor, trying to find a more comfortable position. "What am I going to do with ye, Grace? First, ye blacken my eye, and then ye slice me in the thigh." He chuckled. "I bet ye ne'er knew I was a poet, did ye?"

When he felt her hand pat him, he chuckled. "Ye cannae get enough of me, can ye?"

"Pardon?"

"Och, lass. That isnae my thigh."

≪≫

Grace pulled back her hand as if she'd touched a flame. She was never so thankful for the darkness that hid the blush she knew crossed her face.

"Don't flatter yourself. I was only showing you sympathy and missed your leg." She let out a heavy sigh. "I can't believe I stabbed you. Can you ever forgive me?"

"How angry do ye think Ruairi and Ravenna will be when they find out ye've agreed to wed me?"

"I know you're only trying to distract me."

"Then answer the question."

"Ravenna loves Ruairi. I don't think she'll have a problem with the fact that you're a Scot, but she may have a difficult time understanding why we no longer want to kill each other. All my sister and Ruairi ever saw was us quarreling, and I never told Ravenna about the times when you kissed me. I think this will come as quite the shock."

"Ye mean when ye kissed me."

She swatted him in the arm. "Thank you."

"For what?"

"Distracting me."

"I'd do anything for ye, Grace. And what will ye say to Casterbrook?"

"That is a conversation I'm not looking forward to having. The banns haven't been posted yet, but I did talk to Ravenna before I left about Daniel. She knew I was confused and said she'd support whatever I decided. I was foolish enough to think that Daniel and I could grow to love each other. I hope you understand that I wanted to marry into the aristocracy because that's what my father desired for his girls, but now I realize he only wanted us to be happy. At least I hope that's true."

"A father would do anything for his children. Even though I ne'er knew your sire, he sounded like a great man. He would've wanted the best for ye and your sisters, but I'm certain he wouldnae deny any of ye love."

She leaned against his arm. "Then I'm in luck because I have the best of both worlds. Although you're being an arse for not telling me how you feel, you challenge me to be a better person. I want to be a better person when I'm with you. You and I are like kindred spirits."

"Och, lass. I knew that when ye first arrived at the gates."

"Fagan…"

The light was coming closer and the door swung open. Two guards entered and torchlight illuminated the room. She gazed down at Fagan and felt like she was punched in the gut. Blood had soaked clean through the makeshift bandage and he was covered in muck. He looked much worse than she had imagined.

"Ye're coming with us." One of the guards stepped forward and pulled Grace to her feet.

She shook off his arm. "Get your hands off me. I'm not going anywhere with you."

"Leave her the hell alone," said Fagan. He tried to stand, but the guard kicked him hard on his wound and brought him to the ground. Fagan held his leg and briefly closed his eyes.

"The damn spy sent a messenger to see if ye are hale. He will nae meet with the captain until 'tis confirmed that ye are."

"Fagan…"

"Ye donna have a choice, lass. I beg ye to remember what I told ye."

Grace was escorted out onto the cliffs and up the path. She prayed Ruairi and his men would arrive in time. At least she had confirmation the spy was Uncle Walter. Perhaps she'd have time to warn him about what these men intended to do. But Fagan's words haunted her. He didn't need to remind her that once she was no longer useful to the mercenaries, they would kill her.

# Nineteen

Grace stood in an open field flanked by mercenaries. She hadn't uttered a single word since the guards escorted her from the cave. Not only was she concerned for Uncle Walter, but Fagan did not look well. He needed a healer to properly see to the wound that she had inflicted.

The men were at the ready, their hands resting on the hilts of their swords. To make matters worse, a light rain obscured her view of the forest. She wasn't sure where the rest of the men were lurking and lying in wait, which meant neither did Uncle Walter. She glanced around the tree line praying for some type of rescue from her brother-in-law and his men. Nothing stirred, at least not anything she could see, and that frightened her even more.

"We know ye're there!" yelled the captain. "Come out. Ye can see the wench still breathes. We have fulfilled our end of the bargain."

Something moved out of the corner of her eye, and five men emerged from the forest several hundred yards away. One man wore a dark-colored cloak and walked ahead of the others. Although she couldn't see his face, he was the same size and shape as Uncle Walter. The men approached, and their hands mirrored those of the mercenaries with fingers strategically placed around the hilts of their swords. She had to warn her uncle before it was too late.

"Don't come any closer! They're going to kill you!"

One of the guards whipped his head around, and his eyes darkened. "Shut your mouth, wench!" He imposed an iron grip on her arm, and she cried out in pain.

Two of Uncle Walter's men now flanked him, and the two others stayed back. They stopped when they reached the mercenary captain. Her uncle's men gazed around warily as Uncle Walter stood as still as stone. A few moments passed, and then he lifted his arms and removed the hood of his cloak.

Grace gasped.

"Release my betrothed at once."

"Daniel?"

"Are you all right, my dear? Worry no longer because I am here to take you home."

"She's nae going anywhere until ye hand over the evidence against the Earl of Orkney—which ye have."

Daniel lifted his head haughtily and puffed out his chest. "You see, my good man...that may be a problem because the earl's son, Robert Stewart, was already taken to Edinburgh where he will stand trial for his insolence."

The captain's face clouded with uneasiness.

"Oh, my apologies, you didn't know. Stewart was

not the wisest of men. You see…while his father was already imprisoned for disobeying the king's commands, Stewart also had an accomplice, Patrick Halcro, who talked. And he talked a lot."

The captain shifted his weight. "What the hell are ye rambling on about?" He turned to his men. "Me thinks this whelp likes to talk a lot." When his men laughed in response, Daniel's eyes narrowed.

"If you had any hope of seeing the earl released from prison, it's too late, my friend. I'm afraid his fate is sealed. You see…Patrick Halcro insisted that he acted on the earl's behalf, even though the earl was in prison. The servant girl, Margaret Buchanan, whom one of you killed, read instructions for Halcro written in the earl's own hand. In turn, Halcro gave the letter to Stewart who read it and then tore it into pieces 'for the better,' he told Mistress Buchanan. And why, you ask? So that the letter could do no harm in the future, and because the Earl of Orkney did not want to lose his head for it, she was told. And before she was killed, she told me the contents of the letter."

The rain hardened, and Daniel smoothed back his hair. "I've already given this information to the king's advisors, and now I'm here with you speaking with the authority of the king. The Crown is perfectly aware the Earl of Orkney hired you, but the poor earl didn't expect Mistress Buchanan to talk with me before you killed her. And now I'm afraid you won't be getting paid for your efforts because you're a little too late to bargain anything. So let me tell you how this is going to work. I'll be leaving here with my betrothed, and you'll be leaving here without your heads."

The captain smirked. "If ye havenae noticed, your king's laws arenae observed in the Highlands. And I would have to say that our numbers are far greater than yours, ye English prick. If anyone is going to lose their bonny head, 'tis going to be ye and this English wench ye came to rescue."

Daniel sighed. "I was afraid you were going to say that, but I was hoping you wouldn't be difficult. Perhaps there is still time to change your mind." Daniel raised a fist into the air as armed men on horseback rode out of the forest from all directions. Immediately, Grace recognized the royal badge of the Tudor rose divided by the Scottish thistle, topped by the royal crown. It had been a long time since she'd seen her countrymen, and she'd never been so relieved in her life.

She and Fagan were about to be saved by Daniel and the king's men.

❧

Fagan lost track of how many times he'd cursed Grace. Now that he was injured, by her hand no less, there was little he could do to aid their escape. He prayed Mildmay had thought long and hard before he summoned the mercenaries to bring Grace to him.

His leg was getting worse, and God how he wished he had a healthy dram of whisky to ease the pain right now. But the constant throbbing in his thigh wouldn't be close to the agony he'd feel in his heart if something happened to the lass. He was supposed to protect her, but all he'd done thus far was deliver her into the arms of the mercenaries—twice.

He leaned his head back against the wall and closed his eyes. It would be so easy to just let go and give in to the blackness. But he had every reason to live. His eyelids flew open when the sound of clamoring men echoed through the cave. He held his breath. He didn't think he imagined the noise, but the guards shouldn't be back so soon.

In the distance, metal struck metal, and he realized the men were only having a wee bit of swordplay. He supposed they needed something to pass the time and was thankful they weren't torturing him to satisfy their restlessness.

Fagan shook his head to clear the fog because he swore he'd just heard a scratch at the door. He hesitated another moment to decide whether or not to investigate the noise. When there was another odd sound coming from outside the door, he grudgingly pulled himself to his feet.

Pain shot through his leg, and his breath hitched in his lungs. He willed himself to remain conscious. With his hand, he placed pressure on his wound as he took a small single step. "One dram: nae the better or the worse from it." He inched forward. "Two drams: the better and nae the worse from it." About two more steps and he'd be at the door. He continued to speak through the agony and caught himself before he crumpled to the ground. "Three drams: the worse and nae the better from it. I. Need. A. Damn. Drink."

He reached for the door and leaned his head against the bars. The boisterous guards were still practicing their swordplay in the distance, but he heard a faint whine coming from outside the door.

"Is someone there?" Not that he expected anyone to answer. He paused another moment, and heard another scraping noise. "Who's there? Can ye help me?" This time he heard another whimper—the kind an animal would make.

Something thumped up against the door, and Fagan took a chance by reaching his hand through the bars. He was greeted by a large mass of fur and another whine. "Angus?" A tongue licked him on the hand. "Och, Angus. *'Se balach math a th'annad. An cuidich thu mi?*" *You're a good boy. Will you help me?*

Torchlight was coming closer and reflecting off the cavern walls.

"Fagan!"

"In here! Please, *greas ort!*" *Hurry up!*

Ruairi gazed through the bars, and Fagan had never felt so relieved in his life. When the door swung open, his leg gave out beneath him and his friend caught him. Ruairi draped Fagan's arm over his shoulders and grabbed him around the waist, supporting him. As Ruairi pulled him from his prison, Fagan realized he would've laughed if the situation wasn't so dire because he was the one who'd always saved Ruairi's arse. They moved through the corridor of the cave as fast as Fagan's legs could carry him.

"*Mòran taing.*" *Many thanks.*

"How badly are ye injured?"

"'Tis naught. Where's Grace? Did ye make it in time to help Mildmay?"

"Mildmay? What are ye talking about, and where is Grace?"

Fagan stopped. "Ye didnae see her?"

"Nay. Calum told us what happened to ye, and thank God I was able to track ye here from the signs ye left us. The guards are dead."

"Nae all of them. These bastards wanted Grace because Mildmay holds evidence against the Earl of Orkney. They threatened to kill her unless Mildmay came here and didnae deliver the evidence to Edinburgh to the king. The men took Grace to meet her uncle."

"Are ye able to ride?" As if Ruairi read Fagan's mind, he pulled out a flask and handed it to him.

"Aye."

❧

The captain bristled. "Ye think that ye and the king's men will make us cower at the feet of the English?" He turned to his men. "Kill them all."

Daniel and his men unsheathed their weapons as the captain and his men did the same. Grace fled and didn't stop until she reached the tree line. The men didn't pay her any heed because they were more interested in killing each other. Even though the English had far more men than the Scottish mercenaries, all her nervousness slipped back to grip her. She wanted this to be over. She wanted Fagan to be well again. And she never wanted to hear about or see another bloody spy. How could she have been so foolish in thinking this was the life she wanted to lead?

She. Was. An. Idiot.

Swords were drawn. Blood was spilled. The men on horseback cut down the Scots on foot in less than a minute's time. A man was beheaded, another stabbed through the chest, and a few men were even impaled in the eye. Taunts were thrown like stones, and men screamed battle cries, each attacking their enemy with forceful blows.

Grace flattened her hands over her ears to silence the cries. There was chaos all around her, as if hell was set free on earth. She knew the mercenaries deserved their fate but was surprised by the brutality of her countrymen. She closed her eyes. Even though the battle was over before it had barely begun, it felt eternal. Hands gripped her, lowering her arms, and Daniel gave her a warm smile.

"Are you all right, my dear?"

Grace swatted at him. "How could you not tell me you were a spy for His Majesty?"

"You didn't need to know, but you are safe now and that's all that matters." He wrapped his arm around her shoulders. "I'm sorry you had to see my men bring these mercenaries to their knees, but that's what happens when anyone tries to cross His Majesty—or Lord Casterbrook, for that matter. Come, dearest, let me take you home to England where you belong."

She shook off his hand. "I'm not going anywhere. We need to see to Fagan."

He lifted a brow. "Fagan?"

"Mister Murray, the captain of Laird Sutherland's guard." She glanced around the field of blood as Daniel's men poked the fallen Scottish dogs, making certain they were dead. "Is my sister's husband with you?"

A look of disgust crossed his face. "Why would the bloody Highlander be here with me? And where exactly is his captain?"

She gestured toward the east. "He's injured in the cave where the mercenaries held us. He needs a healer. Do you have one with you? Please, we must move quickly."

"You were held together in a cave? Is that why you call this *man* by his Christian name?"

She pulled him by the arm, leading him away from the scene that would be forever imprinted in her memory. "Daniel, please. What difference does it make what I call him? We are wasting precious time. Please gather some of your men because a handful of guards still keep watch over him."

Daniel stopped dead in his tracks. "I'm sorry, my dear, but I think you misunderstand my purpose."

"Whatever do you mean?"

"The captain of the mercenaries is dead, and the evidence against the Earl of Orkney and his son has been delivered to Edinburgh. These men held Lord Casterbrook's betrothed, and they paid for that mistake with their lives."

A war of emotions raged through her. "I don't understand. Why are you talking this way, Daniel? This doesn't sound like you at all. And why are we still standing here? A man needs our help."

He waved her off. "Didn't I tell you that I wanted to send my own men to escort you home? And I told your sister and her Highland husband the same, and look what happened. You need to listen to me, trust me. As far as I'm concerned, I'm practically your husband. Now that you are free and safe, there is nothing else to do. My men will see to the fallen. Leave that barbaric Highland captain to his fate with the bloody Scots. There is nothing else you can do for him."

Before Grace even realized what she'd done, she raised her hand and slapped Daniel hard across the face. She knew she was in trouble when her palm stung and his eyes pierced her. His voice lowered to a threatening tone.

"How dare you strike me in front of my men! Do you think to play me for a fool? I *saved* you, and this is how you repay my kindness?"

"Your kindness? You would leave a man to die!"

"I would leave a bloody Scot to die." When her eyes widened, he added, "Don't look at me that way. I know you despise those Scottish barbarians as much as I do."

"You attended my sister's wedding."

"Only because you are my betrothed. You said yourself how you couldn't bear being in Scotland and around those men. That's one of the attributes I favor most about you—well, that and the fact you're Lord Mildmay's niece." His voice softened, and he lifted his fingers, brushing back the wet hair that had fallen into her eyes.

"Listen to me, my dear. When the king discovers I have slaughtered the mercenaries, I will be in his good graces. He will no longer confide in your uncle but in me. I will assume your uncle's position and quickly rise as one of His Majesty's most trusted men and advisors. Our future is secure. We will have wealth, power, anything you can imagine."

"Greed..." Her voice went up a notch. "Well, I'm sure my uncle will have something to say about your scheming, Daniel. And just so I'm clear, let me make certain that I understand you correctly. The only reason you wish to wed me is because I'm Lord Mildmay's niece and you want to take his place. Do I have that about right then?"

He dismissed her question and gestured to the fallen men. "This is no place to have this conversation, and this is no place for my future wife to be. You'll come with me now."

Her eyes narrowed. "I'm not leaving here without Fagan."

"As my betrothed, you don't have a choice." He grabbed her arm and started to pull her away.

"Release me at once."

"Only when you come to your senses."

"Daniel, I'm not leav—" When he tightened his grip, she cried out. "You're hurting me."

He stopped and slapped her across her cheek with the back of his hand. "You don't know the meaning of the word."

She lifted her hand to her face and couldn't stay her tongue. "You bastard! You're no better than the bloody mercenaries you've slaughtered here this day."

He chuckled, and his eyes gave her a firm warning. "You will be grateful that I saved you, and you will heel in front of the king's men, my men."

She snarled at him. "I will never marry you, and we are no longer betrothed. And I will *never* heel."

His dark eyes sent a shiver down her spine. "You're too late, my lady. The banns have already been posted, and we will be wed upon your return to England."

The stench of burning bodies hung in the air, and Fagan willed himself not to gag. Once Ruairi and his men saw the billowing smoke over the trees in the distance, they rode hard to reach Grace. To Fagan's dismay, the lass wasn't there. Although the rain had stopped, all that was left were bloodstains on the ground and a bonfire of men.

Ruairi's mount pranced beneath him. "I donna like this. I can understand Lord Mildmay warring with the mercenaries and setting them aflame, but where are Grace and her uncle? Why would they take their leave?"

Fagan gazed into the flames, and his heart sank. "Ye donna think…"

"They arenae in the fire." Ruairi turned his mount and yelled to his men. "See if ye can find a trail." He shook his head. "This makes nay sense. The only reason I can think Mildmay would take his leave is mayhap because he thought ye were dead, but my sister-by-marriage would've told him where ye were. Och, Fagan. Please tell me ye didnae do something foolish and she left ye for dead."

"My laird! We found a man! He lives!"

Fagan and Ruairi galloped across the field to the tree line. Fagan dismounted, and pain shot through his leg. He grabbed the saddle for support as soon as his foot touched the ground. A man lay on the ground with a battle wound in his chest. He gazed up, and when he spotted Ruairi's kilt, he spat.

"We killed all your bloody friends. There is no one left."

Ruairi knelt beside the injured man. "We arenae

mercenaries. I am Laird Ruairi Sutherland. Ye are the king's man, are ye nae?"

"Yes," said the man in a faint whisper.

"What happened here? Where are Lord Mildmay and his niece?"

The man could barely speak. "The mercenaries… did not yield. The last time…I saw the lady…she was safe…with Lord Casterbrook."

Fagan couldn't help it. His voice went up a notch. "Casterbrook?"

When the man closed his eyes and drew his last breath, Ruairi stood. "Mayhap Casterbrook and Mildmay removed Grace from harm's way. I would've done the same for Ravenna. More than likely they circled around to aid ye and we missed them. Why donna we make our way back to the caves?"

"My laird! There is only one trail heading south."

Fagan felt ice spreading through his veins. Grace had left him in the cave and fled with her bloody betrothed.

# *Twenty*

GRACE GAZED OUT AT THE SCOTTISH THISTLE IN THE glade from her seat in the carriage and wished to plant Daniel among the weeds. She tried to understand how her situation had gone from bad to worse. Mercenaries had held her prisoner in a cave, and now she was being held against her will by Daniel, her "betrothed," the man who was supposed to care for her. If this was his way of showing her affection, she'd hate to see how he behaved if he despised her.

Her cheek ached where Daniel had struck her, but the discomfort didn't even begin to compare with the misery she felt about Fagan. She prayed Ruairi had found him in time because she couldn't bear any other option. She couldn't believe this was the second time that she didn't know if he lived or died. She knew one thing for certain. There wouldn't be a third. She was going to take the first opportunity to make her escape.

The king's guard flanked her on all sides of the carriage, although at least Daniel wasn't in sight. But in addition to her impending war with Daniel, she had to admit that she was disgusted with herself. Some bloody spy she would've made. How could she not have known that her husband-to-be was not who she thought him to be? She refused to sit and do nothing. She lifted her hand and pounded hard on the roof of the carriage.

"Lord Casterbrook said we don't stop for anything, my lady," yelled the coachman.

Grace kicked the seat in front of her several times in frustration. "And did Lord Casterbrook tell you that I can't even relieve myself? I *demand* that you stop this carriage at once, or I will jump! Do you hear me? Stop now!"

The man paid her no heed, so she swung open the door. She hung half her leg outside the carriage to make her point. She would've done more, but thankfully she didn't have to take the leap. The coach slowed, not that it was going at a great rate of speed anyway. As soon as the carriage came to a halt, Grace stepped down. The king's guard gazed at her as if she'd gone mad. Who knew? Perhaps she had.

"My lady, I would've assisted you," said the coachman as he climbed down from his perch. His blond locks were windblown and a worried expression crossed his face as if he were a lad awaiting a firm scolding.

"You can assist me by doing as I ask," she said, bristling. "Do you know who my uncle is?"

"Yes, my lady. Lord Mildmay."

"Yes, that's right. And what do you think Lord Mildmay would say if you were holding his niece against her will?" As the man's eyes lit up and he couldn't find his tongue, Daniel approached on horseback.

"Is there something wrong, my dear?" His eyes sent her a private warning. "I should hope not, but if there is anything amiss, please let me know at once so that I can address your concerns."

"You cannot expect me to ride this long without letting me stop and rest my legs, among other things, my lord. A lady has certain…needs she must see to. Besides, your men just fought in battle. I'm sure they're weary. There's no reason to make such haste back to England."

Daniel gestured to a guard. "Let the men know we will rest here for a few moments." He gazed back at Grace with a blank expression on his face, and then he spoke in a steely tone. "And then we will be on our way. We will not stop again until nightfall."

She lifted her skirts and walked away from him toward the trees. Heavy footsteps thundered after her. She knew darned well Daniel was running to catch up with her, but she refused to give him the satisfaction of an acknowledgment. A hand clamped down on her shoulder and spun her around.

"Where do you think you're going?" asked Daniel.

"Unless you want to hold my skirts for me while I see to my personal needs, release me."

He glanced around and then lowered his voice. "Grace, I don't want to quarrel with you. This is no way to start our marriage."

"I agree with you."

When his eyes softened, she realized Daniel didn't understand the meaning of the word "sarcasm." She was about to let him know there wouldn't even be a start to their marriage when he spoke before she had the chance.

His voice was kind, gentle. "I'm glad to hear it, dearest. I knew you'd eventually see reason. When I heard the mercenaries held you, I was mad with worry. Please accept my apologies for my discretion, but I couldn't very well tell you that I worked for His Majesty. I know this must have come as quite a shock." He lifted his hand and smoothed her hair. "But now that you know, you cannot mention this to anyone—not even your sister or Lord Mildmay. You could place me, us, in grave danger by telling someone. Do you understand?"

She hesitated, and her mind raced. She needed a moment to comprehend his words. Was it possible Daniel didn't know about Ravenna and Uncle Walter being spies? She closed her eyes and tried to remember if she ever mentioned her sister or uncle's involvement with the Crown. She didn't think she had. As if she needed any more evidence against him, Daniel's declaration was even further confirmation the man was an idiot. He had no idea who he was dealing with, because once Uncle Walter found out Daniel's intent to replace him as the king's trusted advisor, her betrothed's reputation would be destroyed. And why the man thought she would help him with this foolhardy endeavor was beyond her comprehension.

"Mmm... Then why would you even want to wed me if you're going to be placing me in harm's way?"

"I told you. You're Lord Mildmay's niece. I need you. And if you think hard enough, my dear, you will realize that the only men who have placed you in harm's way have been your sister's barbarian husband and that fool of a captain who escorted you home.

Remember *I* was the one who saved you. I can protect you."

She definitely had learned her lesson because if she'd had her dagger, she wouldn't have thrown it. She would've thrust the blade straight into her betrothed's tainted heart.

◈

"We ride south," said Ruairi. "Once we know that Grace is safe, we will return home. Ye need the healer to see to that wound, but I think 'tis clean enough for now. I donna think it will fester." Fagan reached out and grabbed Ruairi's shoulder as he was reaching for the reins of his mount.

"Wait." He glanced around to make certain no one overheard his words. "There is something I must tell ye." When his friend hesitated, Fagan treaded lightly. "I donna think ye are going to like what I have to say, but ye must know before we take our leave."

*"Sput a-mach e." Spit it out.*

"Grace is to be my wife."

Ruairi's eyes widened, and then he roared with laughter. He returned a brotherly slap to Fagan's shoulder. "Ye must be feeling much better after the new binding on your leg and some whisky in ye. How much have ye had to drink anyway? Come. We donna want them to get too far ahead of us."

"Ruairi… I'm afraid I am nae jesting with ye, and I havenae had nearly enough to drink have this conversation with ye."

"I donna have the patience for this right now. Let us see to Grace, and then we'll get ye home to the healer."

When Fagan didn't move and lowered his gaze to the ground, Ruairi let out a heavy sigh. "Tell me ye're jesting." He glanced up at the sky as if he was asking for some kind of spiritual guidance and then squeezed the bridge of his nose with his fingers. "*Siuthad.*" *Go on.*

"I know that's nae what ye wanted to hear, but I already told ye the truth."

There was a heavy silence, and Ruairi's eyes darkened dangerously. A muscle ticked at his jaw. Fagan knew there was a raging storm brewing underneath the surface, but he wasn't quite ready to face the wrath of his friend, his liege. For the first time since he could remember, he felt like he needed to prepare himself for a thrashing that was sure to come. He was about to be judged, and he was guilty as hell.

"Did ye ruin her?"

And there it was. The question that would tear apart years of friendship, a brotherhood that had existed long before Grace and something that had been established before a certain English spy was ever sent to the Highlands. When Fagan didn't respond, Ruairi repeated his question.

"I asked ye a question and I will nae ask ye a second time."

"Aye, but—"

A fist rammed into Fagan's jaw, knocking him hard to the ground. He let out a grunt, but his pride hurt more than the pain in his face or his leg. Ruairi glowered above him. Awkwardly, Fagan pulled himself to his feet as he eyed his friend. After a moment of silence, Ruairi's steely gaze met his, and rancor sharpened his voice.

"How could ye? I trusted ye. Grace was under my roof, my protection. Ye were *only* to escort her back to England and deliver her into the arms of Casterbrook. What part of 'She is betrothed' did ye nae understand? What the hell were ye thinking? She is my wife's sister! Ye've placed me in a dire situation. She's to be wed to an English lord, and a Highland captain—*my captain*—ruined her! How in the hell do I explain this disaster to her uncle? You know…her uncle who works for the king!"

Ruairi laughed in derision. "And how in the hell do I explain this to my *wife*? After Ravenna kills ye, she'll want to strangle me because I was the one who had insisted that ye be the one to escort Grace home—not Casterbrook or his men—because I was to see to her safety. I only trusted my own men to see to the task. Och, and ye saw to that verra well, didnae ye?" He took a deep breath. "How did this happen?"

When Fagan lifted a brow, Ruairi shook his head. "I know how that happened. I'm talking about ye and Grace. Ye couldnae even stand to be in the same room with one another." Ruairi's face suddenly went grim.

"Donna even think it. I can see it in your eyes. Before ye say another word, ye know me better than that. I would ne'er force myself on a woman."

Ruairi smirked. "I donna know what to believe anymore. I ne'er thought I'd have to worry about ye tupping my sister-in-law either."

"I love her."

Ruairi's eyes widened. "What?" He raked his fingers

through his hair. "Och, this keeps getting better and better. Where did ye put the damn whisky?"

Fagan handed Ruairi the flask, and he took a long swig. "And does she love ye?"

"Aye. We knew ye and Ravenna would be cross with us, but the lass agreed to be my wife. She was going to break the betrothal with Casterbrook when she returned to England."

"I'm glad to see the two of ye thought this through. And just where, pray tell, were ye two going to live once ye wed?" Fagan gave him a wry grin. "Nay… Nay… Ye cannae do this to me. Four lasses? Four Walsingham sisters under my roof? Grace? *Beannaich fèin, a Dhè nan gràs gach là agus gach tràth dha'm thoirt.*" *Bless, O God of grace, each day and hour of my life.* "Because I'm going to need it." Ruairi paused, and his gaze was puzzled. "Ye say ye speak the truth, but there is still something I donna understand. If Grace agreed to be your wife, then why did she leave with her uncle and Casterbrook?"

"I donna know. That's what worries me. Grace would've come back for me. I am certain of it. I think there is something nae quite right about this."

"Damn ye, Fagan. All these years, and ye had to choose my wife's betrothed sister. I told ye to *fuirich air falbh on teine* and ye jumped right in." *Stay away from the fire.* "I want to make sure ye understand something. I am far from all right with the choices ye've made, but if the lass feels the same for ye and ye did take her innocence…" Ruairi scowled. "Oh, hell. Let's take our leave and save your future wife's arse."

❧

The men had stopped for the night, and Grace sat next to the fire. After spending the day in a damp dress, she felt a chill in the air and she didn't think it was from the weather. Daniel laughed with his men, making a toast to their success in overcoming the mercenaries. Her thoughts drifted to Fagan, and tears welled in her eyes. She'd had enough. She wanted Daniel out of her life. She needed Fagan by her side where he belonged. And she wanted to go home.

"Why so grim, my dear?" Daniel's eyes twinkled with amusement as he sat down beside her.

"It's been a long day."

"Why yes, it has. You've had quite an adventure, if I do say so myself, but it's over and done. You have nothing else to fear."

She almost said "you" but decided against it.

"Did you get something to eat and drink? Should you want for anything, all you need to do is ask."

Again, she could've muttered "Release me" but thought it was in her best interest to remain silent. As Fagan would say, she'd possibly make matters worse by opening her mouth. She did the only thing that came to mind. She nodded.

"Your tent is there, my dear." His eyes sent her a private message, and he lowered his voice into a conspiratorial whisper. "I could always join you if you'd like."

"Daniel, you know very well that is not appropriate. With all these men about, that type of scandalous behavior would spread through camp like wildfire. Would you honestly want your men talking about your betrothed in that manner? Frankly, I find your comments ill-mannered."

"I'm sorry if my words offended you, my lady. That was not my intent. I was only jesting with you."

Grace turned her head away from him and closed her eyes. At least she didn't have to worry about Daniel making any unwanted advances toward her. Thank God for small favors because she had more than enough troubles already.

She stood. "Pray excuse me."

He reached out and grabbed her by the wrist. "Where are you going?"

"Daniel, if you insist on plaguing me every time I must see to my personal needs, this is going to be a long journey."

"Of course… But don't wander too far into the trees, because if you're not back soon, I will find you."

Gazing down at the restraining grip that held her, she lifted a brow. "Where could I possibly go with the king's men at my back?"

He nodded and then released her. As Grace ambled into the trees, she thought about her means of escape. If she wanted to get back to Fagan, she needed a horse. Perhaps she could threaten her driver since the man quivered at the very mention of Uncle Walter, but she couldn't very well wander around aimlessly in the dark. Although the blackness provided the perfect cover, she had to see the path to know where she was going. She needed to find the perfect moment.

She brushed down her skirts and was trying to think of all her options when a hard body pressed against her back and a hand clamped down over her mouth. A voice whispered in her ear.

"Donna scream. 'Tis me, *bhana-phrionnsa.*"

Whipping around, she wrapped her arms around Fagan and buried her head in his chest. "Why does this keep happening to us?"

"Shhh… Keep your voice down. Ruairi is here. We've been watching. Where is your uncle?"

Grace stiffened when a dark figure loomed closer. Fagan didn't even turn around. "'Tis only Ruairi and Angus. I told Ruairi everything."

She wasn't sure if that meant about their relationship and thought it best not to ask. "I have to tell you this quickly because Daniel will come looking for me. My *betrothed* was the bloody spy, not Uncle Walter. He said he had already given the information about the earl's involvement with the uprising to the king's advisors. He told me not to tell Ravenna or Uncle Walter about his duties to the Crown because I could place him and myself in grave danger."

"He's already in grave danger," said Fagan.

"Daniel intends to take my uncle's place as the king's advisor. But if he doesn't know that my uncle and my sister are spies, then they don't know that he is. Furthermore, Ravenna would've told me if she'd known about Daniel. She never would've—"

"Ye're right," said Ruairi. "Listen to me. We donna have much time. There are too many of the king's guard here, and I donna know the extent of Casterbrook's involvement with the king. I want ye to delay them along the way for as long as ye can. We will ride ahead and warn your uncle."

"But Daniel intends to mar—"

"Lady Grace!" called Daniel in the distance.

"Go quickly," said Ruairi.

"But Fagan, I need to tell you—"

His lips smothered her words, and then he pulled back hastily. "We'll be together soon."

She watched the men and the wolf step back into the shadows and silently cursed herself for ever wanting adventure. Sitting in a comfortable chair in the ladies solar with a book in hand sounded wonderful right now. If her biggest worry was breaking a nail, she'd even be all right with that.

"My lady!"

"I'm coming!"

As soon as Grace stepped out of the brush, Daniel stood there with a suspicious expression on his face. "What took you so long?" He walked around her and looked back and forth into the darkness.

"I'm a woman. We always take a long time. You should see how long it takes me to dress and do my hair. See what you have to look forward to, my lord?"

"Your efforts are appreciated, my dear. You always look beautiful. When we return to Edinburgh, you will have a chance to bathe and I will make certain you want for nothing."

"Edinburgh? I thought we were traveling to England."

"Once I tell the king about how I killed the mercenaries who were working with the earl and his son, then we will be wed."

"In Edinburgh?"

"I can't think of a better place and a greater reward. After we're wed, you can return to England and tell your uncle and family all about it."

"Oh, Daniel. I'm very disappointed in the decision

you've made. I'm a woman. As such, I need to have my family in attendance. I want the perfect dress made for the occasion so that I'll look beautiful for you. A simple gown just won't do to marry Lord Casterbrook, the king's trusted advisor. My sisters must be by my side. We need to send word to Ravenna to meet us in Edinburgh."

"And have that barbarian Highland husband of hers in attendance? You know he doesn't leave without those hounds of his, his men, and that bloody wolf." He rested his hands on her shoulders. "You've been with that clan for over a month, my dear. Surely you can survive a few weeks without them." When she didn't attempt to mask the sour look that crossed her face, he added, "How about after we return to England as husband and wife, we invite them for a small celebration?"

"And what of Uncle Walter and his family? I don't understand what you need from me."

"Your uncle will be cross when he is replaced by me. You're a strong woman, Grace, and I want him to heel. I want you, my wife, to make him heel."

"What you're asking is for me to betray my uncle, the man who has been like a father to me and my sisters for all these years."

"No, my dear. I'm not asking you. I'm telling you."

# Twenty-one

FAGAN, RUAIRI, AND TEN OF HIS MEN RODE THEIR mounts hard into the night. The pale moonlight guided them on the path, and for once, luck was on Fagan's side. They decided to stop and rest the horses for a few hours before picking up again where they left off. Not even bothering to light a fire, the men lay on their blankets not too far from the path in case an enemy stumbled across them and they needed to make haste.

Ruairi's voice broke through the silence. "Grace and I may have our differences, but she is my wife's sister. I will do anything I can to see her safe. The lass survived the mercenaries, and I have nay doubt will come through this."

"Nae without a few scars." Fagan had his back toward Ruairi, yet he was never surprised that his friend knew him as well as he did. Of course Fagan was awake. How could he sleep at a time like this? Once this was all over, he couldn't wait to hold Grace again in his arms. The two of them deserved happiness. They'd been through enough. But when he continued to ponder the situation, he shook his head. "I ne'er liked that fancy peacock Casterbrook."

"As soon as Mildmay knows the truth, I donna think he or my wife will ever again have the same opinion." Ruairi sighed. "I knew once I wed Ravenna that her family would be as mine, but the king has many spies throughout his realm. In truth, I ne'er would've believed Casterbrook to be among them. I think that makes it difficult to know who to trust and who will stab ye in the back when ye turn."

There was a heavy silence.

"Ruairi, I ne'er meant to place ye and the clan in the middle of this madness. I'm sorry for the mess I've created. If ye must know, I ne'er intended to care for Grace. It just happened. God's teeth, ye'd think I would've known better, especially after the lass blackened my eye and stabbed me."

"When did she stab ye?"

"Somewhere in her mind she decided that an English lady needed to come to the aid of a seasoned Highland captain. She threw her blade through the bars in the door and—"

"Damn. Ye didnae run for cover."

"I didnae have time, and I couldnae move out of the way. I was then fortunate enough to have a weapon and pulled her knife from my leg to stab the man in the chest."

"Och, aye. So the lass saved your life by stabbing ye."

"And unlike with my blackened eye, I would be grateful if ye would keep this to yourself. I'm afraid my pride is spent."

Ruairi chuckled. "Are ye sure ye know what the hell ye're doing with the lass? Ye need to be certain that ye're up for the task. Ravenna was telling me how her sister's been getting into mischief since the dawn of time, and ye know Grace is more than a handful."

"Aye, that she is, but I wouldnae have it any other way. Who would've thought one lass would make me feel the way I do? I cannae change what I know to be true in my heart and believe me, I've tried. I love her."

"Then neither Ravenna nor I will stand in your way, but ye *will* help me with the four lasses under my roof. There are way too many of them for one man to shoulder the burden alone. Do ye understand? Ye need to keep your lass under control. I have enough troubles with my own."

"Aye, well, I can try. Now get some sleep because we're going to need it."

⁓

Once again, Grace found herself confined within the carriage. She couldn't help herself when she snarled at her driver. She had managed to delay their progress some by pretending a backache and demanding stops to attend to her "lady's needs." But with every step, they were still getting closer to Edinburgh and she knew Daniel's patience was wearing thin.

She realized at that moment how much she missed her sisters, even their prodding, lecturing, and mischief making. Men might often complain about the fairer sex, but Grace knew she'd be grateful never to see another one of *them* again anytime soon—well, except for Fagan. All other men were grating on her nerves. She'd been taken against her will, bargained for, rescued, and captured again. Although the carriage was more comfortable than the cave, it was still a prison.

Gazing out at the king's guard, her mind wandered. What was she going to do if she arrived in Edinburgh and Fagan, Ruairi, and Uncle Walter weren't there? She shuddered. How could they be? They thought she was traveling to England. How long could she possibly delay Daniel without him getting suspicious of her? And one more question weighed heavily on her mind: What if Daniel forced her to wed him? She refused to think that way. She was a Walsingham—and not just any Walsingham. She was was the wily Walsingham sister who was always getting into trouble. She'd learned to master that over the years. Perhaps for once she could use it to her advantage.

❧

The men rode hard for a few hours and then stopped to rest the horses by a stream. They wouldn't reach the English border for a fortnight. Fagan had no doubt that Grace would be able to delay Casterbrook, but he hoped she didn't push him too hard. The bastard may be clever enough to spot her ruse, and if that happened, Fagan didn't want her placed in more danger than she already was. She needed to be careful.

Ruairi slapped him on the shoulder. "We're making good time and should be able to reach Mildmay sooner than expected. Come now... I see the look on your face. I remember holding the same expression on mine nae too long ago. Ye know he gave me his blessing before I wed Ravenna. As long as Grace tells her uncle how she feels about ye, I see nay reason why he shouldnae do the same for ye. He does care for his nieces as though they were his own daughters."

Fagan nodded. "That's what worries me. I am nae a Highland laird, only a Highland captain. Mayhap he will nae see me worthy of his niece, a lady."

Suddenly, thundering hooves pounded the ground toward them, and Fagan's hand moved to the hilt of his sword. When he spotted more of the king's men, he stiffened. Ruairi stepped forward, and Fagan counted roughly fifteen of the English. The English guards parted down the center of the path, and when one of the men dismounted, Fagan realized that Ravenna was right. Every time he laid eyes on Lord Mildmay, the man made him think of a pirate, with his dark looks and cool demeanor.

"Laird Sutherland and Mister Murray, to what do I owe this pleasure? I can only assume you were coming to see me for aid with the mercenaries."

"Casterbrook—"

"Yes, whatever are we going to do with Lord Casterbrook, Laird Sutherland?" Mildmay lowered his voice and stepped away from the English guards. "My men have been watching Casterbrook ever since we returned from the Highlands. I had my suspicions, but I did not want to mention this to Ravenna or Grace until I was certain."

"He gave evidence against the Earl of Orkney to the king's advisors," said Ruairi.

"Oh, yes. That he did, but by involving my family, Lord Casterbrook will pay for his carelessness."

Fagan cleared his throat. "He intends to replace ye as the king's advisor. The only reason he wanted to wed Grace was because she's your niece."

When Ruairi elbowed Fagan in the arm, he realized his slip of the tongue by calling Grace by her Christian name. If Mildmay noticed, he didn't comment. He only laughed in response, then ran his hand through his black hair.

"I never cease to be amazed at how young men think they can conquer anything and everyone. First, let us rescue my niece from the mercenaries, and then I'll deal with Casterbrook myself."

"The men are already dead," said Ruairi. "Casterbrook holds the lass against her will. He brings her back to England, but I ordered my men nae to engage the king's guard."

Mildmay turned his head from side to side as if it ached. "Let's remove my niece from the presence of that arrogant whelp, shall we? I don't want her in the clutches of that man any longer than she's already been made to endure. Let's give him a surprise and meet him on the trail."

"Och, aye. 'Tis best to catch him unawares. Let's rescue the lass and kill the bastard," snarled Fagan.

When Mildmay gazed at Ruairi for confirmation, Ruairi nodded. "Ye heard my captain."

❧

"Again, my dear?" An annoyed expression crossed Daniel's face, especially since this was the third time today Grace had delayed their journey.

"I don't know what's wrong with me. Perhaps I

caught something when the men held me in the cave. I didn't have food or water, and I slept on the damp ground for over a sennight. My entire body aches."

"There's no need for apologies. We'll stop here for the night. I would never forgive myself if you became ill on the journey."

She smiled her thanks. "Although I need to rest, I don't think there's any need to further delay the men, especially since we'll be in Edinburgh soon. Do you think you should let them take their leave? I'm sure they want to be home—"

At the mention of the king's guard, Daniel's eyes never left hers. "The men will do as I command, but yes, I see no reason to keep all of them here with us. With any luck, we'll be in Edinburgh sometime on the morrow." He paused. "But I would not want anything or anyone else delaying our travels, and I'd be remiss if I didn't keep a handful of men to escort us." He continued to study her, and she lightened her expression.

"Of course. Whatever you think is best."

As Daniel spoke in hushed tones with his men a few yards away, Grace sat down on a large rock. She smoothed her hair, wanting nothing more than to take a long, hot bath and sleep for days. She could stop Daniel for as many times as it took to reach Edinburgh, but she prayed her delays weren't useless. The carriage ride had provided her with ample time alone to think things through. As soon as she and Daniel reached Edinburgh, he would insist they wed. And the man she loved was in England with no idea where she was. Grace knew she had no other choice.

Tonight she would make her escape.

As the hours passed, she sat with Daniel, listening to his words but not really hearing him. She tried to make an effort to shut him out. His voice was grating on her nerves. In fact, everything about the man was. She glanced at the horizon. The sun would be down soon, and even if it wasn't yet, she decided now was the perfect time.

She stood. "Pray excuse me."

"Stay close."

"I will."

Grace knew Daniel was watching her like a hawk as she made her way into the brush. Once she was out of sight, she didn't hesitate. Making a mad dash through the trees, she did not look back. When she found the trail, she lifted her skirts and ran as fast as her legs could carry her. She'd already made a decision that if she heard the men following her on horseback, she'd dart into the forest for cover until she knew she was safe.

Her breathing was ragged, but she dared not stop. One way or another she would return to Fagan. There was a sharp stab in her ribs but she pushed through the pain. She willed herself to continue. She wasn't sure how much time had passed, but men shouted in the distance.

She stole a quick glance over her shoulder. Horses were approaching. She didn't hesitate and ran into the trees. Her dress became tangled in the brush. As she was pulling her skirts free, she didn't realize that a piece of material was left behind. She tripped over a fallen branch and fell to the ground. She heard the men talking around her and couldn't find the courage to look where they were. She lay flat on her stomach and lowered her head to the ground. She didn't move. She didn't make a sound. Grace had never been so frightened in her life.

"Search the trees. I want her found."

"Yes, m'lord."

She dared not lift her head for fear of being caught. She didn't think Daniel would be kind once he found her, and she wasn't thrilled to be in his company again anytime soon. She was forced to lie in wait, but she'd been in worse situations than this—all within the last few weeks.

"There are no signs of her, my lord."

"Wily minx. She had me dismiss the men only to make her escape, and I played right into her hands. I will not make that mistake again. Take half the men south. She couldn't have gone far. Send the other half north, but I don't think she turned around."

"Yes, m'lord."

Grace closed her eyes and held her breath for as long as she could. She was afraid that if she breathed, Daniel or his men would find her. The sound of hoofbeats galloped off into the distance, but she wasn't a fool. She'd remain as still as a statue until she was certain all the men had left.

Several moments passed, and the trees shielded her in darkness. She no longer heard the men, and she listened very carefully for the slightest sound of one of their mounts. Slowly, she lifted her head. She looked from left to right, and no men were in sight. Finally, God had heard her prayers.

She pushed herself to her feet and brushed the dirt

from her hands. She paused, gazing around at the tall trees and foliage for any sign of movement. Nothing… and that was just what she wanted. As she took a step forward, someone cleared his throat from behind.

Grace jumped.

"The next time you decide to run, you may not want to leave your skirts behind, my lady."

She whipped her head around and shot Daniel a cold look. He stood there waving the material from her dress in an arrogant manner. She gazed around to see four of his men encircling her. He'd never sent his men anywhere. He was clever. She'd give him that.

"And just where do you think you're running off to, my dear?"

"Anywhere away from you, and will you quit calling me that? I never liked it. I will never marry you, and I will never betray my uncle. Go to hell, Daniel."

His eyes darkened. "I have no doubt the devil is holding a place for me and waiting for my arrival, but it won't be today." He closed the distance between them, and Grace refused to be held against her will— again. She didn't care if the man had an army of men at his back. She would not go willingly.

She spun on her heel and ran as fast as she could.

"Well, don't just stand there. Go and get her."

Twigs snapped under her feet. Branches smacked her in the face. Her cheeks stung, her dress tore, and she didn't even notice. She could barely see in front of her, but she would run through the darkness to reach the light.

Without warning, she was pummeled to the ground with a heavy thump. She was trapped beneath a guard, struggling to get free. Fingers wound through her hair and pulled her to her feet. She tried to swing her arms around at the big brute to release her, but he wouldn't budge. She grabbed his hand, fumbling for his fingers and trying to make them let go.

As Daniel approached, he waved his hand in a gesture of dismissal. The guard finally released his hold, but not before he pulled her hair one last time. Grace couldn't help herself. She shot the man a cold smile and kicked him in the shin with her boot. The guard took a menacing step toward her, but Daniel held up his hand to stay his man.

"Now that is no way to treat my betrothed. Let me help you."

Grace gasped when Daniel closed the distance between them and balled his fist into her face. He struck her so hard that he knocked her to the ground. He proceeded to kick her once with his booted foot on the side of her ribs, and she cried out in pain. With all her strength, she held her sore ribs and pulled herself to her feet. Her eyes met Daniel's and she dared not look away. Instead, she couldn't control her burst of laughter. The guards and her betrothed gazed at her as if she'd gone mad.

"And just what do you find so amusing, my dear?"

"Angus is going to tear you to shreds, and Fagan's going to kill you. I shall take great pleasure in watching you die."

Daniel paled when a primal growl pierced the darkness.

# Twenty-two

CASTERBROOK SPUN AROUND AND PULLED A DAGGER from the scabbard at his waist. When he spotted Angus with teeth bared and Sutherland men walking out of the trees and disarming the king's guard, he wrapped his arm around Grace. He placed the blade at her throat, and his eyes darted back and forth between the men. He looked like a caged animal, and that's what frightened Fagan the most.

"Hiding behind my skirts, Daniel? You bloody coward!"

He tightened his grip. "Shut your mouth, dearest! I need to think!"

Fagan stepped from the shadows. "Ye only need to know one thing for certain. Ye're going to die." He gazed at Grace through the darkness, not that he could see her very well. "How are you, *bhana-phrionnsa*?"

"I've certainly had better days."

In the distance, Ruairi and Mildmay made their way behind Casterbrook while Angus stood firm. Two Sutherland guards lit torches and stopped when they reached the edge of the king's guard. They had

Casterbrook encircled, and there was nowhere for the bastard to turn.

Mildmay's voice echoed through the darkness. "I never thought you a fool, Casterbrook, but you've made several grave errors in judgment. You harmed one of my own. You are not worthy of my niece's hand in marriage. And I especially have no idea what in the hell you were thinking with this nonsense about taking my place as the king's advisor." He laughed. "As if you could… You see, I've been in service to the Crown—Queen Elizabeth and then King James's realm—for a very long time. More than likely while you were still a babe suckling your mother's breast."

Casterbrook looked over his shoulder and shifted his weight.

"Let her go," said Fagan. "Naught good is going to come from this. One way or another, ye're going to die."

Casterbrook whipped his head around. "I don't take orders from a bloody Highlander. Stay back, and don't come any closer! I swear I'll kill her! I've nothing to lose! I said, stay back!" Ruairi and Mildmay stopped, but the men were still several yards away.

Grace closed her eyes as a trickle of blood dripped down her neck. Fagan could hear his own blood pounding in his ears. He needed Casterbrook to release her so he could send the Englishman to his maker, but the man continued to hold Grace against him like a shield. Fagan was not willing to take a chance that she would be hurt.

Angus let out another throaty growl, and a look of panic crossed Casterbrook's face. His eyes darted back and forth between Fagan and Angus as if he were deciding which one of the two would kill him first. Casterbrook took a step forward, moving Grace closer to the animal. She was right. The coward was hiding behind her skirts.

To Fagan's surprise, Grace used the wolf as a distraction and bit Casterbrook on the hand. The man cried out in pain and the blade dropped to the ground. Ruairi and Mildmay charged from behind as Grace fell to her knees, fumbling for the dagger.

Fagan unsheathed his sword and ran toward her. "Nay, Grace! For God's sake, do what ye do best!"

When she realized what he'd meant, she stood and placed her boot over the blade. Casterbrook made another attempt to subdue her, but she balled her hand into a fist and rammed it straight into his eye. Fagan was there in seconds and pushed Grace out of harm's way. He thrust his sword into Casterbrook's gut. As he stepped back with the hilt of the sword still in his hand, he lowered his gaze, and his jaw dropped. Another blade came through the man's stomach and missed Fagan by a mere inch. He glanced over Casterbrook's shoulder, and his eyes met Mildmay's.

Only when Ruairi slapped him on the shoulder did Fagan dare pull his weapon from the belly of the beast. He needed to be sure Casterbrook was dead so that no harm would ever again befall Grace. At that moment, he silently swore an oath that he would protect her until he drew his last breath. She was his, and he was hers. As Casterbrook fell to the ground, Mildmay pulled out his sword and stabbed his blade into the grass. He pulled Grace into the circle of his arms.

"My dear, dear niece. Are you all right?"

"Yes, I'm so happy to see you, and I'm so thankful you came when you did."

Mildmay pulled back and lowered his voice. "Now *that* is what it takes to be a spy for the Crown. I hope you have enough sense—"

"Don't worry, Uncle Walter. I've learned my lesson. You may be rest assured that I've had enough adventure to last a lifetime. I don't want to have anything to do with king and country or bloody mercenaries, and you and my sister can keep your spy craft to yourselves."

Not entirely certain how to broach the subject to Mildmay, Fagan lowered his gaze to the ground. To his surprise, a warm body pressed against his, and Grace threw her arms around him.

"Oh, Fagan. I'm so glad you—"

He placed his finger over her lips. "Shhh… I'm here now. 'Tis over." He ran his thumb over her cheek, and her expression was pained. "What's the matter?"

She brought her fingers to her eye. "I'm sore where Daniel—"

A muscle ticked at his jaw, and he wiped the blood from her neck with his thumb. "Nay one will ever touch ye that way again. I give ye my word."

Grace buried her head in his chest. "I just want to go home."

"It's too dark to travel now, Grace. We'll make camp here for this evening, and then I'll see you safely home on the morrow," said Mildmay.

She grabbed Fagan by the hand and pulled him over to her uncle. "Uncle Walter, might I have a word with you?"

Mildmay looked down at their hands. "Mister Murray, is there something you wish to tell me—like when the bloody hell did this happen?"

As the king's guard lifted Casterbrook away, Fagan noticed Ruairi watching them. He gave Fagan a nod of encouragement. Fagan straightened his spine and met Mildmay's eyes, refusing to falter. "I love her. I know that I donna have much to offer the lass, but I give her my heart. In truth, I cannae imagine my life without her—"

"*Grace?* We are speaking of the same woman?"

"Uncle Walter!"

Mildmay shook his head. "I thought you didn't like Highlanders."

"I still don't, but I love this one. I know this makes no sense, especially after the things I've done and said, but it's true. I love Fagan, Uncle Walter. Please give us your blessing."

"And if I didn't, you wouldn't listen to me anyway. You must know that I gave my word to your father that I would look after you girls."

"Ye are a man of honor, and I respect ye for that. I hope ye think the same of me, for I wish Grace to be my wife. I'd give her anything. I'd give my life for hers."

Mildmay rolled his eyes. "Well, let's hope it doesn't come to that." He gazed around at the men. "Where is Sutherland?"

Ruairi walked toward them. "Here…"

"Laird Sutherland, did you know about this?"

"Nae until verra recently."

"I must ask you if you're ready to have the captain of your guard take a wife."

"Uncle Walter, what difference does that make? Ruairi has known Fagan for years."

"Perhaps the better question, Laird Sutherland, is to ask you if you're ready to have the captain of your guard wed my niece?"

Her eyes sparkled. "And just what do you mean by that?"

Fagan cleared his throat. He lowered his lips to hers, but not before he heard Ruairi mumble to Mildmay, "Ye do realize that I'll have all your nieces under my roof, including Grace."

"And I'd like to think you're up for the challenge. Good luck, Sutherland."

༄

Kilts, daggers, and not a single man in the throes of battle—that's what Grace reveled in as she stood in the great hall of her brother-in-law's home. The kilts and daggers belonged to the Sutherland clan, but unlike her sister, Grace had made Ruairi take down those dreaded tapestries before her wedding day.

When her eyes met her husband's, her heart hammered in her chest. Although she'd believed Scottish men were nothing but a bunch of Highland barbarians, they weren't any worse than their English counterparts. Fagan caught her staring, and his eyes twinkled. The man made her feel like he always knew her thoughts, and she loved that about him.

"The ceremony was beautiful. You look lovely, Grace. The blue gown is a beautiful color on you."

"Thank you, Ravenna. I'm aware that you had a lot to do with the removal of the tapestries, and for that, I'm grateful."

"Yes, and you do know that Ruairi demanded I put them all back in their rightful places when the wedding is over."

Grace bumped her sister in the arm. "We'll see about that. Now that they're down, and there are four of us…"

"Please don't push him too far. You know that he'll—"

"What are ye doing now, Wife?"

Grace shrugged. "Nothing."

"I'll leave you two alone."

"Fagan, I'm weary. It's getting late. Is there any chance that we can perhaps escape this madness and go to bed now?"

"This is our wedding day. Ye really want to take your leave and go to sleep?"

"I didn't say that I wanted to sleep. I said that I wanted to go to bed." She gave him a knowing look and laughed when his eyes darkened. She leaned in closer. "Ever since we've told our families that we're to be wed, my uncle, your laird, and my sisters have kept us separated for weeks. Perhaps they were waiting for us to come to our senses, but I think it's been long enough, don't you? In truth, if I don't touch you again soon, I'm going to lose my mind."

He turned on his heel. "I'll make our excuses and be right back."

She gazed around the great hall at her new family. Ruairi cast Ravenna a warm smile from across the room. Torquil was drawing another picture for Kat at the table, and as of this moment, there hadn't been any more fighting between them. And Elizabeth?

Grace glanced around the room. Oh yes. Elizabeth had a flush on her cheeks as she wrung her hands in front of her, sitting across the table from Laird Munro and hanging on to every word the man said. From the look on the laird's face, he was in desperate need of rescue and wanted no part of Elizabeth. Grace supposed he was a grown man and could handle his own troubles because Fagan was making his way toward her and nothing else mattered.

"Take my hand. Keep your head down. Donna look at anyone. We make our escape."

She hastily followed her husband to their new chamber, and when the door closed, she sighed. The room was grand and much larger than her bedchamber in the manor house. It had a stone fireplace that took up the center wall, a small sitting area, and a large wooden bed with tall corner posts. Candles were lit throughout the chamber, and flowers lay on the golden coverlet. Grace smiled at her sister's efforts. She'd be sure to thank Ravenna again later.

Fagan picked up one of the stems from the bed and turned. Grace could not speak as she gazed into her husband's eyes, loving this side of him—the kindness, the desire, the passion. This was the man she had grown so fond of and who had captured her heart. She threw herself into Fagan's arms and brought his lips down to hers. Her calm was shattered by the hunger of his kisses. His firm mouth demanded a response, one that she was more than willing to give.

His lips seared a path down her neck, her shoulder. She laced her fingers in his hair, pulling him close. His gentle touch sent currents of desire through her.

"Mmm… It's been far too long."

He whispered into her hair. "Aye, that it has. Do ye remember how 'tis done, or mayhap ye need me to remind ye, eh?"

She felt the thrill of her husband's arousal as he dropped his kilt to the floor and pressed against her. When he moved his thigh between her legs, the glorious heat nearly caused her knees to buckle.

"Oh, Fagan."

As if he sensed her impending need, he bent down and swept her from her feet, weightless, into his arms. She lifted her hand to his cheek in a gentle gesture, and for a moment, he stood there, holding her and gazing into her eyes.

*"A ghràidh."*

"Now what name are you calling me?"

He chuckled. "I donna want to call ye *bhana-phrionnsa*. I find the name doesnae suit ye any longer. Ye are my wife, and ye need to understand those two Gaelic words from now on because ye will be hearing them from me verra often. *A ghràidh* means 'my love.' Something ye have been since the first time ye blackened my eye."

He carried her and gently eased her down upon the bed. With a fist, he pulled off his tunic and tossed it to the floor. His body covered hers and he ran his exploring fingers over her curves. Her skin tingled when he touched her, shivers of delight sliding sensuously up her arm.

She placed her hand on his rock-hard chest and brushed the tawny hairs. His gaze slowly dropped from her eyes to her shoulders to her breasts. Her gown crept up to her thighs as she moved closer to him. He pulled the fabric upward over her belly, her chest. He lowered his head and his tongue caressed her sensitive nipples, her breasts surging at the familiarity of his touch. His tongue continued to tantalize the buds, which had swollen to their fullest.

When his strong hand seared a path down her abdomen and to her inner leg, she thought she would come undone. He explored her thighs slowly and then moved up. His lips again teased a taut, dusky pink nipple.

He paused to kiss her, whispering his love for each part of her body. The stroking of his fingers sent pleasure jolts through her. Completely aroused now, she drew herself closer to him.

He paused and his body moved partially to uncover hers. "I want to see all of ye."

She wiggled her way out of the delicate gown and let it fall to the floor. She moaned softly as he laid her back down. It was flesh against flesh, man against woman. Her breasts tingled against his hard chest.

"Your first time should have ne'er been the way it was or where. Let me love ye properly. Ye are verra bonny, Wife." His voice was low and alluring. He took her hand and guided it to himself.

Her fingers encircled him, and he moved his body against her. When he reached between her thighs, opening her legs and then inserting his finger, she gasped in sweet agony.

"Och, Grace. Your body weeps for me."

Her desire for him overrode all reason. She didn't want to take it slow. She wanted him. Now. When he recognized her need, he entered her in a single thrust, sending a jolt of pleasure straight through her. A moan of ecstasy slipped through her lips, but he stilled.

"All ye all right? I donna want to hurt ye."

"I know you would never hurt me. Please, Fagan. I need you." The hot tide of passion raged through her, and in one swift motion, he was hers.

Sweat beaded on his forehead and his chest heaved. She surrendered to his masterful seduction, her eager response matching his. When they were roused to the peak of desire, he pulled back and gazed into her eyes. With another heavy thrust, she arched her back, unable to control the cry of delight and feeling of satisfaction her husband left within her as he spilled his seed.

Grace looked up and her heart lurched madly. When Fagan collapsed on top of her, she could feel his heart pounding against her own. There was an undeniable bond between them.

He looked into her eyes, and it was if she could read his thoughts. He gave her a quick peck on the nose, and then he rolled onto his side as she lay panting, her chest heaving. They shared a smile and then both burst out laughing because his breath was as labored as hers.

She ran her fingernails up and down his arm. "That was quite enjoyable, Husband."

"For me as well." He gathered her into his arms

and held her snugly against him. "I'm ne'er going to let ye go."

"I should hope not because I know this is where I was meant to be—by your side, in your arms."

Grace was astonished at the sense of fulfillment she felt. She allowed her thoughts to emerge from their hidden depths, and looking back, she knew Mister Murray was kinder than he wanted anyone to know, especially her. She was a blind fool for not recognizing the truth earlier.

She lay in the drowsy warmth of her bed with her husband, thinking of all the wonderful days yet to come.

READ ON FOR A SNEAK PEEK AT THE NEXT BOOK IN
VICTORIA ROBERTS'S HIGHLAND SPIES SERIES

# Highland Plaids and Petticoats

*Sutherland, Scottish Highlands, 1613*

THIS WAS HIS LAST CHANCE TO TURN AROUND AND
bolt from the gates as if his arse was afire. Against his
better judgment, he kept his eyes forward, his hands
steady, and he tried not to pay any heed to the warning voice that whispered in his head.

Laird Ian Munro wasn't aware of the death grip he
held on the reins of his mount as he approached the
portcullis. He'd sworn that he'd never again set foot
on Sutherland lands as long as the four Walsingham
sisters lived under the same roof as his friend. He
was no coward, but between the troubles with the
Gordon, Stewart, and the damn mercenaries, he'd
made it a point to stay on his own lands.

*Until now.*

Laird Ruairi Sutherland's home was a fortified
castle with round turrets, a square watchtower, and a
curtain wall that was twenty feet thick at the widest

point. Yet, to Ian's surprise, the stone structure wasn't strong enough to hold the wily Walsinghams at bay. He passed the dangerous cliffs on the left and to his right was lush forest. He supposed he could always take a leap to the left if he found himself trapped within the walls with no means of escape.

As he reached the point of no return, his face clouded with uneasiness because the guards had already greeted him from the gatehouse. Ian continued through to the bailey and halted, hesitantly releasing the reins of his horse to the stable hand. Ruairi's captain greeted him with a brotherly slap on the back and a wry grin.

"Munro, how long has it been, my friend?" Fagan Murray's dark hair hung well below his shoulders, and he wore a kilt of green, black, blue, white, and orange, the Sutherland tartan.

"'Tis good to see ye, Fagan." Ian gazed around the courtyard, breathing a sigh of relief that no Walsinghams were in sight.

"Then tell me. Why have we nae seen your face since Grace and I wed? Ye know it has been almost three years since we've last set eyes upon ye."

Ian raised his eyebrows in mock surprise and placed his hand over his heart. "Truly? Has it been that long?"

Fagan lowered his voice and playfully balled his fist into Ian, which was more like a brotherly tap to the arm. "To be truthful, I ne'er thought of ye as a coward."

"I'm nay coward, but as I told ye before, keep your brood here because I sure as hell donna want them crossing the borders to my lands. I have enough troubles of my own."

Fagan laughed. "Come. Ruairi's been expecting ye, and we'll have some food and drink to celebrate your return."

They entered the great hall, and Ian involuntarily burst into a smile. Tapestries depicting swords, shields, and men in the throes of battle remained on the walls. He recalled the time when Fagan's wife, Grace, had insisted that Ruairi remove the wall hangings before her wedding day because she didn't favor them. Ian pursed his mouth in satisfaction as he realized that Ruairi still had his bollocks and hadn't succumbed to the will of the women after all. Perhaps there was hope for his friend yet.

"Munro, I cannae believe ye are standing here in my great hall as I live and breathe." Ruairi's straight, long chestnut hair had traces of red and hung just past his shoulders. A plaid rested over his shoulder and he sported the traditional Sutherland kilt. With his giant sword sheathed at his waist, his friend looked exactly as Ian had remembered him. *"Fàilte. Ciamar a tha thu?"* Ruairi said warmly. *Welcome. How are you?*

*"Tha gu math."* *I am fine.* Ian embraced the man who was like a brother to him. "'Tis good to see ye, Ruairi." Without warning, a hand clasped Ian's shoulder from behind.

"I'm glad to see ye didnae live up to your promise. Ye did set foot on Da's lands again."

"Torquil?" With his reddish-brown hair and green eyes, Torquil was the picture of Ruairi. "Ye have grown. Soon I think there might be a need to fear ye on the battlefield. What age is upon ye now, lad?"

The man who was no longer a boy smiled from ear to ear. "I am fifteen."

A lovely lass stood beside Torquil and she was poking him in the ribs with her finger. "Fifteen, perhaps, but he behaves more like he's twelve." Blond locks framed her oval face and she had sparkling blue eyes. She wore an emerald dress that hugged her young frame.

"Lady Katherine?"

"Yes. It's lovely to see you again, Laird Munro."

Ian shook his head as if he'd consumed too much ale. He couldn't believe so much had changed in three years. The last time he'd seen the girl she had been only nine. Ruairi's wife approached them, and her wealth of red hair hung in loose tendrils that softened her face. Ravenna always looked elegant and graceful, and Ian was glad to see some things hadn't changed.

He kissed the top of her hand. "Lady Ravenna, ye're still as bonny as the day I met ye."

"Thank you, Laird Munro. Although I don't know how much longer I'll appear this way." She lowered her arm and her hands cradled her stomach. "Ruairi and I are again expecting another child. We're hoping for a son to have a brother for Mary."

"*Another* bairn?" He nodded to Ruairi. "Please accept my condolen…er, congratulations to ye both."

Lady Katherine slapped her hands together. "I'm thrilled that I'm going to be an aunt again. I do hope Ravenna has another girl."

Ian didn't know what to say, but Torquil was the only man among them who found his voice.

"Kat, donna even jest about something like that. I think ye might put Da in an early grave."

Ruairi gave Ian a knowing look.

"If it weren't for me and my sisters, this castle—and

the men within it—would be running wild. You should be thankful that you have us here to keep you all in line."

Torquil playfully wrapped his arm around Kat's neck and rubbed his knuckles over the top of her head. "I do like it when ye try."

Ian would be sure to pray long and hard that Ravenna carried a boy, because the last thing Ruairi needed was another cunning female under his roof. If it wasn't bad enough Ravenna was a "retired" English spy, her haughty sister, Grace, had even married Fagan. Oh, and that wasn't all the poor bastard was made to endure. After Ruairi said his vows, he'd taken in all three of his wife's sisters.

Ravenna took her leave from the hall, and Kat wandered off with Torquil. The men took their seats at the long wooden table on the dais, and Ruairi poured them all a drink. He placed a tankard in front of Ian and smiled. "Here. Ye look like ye could use one—or many."

"Och, aye." He lifted the tankard to his lips when he spotted something over the rim. Kat and Torquil sat on a bench…together, close. Ian briefly closed his eyes and shook his head. The two of them used to run away from each other, avoiding the other like the plague. Now he wouldn't be surprised if he saw the two of them holding hands in a wooing gesture.

A growl escaped him. "Something in my gut told me that I should've just met all of ye in London." His mouth pulled into a sour grin, and Ruairi waved him off.

"There's only so much Ravenna and her uncle can

do to keep King James at bay. We've been fortunate that we havenae had to attend court in almost three years. Thank God for small favors. Besides, with the recent passing of Prince Henry, we should pay our respects to the king in order to stay in his good graces. I thought it would be good for us to travel to London at the same time. More to the point, ye know how much we enjoy the pleasure of your company. We always have such a damn good time when we're together." Ruairi held up his tankard in mock salute, and Ian chuckled.

"Aye. I remember all the good times we had with the Gordon, Stewart, and mercenaries, and let's nae forget about the English spies that ye shelter under your roof."

A young woman stepped in front of the dais and cleared her throat. She had reddish-brown hair that hung in loose waves down her back. Her figure was slender and regal, and Ian could've easily drowned in her emerald eyes. But what captured his attention the most was the way the lass carried herself, confident— yet unaware of her true beauty.

She wore a black gown with hanging sleeves and the embroidered petticoat under her skirts was lined in gray. With the added reticella laced collar and cuffs dyed with yellow starch, she looked as though she should've been at the English court rather than in the Scottish Highlands.

"Pardon me, Ruairi. Ravenna wanted me to tell you that we're taking little Mary to the beach. We won't be long. We'll be in the garden until the mounts are readied if you need us."

When the woman's eyes met Ian's, something clicked in his mind. His face burned as he remembered. He shifted in the seat and pulled his tunic away from his chest. Why was the temperature suddenly hot? He felt like he was suffocating in the middle of the Sutherland great hall. God help him. This was the same young chit who had pined after him and followed him around the castle like Angus, Ruairi's black wolf. But like everything else that had transformed around here, so had she. She was no longer a girl but had become an enchantress, still young, but beautiful nonetheless. His musings were interrupted by a male voice.

"Munro, ye do remember Lady Elizabeth, eh?"

How could he forget the reason he'd avoided the Sutherland lands for the past three years?

❦

Laird Ian Munro was still as daunting—and handsome—as Elizabeth had remembered him. His long, red hair hung down to his elbows in complete disarray. His broad shoulders looked bigger than she'd recalled, and wisps of light hair curled against the V of his open shirt. He had a strong, chiseled jaw and green eyes that would make any woman swoon.

For goodness' sake, she thought—prayed—she was over this foolish fancy she'd had for him. After all, she'd been only fifteen at the time. Her brother-in-law often jested that women were terrified of Ian's wild appearance. The man even had a reputation of frightening men on the battlefield by his fierce looks alone. She supposed that's why her family was shocked when she'd shown an interest in him. But there was something about Ian that always drew her in like a magnet.

Elizabeth managed to avoid his gaze. She spoke only to Ruairi and didn't stammer her words nervously in front of the men. Frankly, she was proud of herself. But when her Ruairi asked if Laird Munro had remembered her, Elizabeth made an error in judgment. She met Ian's eyes, and there was a tingling in the pit of her stomach. She found herself extremely conscious of his virile appeal. His nearness was entirely overwhelming. Her pulse pounded and she couldn't breathe. Memories of the past flooded her with emotion.

Irked by her response to him, she was determined to show him she wasn't the same young, stupid, and senseless girl he'd known three years ago. She'd changed. And she needed to let him know that his presence no longer affected her the way it had in the past.

"Laird Munro, what a pleasure to see you again. You look well," she said with as much indifference as she could muster. She gazed back at Ruairi. "Ravenna and Grace are waiting for me in the garden. Pray excuse me."

Elizabeth resisted the urge to bolt out of the hall and not look back. She slowed her pace as much as she could without looking as though she was trying to flee. She was a Walsingham, and her family never ran from anything or anyone.

# Acknowledgments

A very special "thank you" goes out to the following people:

To my agent, Jill Marsal, for keeping me afloat in the murky waters.

To my editor, Cat Clyne, for supporting my dreams.

To the unsung heroes at Sourcebooks—it truly takes a village.

To Sharron Gunn, my resident Gaelic expert, *mòran taing*!

To my family, for their unwavering support and dedication, and especially to my son, who accompanies me to all book signings and lectures. Who would've ever believed a seven-year-old boy would proudly don his kilt and support his mom through the years with so much vigor? I love you, Manny!

To Mary Grace, six books later... We have shed blood, sweat, and tears for Ciaran, Declan, Alexander, Ruairi, Luthais, and Fagan, but you never once doubted me. You continue to push me toward my dreams and to be the best I can be. Your friendship and support mean the world to me, as do you.

To my street team, Bad Girls of the Highlands, you are all amazing. I'm so glad you're with me on this crazy journey.

To my readers, for your posts, emails, and pictures, and for being so incredibly supportive. Thank you for helping me bring my love of Scotland to life.

# About the Author

Award-winning author Victoria Roberts writes Scottish historical romances about kilted heroes and warriors from the past. She was named by *RT Book Reviews* as "one of the most promising debut authors across the genres" and was also a 2013 *RT* Reviewers' Choice award winner for *X Marks the Scot*. Victoria is a member of Romance Writers of America and several local chapters, as well as a contributing author to the online magazine *Celtic Guide*. When she's not plotting her next Scottish adventure, she's dragging her clan to every Scottish festival under the sun. Visit Victoria at www.VictoriaRobertsAuthor.com.

# Temptation in a Kilt
## by Victoria Roberts

### She's on her way to safety

It's a sign of Lady Rosalia Armstrong's desperation that she's seeking refuge in a place as rugged and challenging as the Scottish Highlands. She doesn't care about hardship and discomfort, if only she can become master of her own life. Laird Ciaran MacGregor, however, is completely beyond her control...

### He redefines dangerous...

Ciaran MacGregor knows it's perilous to get embroiled with a fiery Lowland lass, especially one as headstrong as Rosalia. Having made a rash promise to escort her all the way to Glengarry, now he's stuck with her, even though she challenges his legendary prowess at every opportunity. When temptation reaches its peak, he'll be ready to show her who he really is... on and off the battlefield.

"Wonderful adventure with sensual and compelling romance." —Amanda Forester, acclaimed author of *True Highland Spirit*

### For more Victoria Roberts, visit:

www.sourcebooks.com

# *X Marks the Scot*

## by Victoria Roberts

---

### He's fierce, he's proud, he's everything she was warned against.

Declan MacGregor hadn't a care in the world beyond finding a soft bed and willing woman…until he had to escort Lady Liadain Campbell to the English court. The woman needles him at every turn, but he can't just abandon her to that vipers' nest without protection.

Liadain wasn't thrilled to be left in the care of her clan's archrival. It was as if the man never had a lady tell him no before! And yet as whispers of treason swirl through the court and the threat of danger grows ever sharper, her bitter enemy soon becomes the only one she can trust…

---

### Praise for *Temptation in a Kilt*:

"Well written, full of intrigue, and a sensual, believable romance, this book captivates the reader immediately." —*RT Book Reviews*

"Filled with everything I love most about Highland romance…" —Melissa Mayhue, award-winning author of *Warrior's Redemption*

### For more Victoria Roberts, visit:

www.sourcebooks.com

# To Wed a Wicked Highlander

## by Victoria Roberts

— ✧ —

### Torn between his duty and his soul mate, what will this Highland bad boy choose?

When a beautiful traitor is discovered under his own roof, Laird Alexander MacDonnell is faced with a decision he never thought possible. He's sworn to protect his clan, but following his duty will mean losing his heart forever to the woman who betrayed him—his wife.

Lady Sybella MacKenzie is forced to search for her clan's ancient seeing stone under the roof of her father's enemy. But when she finally finds the precious artifact, ensuring her family's survival will mean turning her back on the man who has captured her soul.

— ✧ —

### Praise for *Temptation in a Kilt*:

"An exciting Highland adventure with sensual and compelling romance." —Amanda Forester, acclaimed author of *True Highland Spirit*

"Filled with everything I love most about Highland romance…" —Melissa Mayhue, award-winning author of *Warrior's Redemption*

### For more Victoria Roberts, visit:

www.sourcebooks.com

# My Highland Spy
## by Victoria Roberts

### This Highland laird won't bow to the crown

Laird Ruairi Sutherland refuses to send his only son away to be educated by the English. So he does what any laird would do—he lies to the king. The last thing Ruairi expects is a beautiful English governess to appear on his doorstep.

### But this lady spy might make him...

Lady Ravenna Walsingham is a spy who is sent to the savage Highlands to uncover a plot against the Crown. Playing the part of an English governess, she infiltrates the home of Laird Sutherland, a suspected conspirator.

### If she doesn't betray him first

Ravenna soon discovers that the only real threat Sutherland poses is to her heart. But will the proud Highland laird ever forgive her when he discovers the woman he loves is an English spy?

"Her lyrical prose grabs readers' attention, and the high level of emotional tension simply adds to the depth of the story. This book begs to be read and reread." —*RT Book Reviews*, 4.5 Stars

### For more Victoria Roberts, visit:

www.sourcebooks.com

# Plaids and Petticoats
## by Victoria Roberts

— ❧ —

Don't miss the next book in
award-winning author Victoria Roberts's
Highland Spies series...

Lady Elizabeth Walsingham pined after the same man for years. When she realizes the brawny Highland laird doesn't return her feelings, she decides to stay in England and start anew. She falls for a mysterious thespian at a London play, but little does she know that he has other plans for her family in mind.

Laird Ian Munro spends his time avoiding the young lady who's confounded him for years. When he discovers she's getting too close to a man who's up to no good, Ian soon realizes the lass he's trying to protect is no longer a child but a beautiful woman. But is he too late to capture Elizabeth's heart, or will she see him as nothing more than a Highland barbarian?

— ❧ —

### Praise for *My Highland Spy*:

"A master of Highland romance."
—Becky Condit of *USA Today*

"This book begs to be read and reread." —*RT Book Reviews*

### For more Victoria Roberts, visit:

www.sourcebooks.com

# *Just in Time for a Highlander*

## by Gwyn Cready

---

### For Duncan MacHarg, things just got real

Battle reenactor and financier Duncan MacHarg thinks he has it made—until he lands in the middle of a real Clan Kerr battle and comes face-to-face with their beautiful, spirited leader. Out of time and out of place, Duncan must use every skill he can muster to earn his position among the clansmen and in the heart of the devastatingly intriguing woman to whom he must pledge his oath.

### Abby needs a hero, and she needs him now

When Abigail Ailich Kerr sees a handsome, mysterious stranger materialize in the midst of her clan's skirmish with the English, she's stunned to discover he's the strong arm she's been praying for. Instead of a tested fighter, the fierce young chieftess has been given a man with no measurable battle skills and a damnably distracting smile. And the only way to get rid of him is to turn him into a Scots warrior herself—one demanding and intimate lesson at a time.

---

"Cready's highly satisfying creation is filled with humor, witty dialogue, double entendres, and clever schemes, and a wonderful cast of imaginative characters keeps this twisty story lively to the end." —*Publishers Weekly* Starred Review

### For more Gwyn Cready, visit:

www.sourcebooks.com